A Man Called Moses

A Man Called Moses

The Curious Life of Wellington Delaney Moses

Bill Gallaher

TOUCHWOOD EDITIONS

VICTORIA • VANCOUVER

TouchWood Editions Ltd
Victoria, BC, Canada
This book is distributed by The Heritage Group, #108-17665 66A Avenue,
Surrey, BC, Canada, V3S 2A7.

Cover design: Pat McCallum. Book design: Retta Moorman and Katherine Hale.
Layout: Katherine Hale. Front-cover photograph: Grandpa's Antique Photo
Studios, Victoria, BC. Props: The Command Post of Militaria, Victoria, BC.
This book is set in Cheltenham BT.

TouchWood Editions acknowledges the financial support for its publishing program from The Canada Council for the Arts, the Government of Canada through
the Book Publishing Industry Development Program (BPIDP) and the Province
of British Columbia through the British Columbia Arts Council.

Printed and bound in Canada by Friesens, Altona, Manitoba.

National Library of Canada Cataloguing in Publication Data

Gallaher, Bill
    A man called Moses : the curious life of Wellington Delaney Moses /
Bill Gallaher.

    Includes bibliographical references.
    ISBN 1-894898-04-4

1. Moses, Wellington Delaney — Fiction. 2. Barkerville (B.C.) — Fiction.
3. Black Canadians — British Columbia — Fiction.* 4. African Americans
— British Columbia — Fiction. 5. British Columbia — History — Fiction. I.
Title.
PS8563.A424M36 2003   C813'.6   C2003-910623-3
PR9199.4.G34M36 2003

BRITISH
COLUMBIA
ARTS COUNCIL
We acknowledge the support of the Province of British Columbia
through the British Columbia Arts Council

The Canada Council | Le Conseil des Arts
for the Arts | du Canada

DEDICATION

For Sandi, Kayla and Cameron

ACKNOWLEDGMENTS

Sincere thanks are again due to my wife, Jaye, and to Marlyn Horsdal for her keen editorial eye. Thank you also to John Adams of the Old Cemeteries Society of Victoria for information regarding Ross Bay Cemetery; and a special thanks to the good folks at TouchWood Editions and Heritage House. It is my great fortune to be affiliated with them.

CONTENTS

Prologue 1
Part One 3
   Chapter One 4
   Chapter Two 15
Part Two 23
   Chapter Three 24
   Chapter Four 38
   Chapter Five 50
Part Three 67
   Chapter Six 68
   Chapter Seven 84
   Chapter Eight 96
   Chapter Nine 106
   Chapter Ten 118
Part Four 135
   Chapter Eleven 136
   Chapter Twelve 151
   Chapter Thirteen 161
   Chapter Fourteen 176
   Chapter Fifteen 190
   Chapter Sixteen 203
   Chapter Seventeen 210
Epilogue 223

Endnotes 225
Bibliography 229

Think where man's glory most begins and ends,
And say my glory was I had such friends.
— W. B. Yeats

PROLOGUE

Moses stood at the graveside, just as he had done every year at this time. A light rain had begun to fall; he could hear it splattering off the leaves in the thick foliage overhead. It would be a while yet before it penetrated.

Even at midday the forest was gloomy, a netherworld always on the verge of night. The air was dank and heavy and as still as death. Moses shivered. Death permeated this place, for not only was a man buried here, he had died here as well, violently, at the hands of a cold-blooded killer. Somehow the landscape had memorized it, soaked it up like a sponge so that it had become as much a part of it as the trees and underbrush. Moses could feel its presence. Every time he came here, he felt it. He could not put his finger on it, could not describe it, but it was as if the world had gone slightly out of kilter. He found it unsettling. And though he never knew the details of his friend's death, at a time like this he could easily imagine them.

The sound of the gunshot rolled like thunder among the hills. It surprised the killer but it did not worry him. Others might have heard it, but so what? They would think that it was just someone hunting breakfast. He nudged the body of the man slumped over in front of him, and it was a dead weight. There was no sign of breathing but then there shouldn't be. He'd come up quickly behind his victim and made a clean shot, placing the muzzle of the pistol about two inches from the back of his head before pulling the trigger. Not a second was wasted, smooth and efficient. He had said he was just going into the woods for a piss, so the man hadn't suspected a thing. One minute he was alive, enjoying his first cup of boiled tea and pipe for the day and the next he was as dead as a two-penny nail. There was a part of the killer that was fascinated by this concept. What was it like to not have even the slightest inkling you were about to die, not even a fragment of a second's knowledge? One instant you were alive, your brain full of thoughts, the next you were dead with a brain full of lead. It was interesting, no doubt about that.

He pulled the body over on its back and took a billfold from a breast pocket. Beautifully crafted from leather and embossed with the initials C.M.B., it looked very expensive. Inside, he found $60, which was not nearly as much as he had expected, but better than nothing. He took the money out and threw the billfold into the bush, then took the object that had really caught his eye — a stickpin with a small nugget of gold mounted on it that looked like an angel. He put it in his pocket, grabbed the ankles of the dead man and dragged him away from the campsite, into the bush behind a hummock. After scuffing up the ground with his boot to hide the blood, and obliterating the track made by the body, he struck his tent and stowed his gear in his pack. He doused the fire and, with one last look around to make sure he had left no clues, shouldered his pack and set out on the road to Barkerville, whistling a happy tune. He was $60 richer and that stickpin would no doubt come in handy.

Yes. It must have gone something like that, Moses thought. He had known the killer and it was just the kind of thing the man was capable of doing. But the part that Moses liked best about his flight of imagination was the stickpin. It *had* come in handy. Very handy indeed.

∽ Part One ∾

CHAPTER ONE

Slavery was everything that was wrong with the world, an ugly sore on the sweet face of humanity. It was preposterous that one man could own another and think that it was his God-given right. Yet, Wellington Delaney Moses was once a slave; was once merchandise, just like a piece of furniture to sit on or a plow to turn a field for planting. Like those inanimate objects, his lineage was traceable only back to a sales receipt once kept in a master's drawer. The thought of it sometimes filled him with rage.

He had been born in 1816, to a family also born into slavery, who had known nothing else. Their master was an Englishman named William Eden, whose ownership of 23 slaves attested to his wealth and power. He grew cotton and plantains on a small plantation called Savannah, on Grand Cayman Island's south shore. Down on the beach there were fenced-in areas, or "crawls," in which he captured and kept the odd green turtle. Overfishing during the previous century had nearly depleted the species in the area, but he was able to catch a few that were sold for a lucrative price to ships returning to Europe. Since it was possible to keep the turtles alive for weeks simply by turning them on their backs, they always arrived at their destination fresh. Eden also caught hawks-bill turtles, a species highly valued for their shells.

Like many slave owners in the Caribbean, Eden was a descendant of loyalists who, in the decade following the American Revolution, were slowly driven from their plantations in the southern states. As a reward for their loyalty, the British government gave them large tracts of land in the Bahamas, and even sent ships to transport them. Most took everything they owned, including their slaves, and some even dismantled their manor houses, brick by brick, and took them as well. Eden's father left too late to get land on the Bahamas and ended up on Grand Cayman. Since he had lived near Savannah, Georgia, he named his new plantation after the town.

Eden was a patriarchal figure and was sometimes indulgent with his slaves. Moses, for instance, often played with the Eden children in the master's house. Eden even went so far as to have the teacher, whom he had brought out from England to tutor his children, also instruct his slaves in the fundamentals of reading, writing and arithmetic. He was convinced that English was the language of the future and he urged them to learn it well. They would need it, because he could see that slavery was an anachronism and in its death throes. Britain had already abolished the slave trade in 1807, and there were rumblings that she would eventually end slavery in all her colonies. Meanwhile, Eden oversaw his plantation from one of the finest stone houses on Grand Cayman, which Moses' ancestors had helped build for his father in 1780. The slaves, as they always had, continued to live in single-room, thatched-roof dwellings, regardless of the size of their families.

In time, the stone house would become known as Pedro St. James Castle, and for Moses, his parents, and all the other slaves, it would come to symbolize both their captivity and their freedom. It was there, in 1831, that democracy first came to the island, and where the Slavery Abolition Act was read four years later. Moses had just turned 19 years old and he wept tears of joy. For his parents it was a day of excitement and dismay as they faced an uncertain future shaped by their own decisions.

Though Eden had offered his father work, Moses and his older brothers begged him to turn it down. True freedom, they believed, could only come from severing all ties with the plantation. Eden may have been benevolent, but he had still been a slave owner, and to Moses that was unconscionable. He was angry enough to feel that some kind of retribution was necessary, and might have sought it had his father not cooled his temper. Revenge was for the petty-minded, his father had said. So they quietly packed up their few possessions and moved as far away from the plantation as the small island would allow, up to the north end of West Bay. What the landscape there lacked in character it made up for in colour. Green and blue parrots flitted among tracts of mahogany and pine trees, and purple bougainvillea, blue hydrangea and red and white oleander grew to astonishing heights. Blue iguanas sun-bathed on black rocks, and green palms bent over beaches of sugar-like sand washed by emerald water. Not far away there was a strange coral formation that looked like Dante's Inferno. Everyone called it Hell.

Moses and his family set to work building a small mahogany-frame house, more than twice the size of their quarters at Savannah, with plastered walls and a palm-thatch roof. It sat among oleander bushes as high as the ridge of the roof, and the family lived well there, fishing and growing yams and manioc. They also raised agoutis, a rabbit-sized rodent, for meat, and there were plenty of breadfruit and mango trees about. The family logged and sold some of the mahogany trees to shipbuilders in Georgetown, and supplemented their income by salvaging wrecks. The Caymans lay right on established sailing routes and countless vessels foundered on the treacherous reefs, some with a little help from native "wreckers" who lured them in.[1] The ships provided much bounty for those who were swift and daring.

In 1838, within the span of a month, two hurricanes struck the islands. While the first caused considerable damage, the second one was much worse. It attacked the islands like a crazed beast, destroying a hundred homes on Grand Cayman alone, knocking many of them flat, smashing the walls of others and sending their roofs flying. Most of the turtling fleet in Georgetown harbour was wiped out, thrown up on shore like driftwood, and the docks were smashed into kindling. Buildings along the harbour front were torn apart as if they were paperboard. When the storm subsided, and Moses and his family came out of their hiding place, all that remained of their house was the mahogany frame. Without a word of complaint, his father began clearing up the mess that had once been their house and spoke only of how they would rebuild it, stronger and better.

Hurricanes were regular visitors to Grand Cayman and contributed to the island's schizophrenic nature. On the one hand, it was a tropical paradise; on the other, a place of appalling violence. Nevertheless, the islanders had learned how to survive them, although the recovery process was always difficult and expensive. Every time one hit, Moses swore that it would be his last, that he would move somewhere far beyond their reach.

It was not only the hurricanes that made him think about leaving. For a long time Moses had considered doing something different with his life, something that would be more satisfying than living on a small island that both confined and bored him. In Georgetown, he learned of a British merchant ship returning to England and found passage on it as a mess boy. His family was at odds with his decision and tried to dissuade him, but Moses was resolute. When the ship sailed from Georgetown harbour during the summer of 1843, he felt unfettered at last.

They steered a course northeast for the Gulf Stream, and let the westerlies blow them across an empty, benign ocean toward Europe. Five days out of England, Moses had his first taste of heavy weather at sea. For a while, the ship made headway under reefed sails while the cold, grey waters of the North Atlantic cascaded across her deck. Beyond the immensity of the waves, the thing that frightened Moses most was the noise of wind and water: it was unceasing and almost deafening. And just when Moses thought things could not get any worse, they did. The wind shrieked louder than a man could scream and the sea went mad. The ship plunged into deep troughs, her timbers groaning like an injured animal as she bottomed out and climbed up the far side. Moses wondered how any object made from mere human toil could withstand such punishment. At dawn on the second day of the storm, a monstrous wave, much bigger than all the rest, appeared astern, as if the sea was not satisfied with the job that it was doing to destroy them. The curling wave crashed on top of them with the sound of a hundred cannons booming simultaneously. The ship seemed to be completely under water and the mizzenmast snapped off at the first step. A tangle of ropes, canvas and wood crashed onto the quarterdeck, nearly wiping out the helmsman.

Moses was below decks, heard the booming wave and felt the ship shudder and wallow. For a moment, time seemed to stop and he was certain that the end had finally come. Fear congealed his blood and he could not move. This was nothing like the hurricanes on Grand Cayman, where he at least had a place to hide. The second mate, on his way topside, saw the terror in Moses' eyes and grabbed his shoulders with calloused hands. He leaned close enough that Moses could smell his foul breath.

"You've a right to be scared, lad," he shouted, "but the sea's no place to let it get the best of you. You need to keep your wits about you out here. Now follow me!"

The mate spun away and Moses had to use every ounce of his will to follow. The deck was a cold, watery hell. He crawled onto the quarterdeck and joined the crew cleaning up the jumble of wood, rope and canvas while the ship punched her way northward on the still-mountainous waves. The work took his mind off the maelstrom around him and helped to calm him down. Once everything was secure, he returned to the main deck and the jackline, a rope that ran between the quarterdeck and the forecastle. He wrapped his arms around it and stayed there until he had full control of himself; until he had accepted that his death, whether it came now or later, was a part of the natural order of the world and that in nearly all instances he would have no say in the matter. Then he went below and tried to stop himself from shaking from the cold.

After the rogue wave, the storm seemed to give up trying to annihilate them. The sea subsided and a welcome sun broke through the overcast. The weather steadily improved over the next couple of days and gulls visited the ship. Soon, England was a dark smudge off the starboard bow, and when the lookout shouted, "Land ho!" the excitement among the crew was palpable. Having weathered a ferocious storm with these men who spent their lives at sea, Moses felt a modest kinship with them and there was no small degree of pride in it. The ship limped into Portsmouth harbour on a glorious summer day with at least one of the crew wiser than when he had first come aboard.

Before they left Georgetown, the captain had told him that if he worked hard there might be a job for him as a manservant with a well-connected family in London. He did not like the thought of being a servant, but it was a salaried position and, like his job as mess boy, a means to an end: he reasoned that the experience of going to England and the opportunity to learn English in its native home, would make it all worthwhile. So he never let the captain's eye catch him being idle, even for a moment, and found himself employed by the Cracroft family as a result. Mrs. Cracroft was the sister of the explorer John Franklin, whose expeditions to the Arctic were one of the leading topics of conversation among the privileged classes. He lived below stairs with a small staff that catered efficiently to the Cracrofts' comfort and they, in turn, treated the staff with respect. Moses laboured tirelessly to improve his English, until his accent was that of the Cracrofts' with just a thin Caribbean edge.

The verdant English countryside impressed him, as did its rich, fertile soil. His first view of London amazed him, the endless rows of buildings of brick and mortar, wood and plaster and stone; the sheer size of the place and the teeming crowds of people, nearly all of them white. He had never felt so black in all his life and the stares he received ranged from the mildly curious to the sneeringly malevolent. There was a bookseller within walking distance of the house and he frequented the shop often, purchasing periodicals containing the works of Dickens, Thackeray and other authors, which he read voraciously. Despite such amenities, he soon found

London a dreary place, grimy, cold and damp; there was often an unhealthy stink in the air and he felt fatigued and irritable much of the time. Mrs. Cracroft sensed his mood and told him that if he wished, she could probably get him a berth as mess boy on her brother's next expedition to the Arctic. Moses gave it considerable thought and almost accepted the offer, but in the end he declined, because he could not imagine living in a world of perpetual ice and snow, never mind the long, dark days. It was not the sort of adventure he was looking for. Instead, he quit England and in 1846 worked his way back to Georgetown. He heard later that Franklin never returned from the Arctic.

It felt good to be back in the sun again, good to be amongst his family. Moses regaled his parents and brothers with stories of London, of serving aristocrats, and how they could be as dim-witted as anybody else. He slipped easily back into the routine of island life, which did not take long to start wearing thin again. Then another hurricane struck.

The Moses family home survived, but many others did not, nor did any of the ships in Georgetown harbour. Even worse, the lower parts of the island were flooded with seawater that contaminated most of the wells. During the ensuing dry season, Moses and his family had to canoe 14 miles to the well in Bodden Town for fresh water, and it was nearly a year before their own well was fit to use again. Every time he made that trip, he cursed the island and wished he were somewhere else. He grew moody, bickered often with his brothers and argued with his father, something that would have been unthinkable before. He hated how his father still saw William Eden as a benefactor.

"He was a slave owner, Father," Moses said. "A man can't be both." He knew that his father always tried to make the best out of any bad situation, and he loved him dearly for it but on this subject, he would give him no latitude.

"But he fed us well and didn't overwork us, and you and your brothers have a good education because of his thoughtfulness and generosity."

Moses sneered. "The fact that we are considered an inferior race is due solely to his owning us."

His father was indignant. "It's more the other way around. Either way, I don't happen to feel inferior."

"You don't feel inferior because men like Eden have lodged it so firmly in your mind that you're completely unaware of it. You believe what he taught you, that it has always been a black man's lot to serve a white master."

"Say what you will, he prepared us well for emancipation."

"But we were not freed until the proclamation was read, which tells me that he wouldn't have done it unless he had to. Nor would we have been freed if Eden had been able to get to Jamaica and register us as apprentices." Moses was referring to a law that allowed owners in British colonies to keep their slaves for five to seven years after emancipation. All that was required was the owner's presence in Jamaica, prior to the proclamation, to register his slaves as "apprentices." Those who could not make it, and thus lost their slaves, petitioned the British government for compensation. Eden was not one of these, but Moses did not know that, and went on, adding, "I think he prepared us *not* to seek revenge once we had achieved freedom. He was protecting his own interests. Nothing more."

The argument continued and resolved nothing, ending only with both father and son feeling utterly frustrated. Afterward, Moses felt guilty, for he had not meant to be so disrespectful.

Moses' frustration ate away at him. One night he went into Georgetown, which was little more than a collection of shops, warehouses and bars that catered mostly to fishermen and sailors, intending to get drunk. He ended up at a bar near the wharves that had a reputation for roughness. A British sailor insulted him, which proved to be a serious mistake on the sailor's part. Moses flew into a rage and the next thing he knew, others were pulling him off the man, who lay unconscious and bleeding on the floor. When Moses sobered up, he could recall everything prior to the fight and everything after, but of the fight itself, he remembered nothing. It horrified him that he had nearly taken a man's life without even being aware of it.

Months passed, like stones grating against each other. One morning, just as Moses had awakened, he heard his father get up and go out to the pit that the family used as a latrine. Moses also had to go and waited impatiently for his turn, listening to the parrots squawk and flap among the trees. When his father did not return within a few minutes, he went out to see what was taking so long. Moses found him curled up on the pathway, dead, his face purple, clutching his chest as if he were cold. He had always looked so youthful and strong that it seemed as if he would live forever, and Moses could not believe that the lifeless form on the ground was his father. He shook his shoulder as if trying to awaken him. His mother and brothers came out and found him there, tears streaming down his face, trying to rouse his father back to life.

Moses was devastated. He began to think about his own mortality, something that he had not given much thought to since his voyage to England. What had he accomplished so far in his life? Apart from going to England, he could not name a single thing of significance. He was 34 years old, a bachelor, did not even have a lover — available women were scarce on Grand Cayman — and his prospects were practically nil. His life was as stagnant as the swamps in the interior of the island. When his mother died within a year after his father, Moses knew what he had to do. He feared that he would be found one day, dead on the same path to the same latrine as his father, with nothing at all to show for his life. Consequently, he found himself in Georgetown more and more often, gathering information on far-off places from the crews of ships anchored in the harbour.

News of a major gold strike in California had been on everyone's lips in Georgetown harbour for some time. Apparently, miners were making great fortunes with the turn of a shovel, and Moses had learned at an early age how to work one of those. An added incentive was the climate, which was said to be second to none. It was a gamble, no question about that, but California looked as good a place as any for a man to make a new start. Moses began preparing for his departure.

"Why do you want to break up the family any more than it already is?" his eldest brother, Kensington, demanded to know. He had become the patriarch since their father died and now that the family unit was smaller, it was important to him that they stick together. "And why would you even consider going to a country whose people enslaved our family in the first place? One that is still a land of white masters and black slaves."

"But I'm not going to where the slavery is. I'm going to the opposite side of the continent, where coloured people are as free as you and I. Perhaps even more so, because they're not imprisoned by water. I can't go to the beach these days without feeling the limitations this island imposes on me. Good Lord, you can walk the length of it in a day and stop for lunch along the way! But it's not only that. I don't want to be around here when the next hurricane comes along to blow us all away."

"But the uncertainties, Wellington. How can you leave here for little more than uncertainties?"

"It's the uncertainties that make it worthwhile. Besides the sea, it's the *certainties* of this island that imprison me. I'm bored, Kensington, and I've been bored since I got back from England. I need to do something else; go somewhere else. What's more, I'm a free man and I can come and go as I please, so don't make me beg for your approval. I'll go with it or without it."

He immediately regretted the ultimatum, but did not retract it.

"If you go, it'll be without it," Kensington said.

Afterwards, Kensington spoke to him only when it was required. On the day Moses left, his younger brother, Lancaster, hugged him, but Kensington had found something to do that took him away from the house. Moses was hurt, and he would never think of that moment without wishing that he and his brother had been less stubborn and uncompromising.

Despite the bad feelings surrounding Moses' departure, he stepped out briskly, down the Georgetown road. He carried a knapsack over his shoulder, stuffed with a change of clothes and some toilet articles. Tied on top was a blanket. His life savings were safely tucked away in a hand-made money belt around his waist. Each step that brought him closer to Georgetown was lighter than the last. In his mind, he had thrown open a cell door and was walking out a free man. He reached town so lost in thought that he was hardly aware of the seven miles he had just walked.

Fishing schooners and ketches lay at anchor in the harbour while some were tied up alongside the docks. As the turtle-fishing season was just about to get under way, Moses looked for a turtler bound for the Nicaraguan coast where he hoped to find passage on a ship to Panama. He would then cross the isthmus by foot and take another ship to San Francisco. When he asked around, several people warned him not to take that route. Panama was rife with cholera, and he would be far safer on the alternative route through southern Nicaragua. Greytown was the place he needed to go, but the closest a turtler could get him was Bragman's Bluff, about 200 miles north.[2] The captain who agreed to take him maintained that packets ran up and down the coast and that he should not have any trouble getting to Greytown. That was enough assurance for Moses. In the morning, when he sailed, he thought it an interesting irony that the Eden family owned the vessel on which he had bought passage.

CHAPTER TWO

They had set sail on the remnants of a night breeze, as a slender streak of dawn expanded upward from the rim of the sea. The turtler was a sturdy craft, schooner-rigged and built in Georgetown from the finest Cayman mahogany. She craved the wind and when it rose with the sun, she embraced it like a long-lost lover.

Moses was not the least bit surprised to see how quickly the island disappeared behind them. Its highest point was 140 feet above sea level; one moment it was there, the next it had dropped below the line of sea and sky, "sunk out" as one of the crew said. Ahead lay Nicaragua, less than 400 miles to the southwest and, if the winds held, as they usually did this time of year, they would be there in less than three days.

The schooner sliced through acres of sargassum weed that looked like clotted blood in water that was the deep blue of the night sky at sunset. Like some of the other half-dozen crew members, when they were not on watch, Moses spent most of the time trying to avoid the searing sun that felt hot enough to boil the sea. Once, he threw one of the ship's trolling lines over the stern, after baiting the hooks with small pieces of canvas smothered in animal grease, and caught a small tuna. The steel-blue fish shot from the sea like a bullet, shaking madly to lose the hook lodged deep in its mouth, the water droplets that exploded around it sparkling in the sunlight like splintered glass. He hauled it in without ceremony and one of the crew swiftly gutted it and cut big steaks off for dinner. The rest was cut into smaller strips that were dried on the cabin roof in the hot sun.

During the evenings Moses helped mend nets, and talk among the crew always seemed to end up on turtles: how many so-and-so's vessel brought back last season, and how many could be expected this season. The catch per boat was usually about 125 per season and with two seasons a year and 20 schooners fishing, that meant about 5,000 animals were taken back to Grand Cayman, where they crawled until they could be shipped overseas. It also meant about $1,500 income per boat, most of which went to the owner, who in this case was William Eden. It was always a dangerous job, because the Mosquito Banks, where the best turtling was, were treacherous, and one never knew what kind of weather would turn up during the long hauls between the island and the Nicaraguan mainland.

When the crew called it a day and went below, Moses usually sat for a while with the helmsman before turning in himself. It was not so much the conversation he enjoyed as it was just watching the widening wedge of the phosphorescent wake spread out behind them. Every mile of water that the bow pushed aside was spewed out in that wake, offering a visible sign of their forward progress away from Grand Cayman. It made him feel something he had not felt for a long time: free.

He could scarcely believe where he was. Above him, stars fell with startling regularity, and the night was warm enough that when he finally went to bed — a pallet on the forward deck — he did not need his blanket. The thought of tomorrow and the others following it flooded his chest with excitement, but eventually the boat's smooth motion, as it rose and fell on the restless sea, and the sound of the water hissing past her sleek hull, lulled him to sleep.

On the morning of the third day, they were off the Mosquito Banks, having stayed well out to sea to avoid the reefs that only a fool would try to navigate at night. The helmsman swung the bow due west for the coast. The dark blue water turned light blue and they smelled the land, the mustiness of decaying vegetation, long before they saw it. Then a dark, uneven band that was visible on the horizon eventually became Nicaragua. A mile from shore the blue water turned green and the shore became a low sandstone bluff that acted as a seawall protecting the town behind it. Moses watched as a frigate bird, with a wingspan of at least seven feet, attacked a booby in midair, dislodging a fish from the smaller bird's mouth, then swooping down to catch the morsel before it hit the water. He felt sorry for the booby but it was the way of the world, the big and strong taking advantage of the small and weak. There never would have been slavery, otherwise. The turtler eased alongside the pier at Bragman's Bluff, one of a few sleazy, steaming port towns dotting the Mosquito Coast.

Much of the town consisted of small, thatched-roof dwellings built on stilts because of the constant flooding in the area and the snakes. Near the pier, a few businesses surrounded a small marketplace. All the buildings were beaten into submission by the heat and the humidity; livestock, mostly hogs, roamed freely through the town. Moses took a room in a run-down hotel with no more than a half-dozen rooms. Outside, black mildew crept up its once-white walls, and inside the air was hot and lifeless. His room was in the back and smelled of the garbage and waste thrown out behind the building. He slept on the floor with the cockroaches rather than in the flea-infested bed. During the sweltering days he waited, with more patience than he knew he had, for a southbound packet. Each afternoon iron-grey, rain-heavy clouds formed and pressed down on the town, then spilled their contents in a deluge that turned the streets into mud. By noon the following day they were baked hard as concrete again in the oppressive heat.

One evening, at a bar near the pier, he met Evaña, a young and beautiful *mestizo*.[1] Because England had controlled this coast for many years, and there were still a few Englishmen around, she knew a smattering of the language and offered herself to him for what he considered a mere pittance. They went back to his room in the rain and he was glad there were hardly any people in the streets, although he felt eyes peering at them through shuttered windows all the way. They made love among the fleas. She giggled at his inexperience, his fumbling, and when he was premature she was not surprised. But he paid her again and he was better, and it seemed to him a wonderful contradiction that he felt as if he'd lost his innocence and regained his youth at the same time.

He saw her for the next two nights and on the fourth night, he checked out of the hotel and moved into the one-room shanty in which she lived. Between long sessions of love-making he told her of his dreams, but she understood only his passion, for she did not know half the words he used. In the mornings, they went to the market and he would buy fresh fruits and vegetables to see them through the day. He did not feel ashamed to be with her any more, and was proud to have her take his arm.

It was a full week before a packet that was going in the right direction arrived. He had gone to the dock one afternoon on his own, just as the vessel arrived. The captain said it would depart the following morning and Moses made arrangements to be on it. Evaña was crestfallen when he returned with the news. That night, as they made love for the last time, her arms and legs were like vises, and if she could have held him captive there forever she would have shamelessly done so. When he kissed her goodbye in the morning he tried to press some money into her hand, but she would not take it. Because lying was easier than the awkwardness of truth, he told her, "When I make my fortune, I will come back for you."

She nodded and put her head on his chest. There were tears in her eyes because even though she hoped with her heart that what he said was true, she knew in her mind that she would probably die a prostitute in Bragman's Bluff.

Moses was nauseated during the trip south as the small steamer bobbed in the long swells that rolled over the banks toward the Mosquito Coast, the residue of a storm that had passed through the central Caribbean. It rained most of the way, so the coastline was hardly visible. They stopped at three port towns, which looked exactly like Bragman's Bluff, to load and offload freight and passengers. They stayed overnight in these ports as the reef-dotted banks were no place for a ship after dark. Four days later the vessel dropped its chain in Greytown harbour, among other ships, and a lighter came alongside to transport the passengers and cargo to shore.

The village had the appearance of something hastily thrown together, as much of it had been, in order to accommodate miners travelling to and from the goldfields. The stable population of about 500 was largely Indian, but there were also many black Americans, ex-slaves and freemen, who ran most of the town's businesses including five of its eight hotels. The streets were crowded with travellers, many of them Americans who had sailed out of New Orleans and New York and, like Moses, had come this way because of the cholera epidemic in Panama. Others were going home. They had had enough of the hardscrabble life on the creeks of California and left while they were still able to afford it. A few even had small pokes of gold dust, but they were a distinct minority. The news they brought was not entirely dismal. Though gold was becoming more difficult to find, California was growing and a man with an eye for business could still make plenty of money. That was enough good news for Moses to keep his spirits up, but he still intended to try the goldfields.

He found that many of his fellow travellers were from the northern States and were tolerant of his skin colour; some were even cordial to him. Others were openly disdainful and he presumed they were from the slave states. He reckoned that they would much rather see him picking cotton on some sprawling plantation than as a free man who shared the same lofty ambitions as they. He bought a backpack from a miner returning from the goldfields and enough hardtack and tea to last him on the trail, then took a room for the night in one of Greytown's flea-ridden hotels.

In the dining room, he stood in a short line to purchase a ticket for supper. Prepaying for meals was common practice and he presumed it was because the food was so revolting that most people would refuse to pay for it afterward. He had scarcely enough time to take his first mouthful when he was interrupted by the landlord ousting a young black man for sitting at a table reserved for whites. Such an incident would not have surprised Moses had the proprietor been white, but he was black himself. Moses was appalled, as were the whites at the table who were apparently friends of the young man. They left with him. So did Moses, following them to a hotel owned by a white man who was not concerned with segregating his customers. The meals there were even less appetizing than those served at the black's hotel, but Moses felt good about sticking to his principles, which more than made up for it. After dinner, instead of paying for another room, he went to the edge of town, slung a hammock between two trees, and slept the sleep of the just.

In the morning, he was able to team up with some friendly Yankees and together they hired a *panga*, the local term for a dugout canoe. It was about 30 feet long with a thatched shelter arching between its gunwales to protect passengers from the elements. Their route was up the San Jaun River, part of the proposed route for the Nicaraguan Canal, which would ultimately link the Caribbean Sea with the Pacific Ocean.[2] They spent eight days working their way against the current, until the river was no longer navigable, then took to a rough, slippery trail that turned and twisted uphill for most of the way. It poured rain at some point every day, usually in the late afternoons, but the jungle canopy was effective at dispersing the water so that it was not drenching on the men below. Moses worried about stepping on one of the many poisonous snakes of Nicaragua, but never saw anything more dangerous than the men he was with. They walked for two and a half days and came to the village of San Carlos on the south shore of Lake Nicaragua. There they waited three days for a sternwheeler that would take them north to Granada. When it finally arrived, it was so decrepit-looking that Moses feared it might founder at the dock.

The 80-mile trip up the lake was worse than the trip down the coast, since the waves never seemed to know which way to go and the vessel was tossed about like a toy boat on a windswept pond. Unable to find an inch of space anywhere on the deck, Moses and his companions slept on the cabin roof. Rumours flew throughout the journey that there were 10-foot freshwater sharks in the lake, and sawfish as big as pangas.[3] Fortunately, the vessel did not stray far from shore, just in case there were problems, but the rumours only compounded everyone's anxiety. Many disagreeable things could happen to a man during a swim to shore, even though it was only a short distance. It was not until Granada loomed on the horizon that the men felt reasonably safe.

Moses thought the Spanish colonial city was quite lovely, but he did not see as much of it as he would have liked. Early the following morning they climbed into oxcarts and rode north to El Realejo, a seedy town enhanced by the ruins of an ancient Indian city. There they rented beds at the Hotel American, which was nothing more than a barren room slung with 40 to 50 hammocks that was a breeding ground for mosquitoes. The travellers were all but eaten alive. In order to get dinner they had to buy tickets from the owner, and soon discovered why the meal was pre-sold; the food was so appalling that most were wishing they had eaten the tickets instead. They left the next morning, glad to be on their way, and walked down a well-used jungle trail to a small river where they hired another panga to take them to the Pacific coast.

A steamer out of Panama, bound for San Francisco, picked them up. As there was no dock, the ship stood idle in the offing while a jolly boat came in to shore for the passengers. Even so, rocks prevented the small vessel from coming all the way in and some of the men were carried out to it on the backs of natives. Moses chose to wade out on his own.

Normally, such ships were packed to overflowing, but because of the epidemic in Panama there was saleable space left.

Moses was relegated to a small area below decks with several other blacks, most of whom resented having to make room for one more body. The accommodations were stiflingly hot, the most deplorable Moses had ever experienced, even as a mess boy on his trips to and from England. He imagined that this was how the old slave ships used to be, only with shackles. He spent as much time topside as he could, but the sun was fearsomely hot even with the breeze that streamed along the deck. The farther north they sailed, the more tolerable it became until at last the ship turned through the Golden Gate, chased into San Francisco Bay by a cooling, late afternoon fog. Past Alcatraz Island, they came upon an astonishing sight: scores of abandoned ships crammed in the harbour, deserted by crews gone looking for gold. Beyond the forest of masts was the city itself, the flanks of its many hills strewn with multi-storeyed buildings, both brick and wood. In the grey light of the dank sea fog, it seemed to Moses the most dismal place he had ever seen.

∽ Part Two ∽

CHAPTER THREE

"**O**ver here, boy, and take these bags!"

The speaker was a portly, well-dressed man in his fifties and he was directing his order at Moses, whom he presumed to be a porter.

"Take them yourself, sir," Moses replied. "The exercise will do you wonders."

It was not exactly an auspicious welcome to California, but at least none of the whites seemed ready to clamp him in chains and auction him off, as Kensington had suggested. Generally, everyone was going about their business and paid little attention to him. He worked his way through the crowds along the wharf, which jutted out more than a half-mile into the bay. The harbour front consisted mostly of slop shops outside which hung colourful, ready-to-wear clothes that were sold cheaply to sailors and new arrivals alike. It looked as if all the townspeople had washed their clothes at the same time and hung them out to dry. Beyond the shops, Moses entered the city proper and went looking for a place to stay.

Montgomery Street, the city's main thoroughfare to all appearances, was lined mostly with banks on one side, and many of these buildings looked brand new. The boardwalks were crowded with miners and would-be miners, many long-haired and bearded, wearing scruffy clothes with floppy hats and jackboots. Everyone seemed to be in a colossal hurry. In the windows of the few hotels and stores he passed were crudely penned signs that read "Coloureds not welcome" and "No Negroes." On a corner of Commercial Street, Rowe's Olympic Circus housed an entertainment troupe, and the painted pictures of the minstrels out front were obviously of whites in black face. He threaded his way up Commercial, raucous with music since every building was either a gambling hall or a saloon, then along Kearny until he reached an area where Orientals and blacks seemed to predominate. There, he found a room with board for $12 a week in a modest hotel owned by blacks. No one seemed the least bit curious about his accent; he supposed it was because the city was full of men with even stranger accents. The desk clerk said only that if Moses valued his life, he should not walk the streets alone after dark.

Still determined to try his luck on the creeks, Moses set out the following morning to outfit himself. The fog was just beginning to burn off under the heat of the California sun and the streets were already busy with pedestrians and wagons of all kinds. The first item on his list was a good pair of boots and, after asking around, he was directed to the Boot Emporium on Clay Street, owned by two of San Francisco's most successful black businessmen, Mifflin Gibbs and Peter Lester. They had the best selection and he would, without a doubt, find something there.

A bell tinkled as he entered the store, and he was delighted by the array of boots and shoes that were on display. He was greeted by a man about 30 years old, of medium height, with ramrod straight posture and a determined look in his eyes that had little to do with selling boots.

"Good morning, sir. I'm Mr. Gibbs. May I be of assistance?"

Moses told him what he wanted and while Gibbs went off to bring a selection of boots for him to try on, he sat down and breathed in the wonderful aroma of new leather and polished wood floors. The doorbell tinkled again as another customer entered, this time a white man. A large black man, whom Moses assumed was Lester, came out of a back room and greeted the customer cordially. The man said that he had had an eye on a pair of boots in the window and asked if Lester would hold them while he went to the bank for money. Lester assured him that he would and the man left, saying he would be back soon. Just then, Gibbs came out of the back room with an armful of boots.

A few moments later the doorbell tinkled again and another white man entered. He said he was a friend of the first man and had been instructed by him to purchase the boots that Lester had been asked to put aside. Lester politely said that he felt he should only sell them directly to the person who ordered them. The man assured him that all was aboveboard and that his friend would appreciate Lester's co-operation in the matter. Reluctantly, the proprietor sold the boots to him and the man left. Moses was just trying on the last pair of boots when the doorbell sounded once more. This time it was both men. The first man waved a cane in Lester's face and demanded to know why he had sold the boots to the other man.

Lester was perplexed. "But your friend here said that you had instructed him to obtain the boots for you, sir!" Just as it dawned on him that he was the victim of a cruel trick, Lester was struck with the cane. He stumbled back trying to avoid more blows, tripped, and crashed to the floor, knocking over a small display of boots. Both Gibbs and Moses rose to their feet to assist Lester, but the second man pulled out a gun.

"Another step and you'll be dead!"

While Gibbs and Moses were held at gunpoint, the first man beat Lester until he was bloody. Moses watched, barely in control of himself, a sick feeling in his stomach, but he could not tear his eyes away. All Lester could do was put up his arms to try and ward off the blows from his head because he knew that if he fought back his death was certain to follow. He moaned and writhed on the floor but would not beg his persecutor to stop. When the beating finally ceased, the man stood over him, panting, his face glistening with sweat. "Let this be a lesson to you," he said. "You might be a free man here but you're still a nigger, and you're acting way above your station." Then he and his companion strode from the store, slamming the door so hard it rattled the window glass.

Moses and Gibbs ran to Lester. He was dazed; his face a mass of bleeding cuts and welts, his eyes welling with tears. They helped him to his feet and over to a chair. Gibbs locked the front door, then went to the back room and returned with some alcohol, iodine and swabs. He cleaned the cuts out as best he could with the alcohol and swabbed them with iodine. Lester moaned from the pain of the treatment and the iodine's wicked sting. He told Gibbs and Moses that he did not think anything was broken.

"Surely this is a matter for the police," Moses said, surprised at how calm he sounded, when what he really wanted to do was chase the men down and hurt them as badly as they had hurt Lester.

"Perhaps in your country," said Gibbs, "but not here. This incident is of no interest whatsoever to the sheriff or to the vigilantes. They can't keep up with the white men who are beaten, robbed or even murdered, never mind trying to make time for injustices to black men. At any rate, they would probably laugh in your face if they didn't beat you first for asking."

They moved to the back room, away from the windows of the shop, and Gibbs retrieved a flask of brandy from a desk; he found three shot glasses, and with a trembling hand poured drinks. He sighed. "The perfect medicine for all parties during times like these, the injured and uninjured." All three drinks were gone in single gulps.

Moses felt shaken. Never, in all his years as a slave on Grand Cayman, had he seen such a cold-blooded, brutal beating. He was both appalled and terrified that it could be carried out with impunity. He introduced himself and apologized for his naiveté, adding that such incidents were unheard of where he came from.

"You may find yourself wishing you had stayed at home, Mr. Moses. California is not a slave state, but insofar as the black man is concerned, it's not much better."

"But the fact that it's not a slave state and there is no ban against blacks seems to suggest that legislators here must at least have *some* abolitionist leanings," Moses responded.

"Ah, if that were only the case. But the reality of it is that blacks are not banned because many of the legislators *are* from the slave states. If they banned blacks then they, and others of their ilk, could not bring their slaves here to work for them. There must be 2,000 blacks here in San Francisco and up in the goldfields, and many of them are still slaves."

"But how is it possible to own slaves in a free state?"

"It's simple. The owners get around it by calling them indentured servants, or house servants, but they are slaves, no more, no less. Granted, some owners pay their slaves a small wage and if they can save up enough money they're allowed to buy their freedom. But such cases are few and far between."

Gibbs went on to explain that he himself had been born a free man in Philadelphia; nevertheless, he had been discriminated against at every turn in the road. He had travelled through New York State with Frederick Douglass and the two men spoke out against slavery, but the negative reaction they invariably received depressed him.[1] He had felt at loose ends until one day an abolitionist friend said to him "What! Discouraged? Go do some great thing." So he threw all caution to the wind and borrowed enough money to buy steerage-class tickets to Panama and on to San Francisco. Gold was what he sought, but it did not take him long to discover that gold mining was mostly a white man's enterprise. Oh, there were black diggings on the creeks all right, but most were in non-productive areas. The best claims belonged to the whites. He tried to get work as a carpenter here in the city, and did, but all the whites walked off the job. He then started his own business as a bootblack which, in a city with no short supply of mud, turned out to be a bonanza. In less than a year he had enough money to open a clothing store, which was even more lucrative, and a few months later he and Lester opened the Boot Emporium. "From nothing to this in a year and a half," he added. "Plus I've paid all my debts."

Gibbs poured another round of brandy and asked Lester how he was faring. Lester tried to smile but it was too painful. "I'm alive," he mumbled, "if one can call this living."

"Now take Mr. Lester here," said Gibbs. "He was a slave in Virginia until relatives in the north purchased his freedom. But at moments like this, one wonders about the authenticity of that freedom. We are only valued for the services we provide so, in one sense, we now have many masters instead of one. We cannot vote, nor can we testify in court, which, of course, means that even if they caught the men who assaulted Mr. Lester, we could not testify against them.[2] We can't even take advantage of the First Amendment of our constitution, which says that citizens have the right to petition the government for change. We are not citizens, nor are we entitled to citizenship. Yet they demand taxes from us as readily as they do from everyone else. The whites seem to have forgotten that they fought a revolution over taxation without representation. They are a strange breed, Mr. Moses. They harbour some strange notion that the colour of their skin somehow makes them superior, and I can't for the life of me understand why. So many things they do make it quite apparent that they are not. Was not the attack on Mr. Lester the work of savages?"

"Indeed it was," said Moses. "So why do you stay?"

"Because they want to drive us out so that they can have California to themselves. They don't deserve it any more or less than we do, so we're not leaving. At least not without a fight."

The conversation turned to Moses when Gibbs said that it sounded to him like a slave name.

"It was my grandfather's name, given to him by his master in Georgia, who liked to name his slaves after biblical characters. It was, of course, grandfather's first name, his last being 'Eden' after his owner. But when my father could see the end of slavery, he made Moses our last name and named my brothers and me after British dukes. He thought it would lend us an air of respectability."

Gibbs smiled. "So, in a way, you've returned to the land that enslaved your family."

"In a way. But I'm now a free man and intend to remain that way." He went on to tell Gibbs of his life as a slave on Grand

Cayman, dragging bags of cotton behind him, and how he wept for joy on the day his freedom came. He spoke of the dead end that he, like Gibbs, had been confronted with, and how he resolved to do something more with his life than spend it on a speck of coral in the Caribbean. He had come here for a change; and he had also come for gold.

"You'll find your gold, Mr. Moses, but my advice to you is to not waste your time looking for it in the goldfields. The gold rush for blacks is right here in San Francisco and I'll tell you how to go about acquiring your share. The one service in town for which there is a great demand is barbering. I have a friend who can teach you the tricks of the trade, how to wield a razor without cutting a man's throat, even though you might like to, and how to shampoo the tangles out of a white man's hair and massage his scalp so that he'll be back for more. It shouldn't take much to open a small shop, and I can help you find one. I guarantee that if you can learn to cope with the fear of living in this lawless place, your business will be expanding before you know it. In the meantime, you can join us in our fight if you like. You seem like a good man, and we can use all the good men we can get."

"I'll take you up on your first offer," said Moses. "As for the second, I would need time to get established before I could get involved, but get involved I will. You can count on it."

The two men shook hands firmly.

"Right. I'll set up a meeting and send a message to your hotel with the details."

"Thank you," Moses said. "I look forward to it." Before taking his leave, Moses asked Lester if he was feeling any better.

"The brandy seems to be working wonders," the big man winced. "Fortunately the supply is unlimited."

Out on the street the sun had burned the fog away and the city had come fully to life. Drays rattled by, loaded with all manner of goods, from produce to hardware, while some loads were sheeted over with canvas. One dray, hauling a large load of lumber, was pulled by four truly magnificent horses with silver-studded tackle. Moses had walked a block before he realized that he had not bought the boots he had set out for. It hardly mattered, though; he would not be needing them just yet. He felt tremendous excitement and was near to bursting with energy, due partly to the assault and partly to his good fortune in having gone to the Boot Emporium in the first place. He only wished that his good luck had not been tied so closely to Lester's bad. Nevertheless, he looked forward with great anticipation to his meeting with the barber. He was certain that he had enough money to open a shop and Gibbs' offer to help him find one was exceedingly generous.

Moses did not think for a moment that the businessman would renege on his offer, as there was nothing about him to suggest that he was the kind of man who would say one thing and do another. At any rate, thanks to Gibbs, Moses felt that he'd come to the right place, that he now stood on the threshold of something, if not great, at least challenging. He nodded at passers-by, white and black, whose eyes he happened to catch, but for the most part everyone ignored him, particularly the whites. He was bothered only a little by it. He had discovered at an early age that blacks often disappeared in the presence of white folks, and this was demeaning only some of the time. Most times it was for the better. Besides, he had resolved not to let such things wear him down, because it seemed to him that it was not so much his problem as it was theirs.

∽∾

Gibbs proved to be as good as his word. Three months later Moses was working full tilt in his own shaving saloon. He had more customers than he could handle, and if business remained as brisk, he was determined to open a bath house as well. So far he had been able to install a marble sink and buy a new, velvet-covered chair that had a screw-type adjustable headrest. It was said that he gave the best scalp massage in town, a claim that was fully supported by advertisements in the shop window. He lived as frugally as he could, and to that end had taken a small room in a boarding house run buy a sweet, matronly black lady named Mary Ellen Pleasant. In the meantime, he had become firm friends with Gibbs and Lester, and still thanked his lucky stars that he had been directed to them first off. Now, he supposed, they finally wanted to find out whether or not he was ready to get involved. A meeting of the antislavery coalition had been called by Gibbs and Lester, and Moses had been invited to attend.

Tobacco smoke hung as thick as fog from the ceiling of William Hall's billiard parlour on Clay Street. A sizeable crowd had assembled, all men, and all wore solemn faces. Lester had only just fully recovered from the assault and his face still bore several scars. So did his soul, for he had vengeance in his heart and wanted to find a way to punish the two men responsible, not to mention anyone else whose skin was white. Gibbs was concerned enough that he thought a meeting should be called before something happened that black men everywhere would regret.

Lester was the first to speak and he outlined his scheme for kidnapping his attackers, whose identities were known, executing them, and disposing of their bodies in some remote place where they would never be found.

"Do you think for one moment we would get away with that?" This was asked by Nathan Pointer, who had been Gibbs' partner in the clothing business. Moses had met him some time ago and found him to be an inscrutable man with a woeful lack of personal charm. "All we'd succeed in doing is bringing everything we've managed to build here tumbling down around our shoulders. I agree that the perpetrators should be punished but it must be done by lawful means. Otherwise we are no better than they are."

There was a mixture of derisive laughter along with murmurs of agreement. Moses reckoned that this was as good a time as any to let others know that he was here, and spoke out, "How would you propose doing that when we have no recourse to the law?"

"We take one step at a time. We start out by using the First Amendment to petition the government to repeal the law that says blacks cannot testify against whites. If we manage to get that one law changed, it will be a giant step forward for us."

There was even more laughter and Lester said, "Have you forgotten, Mr. Pointer, that only citizens can petition the government and that we have not been afforded that honour?"

"I'm well aware of that," Pointer answered. "But even though we are not citizens, it's important that we *act* like citizens. Just as we must act like free men even though we are really not."

The discussion went on for some time, back and forth, until it was decided that vigilantism was not the answer and that no matter how frustrating the process might be, they must work within the law. To that end they would write up a petition and have it signed by as many townspeople as possible and submit it to the government. If it was ignored, they would do it again and again, until the matter was dealt with in a way acceptable to all parties. Gibbs and a few others worked on the wording until it was done to their satisfaction. Then a vote was taken and a large majority approved it.

Later, Gibbs asked Moses to join him and Lester at the Emporium for a nightcap, and the three men walked the short distance to the store in silence. A cold, dense fog had rolled in from the sea and transformed itself into minute droplets of water on the men's coats. Inside the store, the smell of leather had become Moses' favourite. It was such a masculine smell, so opposite to the *eau de cologne* he used at his shaving saloon. Once drinks were poured, they saluted the evening's progress. Lester's hate and anger had not abated, but he grudgingly admitted that the right course of action had been taken.

"What are your thoughts, Moses?" Gibbs asked. Now that he and Moses were friends and there were no whites around, Gibbs relaxed his rule that all blacks address each other by the title "Mister," which he thought showed good breeding and was the first sign of being a gentleman. "Are you ready to get involved?"

"Well," said Moses, "My first thought is that I'm not sure I've ever appreciated my British citizenship so much as I have tonight. As for getting involved, I am ready indeed. What can I do to help?"

"We are grateful that you will help, but I warn you that your involvement may one day land you in jail and get you deported as well. There's even a chance that your rights will be ignored entirely and you'll be shipped to New Orleans and sold into slavery."

Moses was rocked by this last piece of information. He felt he could withstand a jail sentence, and if the worst thing that happened to him was that he had to spend the rest of his days beyond the boundaries of the United States, then so be it. But he would rather die than become a slave again. Clearing his throat, he looked Gibbs in the eye and said, "If the only kind of freedom available to a slave is death, then how can we rightfully enjoy ours?"

"I would like to show you something." Gibbs rose from his chair and picked up the oil lamp on the desk. "Come with me," he said, and went over to a wall against which were floor-to-ceiling shelves of stock for the store. He gave the lamp to Moses, reached in behind a pair of boots and, grasping something that Moses could not see, pulled on it. A section of shelves swung smoothly away from the wall. Behind it was a door. Taking a key from his vest pocket, Gibbs inserted it into the lock and turned it. There was a muffled click as the bolt slid back. He pushed the door, which moved silently on well-greased hinges. He then took the lamp from Moses and held it in the doorway. In the shadowy light a narrow room was revealed, containing two bunk beds and a small table upon which sat an unlit lamp. On the end wall was a door that appeared to lead into the alley. He looked at Moses. "Welcome to the San Francisco terminus of the California Underground Railroad."

Moses was astonished. He knew that both Gibbs and Lester were passionately committed to the antislavery movement; indeed, both invited slaves and servants into their homes and lectured them on their rights and taught them antislavery songs, but this took him completely by surprise. Anyone caught helping a fugitive slave was subject to a $1,000 fine and six months in jail, if he survived the vigilantes.

"How does it work?" asked Moses.

"Word is passed around to slaves in the goldfields that if they choose to escape there is a network of support for them. They are given a time and place to meet an agent who escorts them to a safe house. From there they are eventually smuggled to a church basement in Sacramento. Someone from San Francisco, sometimes me or Lester, takes a buckboard up there to collect them and bring them back here. That's the most dangerous part of the operation. The road is well travelled and you never know who you're going to run into. Once they get here we spend as much time as we can teaching them how to act like free men and women."

"How do you do that?" Moses interrupted.

"We bring in white abolitionists and teach the runaways to look a white man in the eye. This is not as easy as it sounds, since most of them have been taught from birth that looking into a white man's eyes is a good way of getting a riding crop across the face. Then, they have to learn to speak with the confidence of a free man, and that's no easy task either. In other words, in a matter of days they have to shake off habits that have been developed over a lifetime. I tell you, Moses, it's sometimes heartbreaking to watch."

Gibbs pulled at his collar, bothered by the thought, and continued. "We also buy them clothes from the slopsellers on the waterfront, and Lester and I provide them with a pair of inexpensive shoes. Those who want to stay are given forged papers, and those who want to leave are given a bit of money and put on a ship to Mexico or Central America. It's not difficult to find a corrupt ship's captain or some employee who can be bribed to take them on board."

"There must be considerable expense involved."

"More than considerable, but there isn't a black businessman in town who doesn't contribute to the fund. So do ordinary working men and a few white abolitionists as well. Needless to say, the whites have to be extremely careful. Life can be made difficult enough for them for just speaking out against slavery, let alone being caught actively helping us. You'll probably be surprised to know that your landlady, Mrs. Pleasant, is one of our biggest contributors. She has turned a sizeable inheritance into a small fortune by making loans and speculating in real estate, and is very generous with it."

Moses was indeed surprised. Mrs. Pleasant, of all people! He would never have guessed that behind that sweet, mother-like exterior beat the heart of a shrewd businesswoman who was subsidizing the Underground Railroad. But if she was involved, then the network required to make the railroad work must be extensive indeed.

"Why do you risk your freedom, and probably your life, for this?"

"I would like to say that my reasons are entirely altruistic, but that wouldn't be quite true. A good part of it is guilt."

"Why guilt?"

"Slavery in America is not like slavery was on your small island, Moses. Think of it this way. One black man is born in Pennsylvania and another in Maryland. All that separates them is an arbitrarily drawn, imaginary line. Call it the state line if you wish, or Mason and Dixon's line — either way it isn't any thicker than the milestones used to mark it. But the man north of the line leads a life of freedom, the one south of it a life of servitude.[3] He starts work with the rising of the sun and quits with the setting of it, and in between he gives over every one of his waking moments to a man who legally owns him and who has complete power over him. He even has to ask permission to carry out his natural bodily functions, and if the overseer is in a foul mood, God help him. He does not get paid for his labour; in fact it is illegal for him to have money in his possession. Usually all he gets in return for his hard work is a shanty to sleep in and enough food to make sure that he's capable of working the next day. If he steps a single foot off his owner's land without permission, there'll be dogs after him. Meanwhile our man from Pennsylvania, though generally despised for the colour of his skin, has no such misfortunes and lives a life of relative ease. I'm that man from Pennsylvania, Moses. Because of some strange lottery played by God, I was lucky enough to be born north of that imaginary line and I am free, while an unlucky brother, through no fault of his own, is not. Sometimes I find the weight of that thought unbearable."

Moses was moved by Gibbs' words, and his admiration for the man soared. "So how can I help?" he asked, still unsure about the reality of what was transpiring.

"Well, now that your business is flourishing you can make monthly contributions to the antislavery fund. We not only need money to help slaves escape, we need it to buy slaves that are for sale, so that we can set them free. That's always an expensive venture, but worth every penny. Just last month we bought a slave named Charlie Bates for $750 and set him free. That's a lot of money, but if you could have seen the look on his face when he was told that he was a free man, you would have paid 10 times the price. We are also told that there's a 12- year-old girl for sale up in Sacramento and we intend to set her free too, regardless of the price. The child should be in school, not up to her neck in someone else's dirty laundry and God knows what else. So you can see why we need the money. We do not ask you to bankrupt yourself for the cause, since the more successful you are, the better off all blacks will be. Naturally, all contributions are voluntary."

"You have my commitment," said Moses. "Is there anything else?"

"Yes. How would you like to take a ride up to Sacramento with me?"

CHAPTER FOUR

Rain pelted down on Moses and Gibbs as they sat in the buckboard wagon and waited to board the first ferry of the morning to take them across the neck of San Francisco Bay. A slip had been built at the foot of Market Street to accommodate the steam propeller ferries that, weather permitting, ran across to the east side of the bay. Though it was raining, the visibility was good and the water only slightly choppy, and now the *Kangaroo*, a small, barge-like vessel, was arriving from its berth at the California Street wharf. It thumped against the landing, and chains rattled as a ramp was winched down. The two men jumped down from the wagon and each took a horse by the halter to lead it up the unstable ramp onto the deck. They were followed by a miner and his pack mule and, as there was no one else about, the captain waited only a few moments before hauling up the ramp. Forty minutes later the *Kangaroo* had reached the opposite shore and was unloading its passengers. Gibbs clucked at the horses and the buckboard rolled north on the road that wound along the base of the hills, leaving the miner and his mule far behind.

Underneath tarps thrown over their shoulders like ponchos to keep them dry, Moses and Gibbs were dressed in labourers' clothes. Both wore black, floppy-brimmed hats that dripped rain, and cowhide gloves.

"It usually dries out, farther inland," said Gibbs. "In the meantime, the rain is partly a blessing. No one will pay much attention to us in it."

"It looks a little brighter off to the west," Moses said, "so this weather might be short-lived." He had not felt this cold since he had sailed the North Atlantic, but he was not about to complain. They were going to pick up a man and a woman, probably a husband and wife who, he would wager, were a lot worse off than he.

They passed through a small community, and the wagon rolled along the narrow road at a good pace despite the muddy conditions. Tree- and chaparral-covered hills loomed above them to their right, and the headlands of the Golden Gate could be seen in the far distance to their left. They trotted along, wordless, the only sounds the splat of the horses' hooves in the thin layer of mud, the clatter of the wheels striking rock, and the creak of the wagon's springs. Moses drifted off into a nebulous world of thought. He had come a long way from Grand Cayman, in more ways than one, and knew that if his brothers could see him now, they would be proud. They would know that his leaving had been worthwhile, that a selfish decision had taken on selfless overtones. Moses wanted more than anything to write and reveal what he was up to, but it was too dangerous. Letters were not always deliverable and might fall into the wrong hands.

"Wagon up ahead," said Gibbs, interrupting Moses' reverie. "It looks like a freighter with just a driver, but we'd best be on our toes anyway. Remember to smile if he's white, and don't look him in the eye. Not only do they not like it, they remember eyes, whereas one black face is just like another to them. Oh, and remember where your pistol is, but don't reach for it unless I go for mine."

Before they had left, Gibbs had showed Moses the two pistols concealed beneath the seat, one on each side, where they could be reached quickly should they be needed. There was also a rifle on the floor at their feet. Moses had never used either weapon, and prayed he would not have to now. As the freight wagon neared, Gibbs pulled the buckboard off the road into a swampy area, hoping they would not get stuck. The freighter approached, driven by a thin white man with a sharp face and a red beard. He held the reins in his left hand and had a rifle in the crook of his right arm, pointing downwards, but ready to be brought up into firing position if it was needed. He looked at the two black men warily. Gibbs touched his hat, smiled broadly and looked at the man's chest. "Good mawnin, suh!" he said. "It be a fine mawnin' even with the rain." Moses put on his best smile too and tried to look vacuous.

The driver merely nodded and the freight wagon trundled by. Moses breathed a sigh of relief. Gibbs coaxed the horses forward and they strained to pull the wagon from the muck. The wheels came loose with a sucking sound and Gibbs directed the animals back onto the road. By the time they reached Port Costa they had passed two more wagons carrying white men, and Gibbs and Moses had gone through the same routine. The buckboard was wheeled well off the road in deference to them, regardless of the conditions, and the two men pasted sycophantic smiles on their faces while Gibbs spoke like an uneducated labourer.

They crossed over to Benicia on a small ferry that plied the narrow strait and carried on toward Sacramento. Ten miles farther on, they stopped and set up camp for the night, pulling the wagon out of sight among some barren hills, and putting up their tent in a rare stand of trees.

Setting off early the next morning, they made good time under clearing skies and over a dry, flat road, past a Spanish *ranchero* that was one of the last in the area. By mid-afternoon they had reached Sacramento. As they approached the outskirts of town, traffic was heavier and Moses and Gibbs made sure not to offend anyone. Avoiding the town centre, they took side streets lined with clapboard buildings interspersed with a few brick ones, until they came to the African Methodist Church, sitting off by itself in a copse of sycamores. They pulled around to the rear of the church, to the small manse which was attached. The wagon had hardly stopped when out the door came a pleasant-looking man with greying hair, dressed in the black garb of a preacher. He was the Reverend Barney Fletcher.

Fletcher was an ex-slave from Maryland who had earned enough money at the gold diggings to buy his freedom. Then he worked nearly every waking hour, selling newspapers, shining shoes and at whatever other jobs he could find until he had enough to free his wife and children. He was now doing what he had always wanted to do, which was to preach the gospel and help others climb out of what he called "the dark pit of slavery."

After being introduced to Moses, and handshakes all around, he invited the two men to come inside once they had tended to the horses. Later, they were greeted in the manse by Mrs. Fletcher, a bird-like woman with frizzy, grey hair, who introduced herself to Moses. She bade the two men welcome and asked if they would like tea and something to eat. Her husband interrupted and, in a kindly voice with a slight drawl to it, said, "I think, Eliz'beth, that perhaps a small brandy is in order for these gentlemen. After that long trip I'm sure their mouths are as dry as Georgia cotton, so if you'll bring just enough to clear out the dust, why, I'm sure they'll be beholden to you."

While Mrs. Fletcher went off to get the brandy, the minister explained the background of the runaways hiding in the church basement. "The family's name is Turner, and Mr. Turner's story's about the same as mine, 'cept his took such an awful twist that every time I think of it it makes my heart flip. God works in mysterious ways, gentlemen, ways that I've been studyin' hard and ain't quite been able to get hold of yet. Anyway, Mr. Turner's owner is a lyin' dog named William Bennett — walk way 'round that man if you happen to cross his path — who promised him that if he worked hard on the diggin's he would be freed. Now, bein' in his sixties, this was a real trial for Mr. Turner, and he worked himself near down to skin 'n bones before Bennett finally kept his word. Mind, Bennett still had Mrs. Turner and their two boys, so Mr. Turner took himself off to San Francisco and in no time at all made $3,000 as a bootblack. That, of course was exactly how much he needed to buy his family out of bondage. I don't know that there was a happier man on this earth when he went back to William Bennett to claim them.

"But that white man did what every free Negro in California is afraid of. He claimed that his ex-slave was a fugitive and had him arrested. Now, I don't need to tell you two gentlemen that even though Mr. Turner had written proof of his freedom, he was not allowed to present it as evidence in court. The judge returned him to slavery, and to add a boil on a bruise, Bennett also got the $3,000. So Mr. Turner was a slave again, only this time to a liar and a thief, and there was only one road left open to him and his family. His two sons, big, strappin' boys they are, headed off into the hills, plannin' to find some black diggin's where they could hide out, but the Turners are too old for that kind of runnin' and needed our help. So now they sit in the church basement, as free as you and me, but called runaway slaves, thanks to that scoundrel William Bennett and the short-seein' eyes of the law. There is evil afoot in this world, gentlemen, and it comes in many guises, but none more foul than men the likes of him. He'll roast in Hell for his deeds, of that I'm certain, and the good Lord will surely forgive us if we gloat from the comfort of Heaven."

Mrs. Fletcher had brought in the brandy and glasses, and her husband poured generous servings. He held up his glass and said, "To the day that *all* men are free." They clinked glasses together and drank them empty.

"Now, come and meet your passengers," said Fletcher, and then to Moses he added, "Just a word of advice, Mr. Moses. It's important to address these fine folks as 'Mr. Turner' and 'Mrs. Turner.' They've earned that much respect. It's also the first step, though it ain't much bigger than a baby's, in givin' 'em a measure of dignity."

Gibbs and Moses followed the minister into the church. At one side of the altar was a small storage room containing some extra chairs and a table. Fletcher tipped the table on its side and removed a small piece of floorboard, under which was a handle.

Lifting on the handle he raised a trapdoor cleverly concealed by the board seams. The faces of an elderly man and woman peered eagerly up.

Fletcher looked down and smiled. "I've brought you your conductors," he said.

The three men climbed down the ladder into a fairly large room lit by two lamps. There were several beds, two tables, and a partitioned-off area in the corner that contained a chamber pot. It was cool in the room, but not cold, and the Turners were dressed warmly.

Turner was bent from a lifetime of hard work, with a fringe of grey hair around a bald pate, and a white beard. Sadness seemed permanently etched in his face. Mrs. Turner was diminutive, her white hair curled tightly against her head. Both were frightened, completely out of their element here in this basement, which was only a stopover on their journey to freedom. After introductions, Gibbs outlined the trip to San Francisco.

It had been planned so that at least one day of travel would be on a Sunday when there was usually less traffic on the road. In the early hours of the morning the Turners would be moved from the basement to the manse, and during the morning service Gibbs and Moses would sneak them onto the buckboard. In the back was a large tarp which they would hide under until they were well away from the town. After that they could come out and enjoy the fresh air. At the first sign of an approaching wagon, they were to crawl back under the tarp and keep as still as the dead. If anyone approached on horseback, Gibbs would pull over and his passengers were to leave the wagon and hide in the bushes on the side of the road. Once the danger had passed, Gibbs would double back and pick them up.

Gibbs was concerned about the couple who, though strong in spirit, seemed frail of body. He looked Turner in the eye. "This won't be an easy ride, Mr. Turner. Are you up to handling it?"

"Yes, sir," Turner replied. "Life itself ain't been an easy ride lately, but I reckon we can take a bit more. Besides, we is free niggers, bought and paid for, and ain't neither of us gonna die slaves, particularly slaves of a devil man."

A band of sweat broke out on Moses' forehead, caused by the heat of anger. Hatred rose like bile in him. If he could have gotten his hands on William Bennett they would have been around the man's throat, squeezing the life out of him, and to hell with the consequences. Because of that blackguard these lovely folks would probably never see their sons again, and would live their declining years watching their every step, instead of watching their sons do well and their grandchildren grow up. His mind still grappled with the evil thing slavery was. Where, he wondered, had the idea sprung from, that some men had the right to hold others in bondage? Surely it must have come from the most depraved of minds.

Moses scarcely slept at all that night, thinking of the Turners and the return trip to San Francisco. If the truth be known, despite his anger, he was frightened himself and had no idea how he would respond in a crisis. Would he be able to keep his wits about him or would he succumb to a blind rage? Would he be able to shoot someone, if need be? He did not know. What he did know was that no one was going to deny the Turners their right to freedom, not while he was able to fight for them. So resolved, he fell into a fitful sleep and dreamed of cloaked horsemen riding down on him as he ran for his life on legs of stone. He awoke as the horses' hooves were trampling him, and it all seemed so real he was surprised that he could move freely, that he was not a rack of broken bones. Outside, a cock's crow greeted the dawn, and a dog barked. Gibbs was stirring. It was time to find out what the day would bring.

The Turners were brought into the manse where Mrs. Fletcher had prepared fresh bread and eggs for everyone, and steaming cups of coffee which the men laced with brandy. Before eating, they bowed their heads in a prayer led by Reverend Fletcher: "Oh Lord, I believe that it's your hand that makes the smallest sparrow fall and the tallest mountain rise, so I beseech you, Lord, to take these good folks in that very same hand and carry them safely along the road laid out before them. We thank you, Lord, for you are the resurrection and the light, and he that believes in you, though he may die, shall live on, and whoever lives and believes in you will never die."

"Ah *believe,*" Mrs. Turner whispered.

There was a gentle chorus of "Amens" by the others, followed by a moment of silence as all were lost in their own thoughts. Then Gibbs and Moses excused themselves and went outside to ready the buckboard.

Later, Fletcher said his goodbyes, wished everyone God speed, and left to greet his flock, now beginning to arrive at the front of the church. When they could hear the voices of the congregation singing "We shall be rejoicing, bringing in the sheaves ...," Gibbs and Moses took one last look around to ensure there were no prying eyes, then hustled the Turners out to the wagon and held up the tarp for them to crawl under. Mrs. Fletcher was on the porch, dabbing the tears from her eyes, as Gibbs shook the reins and the wagon lumbered out to the road. They set off at a trot for San Francisco.

The buckboard pitched, rolled and bumped over the road west, and Moses felt sorry for the Turners, who had to grip the sideboards so that they were not tossed around like rag dolls. No matter how hard they hung on, it was a jarring ride for them. The only way to make it easier was to slow down, but speed was absolutely paramount. The less time spent in transit, the less likely they were to run into trouble.

High cirrus clouds streaked the sky in mare's tails and a bright sun, warm for so early in the year, shone down on the travellers. Gibbs pulled over to let by a dray that was driven by a white man. The Turners hid beneath a tarp while he did his obsequious black man routine, and they got under way again without incident. About an hour down the road Moses spotted mounted riders in the distance, coming toward them. Gibbs quickly pulled the wagon off to the side and Moses told the

Turners to get out as quick as lightning and hide deep in the bushes. "Stay there," he said, "until you hear us call for you." Keeping low, the Turners scrambled over the back of the buckboard with an agility that surprised Moses, and disappeared into the bush. Gibbs drove on.

Farther down the road, a group of five men reined up beside the wagon and Gibbs had no doubt they were a posse looking for fugitive slaves, probably the Turners. The leader was a flat-faced man with an unruly beard and narrow eyes that glared out from beneath the brim of a 10-gallon hat. He pulled out his rifle and aimed it at Gibbs. Before he spoke he spat out a gob of tobacco juice.

"You boys had best have some papers sayin' you're free niggers," he said.

"Why, yes suh," said Gibbs. Since they could not afford to be identified by their real names, he and Moses presented the forged papers they carried. The man looked them over carefully, then handed them back.

"You ain't transportin' nothin' illegal are you, boys? Hidin' it somewhere that we can't see?"

Another man, a pimply-faced youth, had ridden around to the back and without warning fired a rifle shot into the rumpled tarp. Moses and Gibbs nearly jumped out of their skin. The shooter reached over with the rifle barrel and flicked the tarp aside. "Too bad," he said. "Ain't nothin' here."

"Tell us the truth now, boy," the first man said to Gibbs, "and we might go easy on your black hide."

"The truth of the matter is, suh, we's jest on our way back to Frisco, after deliv'rin' goods to the Meth'dist church up Sacramento way. The Rev'rend Mr. Fletcher will vouch fo' our awth'ntic'ty, if it's no trouble to you askin' 'im, suh."

"What kind of goods?"

"Why, hanged if ah knowed, suh. It be just some boxes from Mr. Johnson's gen'ral store in Kearny Street down Frisco way. Ah 'xpect he'd vouch for us too, if'n you asked. Paid us twenny dollar, fo' our good work, he did. Why, ah have thet right here in mah poke, where it be safe an' sound, jest waitin' to quench our t'irst when we 'rrive back home."

"Ain't no dumb-assed nigger worth $20," growled one of the men. "It'd jingle a whole lot better in our pockets."

"Dig it out," said the flat-faced man as he put the rifle barrel against Gibbs' face.

"You mean mah poke, suh? Why, you ain't plannin' to rob me, are you, suh?"

The man whipped the rifle across Gibbs' mouth. His lip split and his head snapped back. Blood trickled down his chin. Moses was stunned and saw red, and wanted to reach for the gun but they were clearly outnumbered. He also remembered that Gibbs had said not to reach for it unless he went for his first. But he knew without a doubt that he could kill these men.

"This ain't no robbery, boy, and you'd best remember that. This is just relievin' you of a burden you don't deserve or need. You get my meanin'?" The man let go another gob of tobacco juice that spattered on Gibbs' pant legs.

"Yas suh, I unnerstan'. Thank you fo' clearin' that up fo' me." Gibbs reached under the seat for the sack of coins. He had to exercise every ounce of his willpower not to pull out the pistol hidden there and shoot the man in the face. He grabbed the sack and handed it respectfully to the man.

"There it be, suh, an' don' it look much better in yo' hands than mine!"

"Get this wagon outta here," the man snarled, "and get your black asses back to Frisco before they're shot off."

"Yas suh!" said Gibbs and, flicking the reins on the rumps of the horses, shouted "Geeyup." He held them at a trot, resisting the urge to go galloping off. Moses was shaking from both fear and fury, and had to force himself not to look back. He waited until he felt it was safe, and then turned, half expecting to see the posse thundering down on them, as in his dream. Instead, he saw the riders disappearing in the opposite direction, off, he presumed, to spend their bounty in the bars of Sacramento. Barely able to speak, he told Gibbs it was safe to pull over.

"We'll give it a few minutes," Gibbs said, touching his lip, "then go back for the Turners. Are you all right?"

Moses nodded. "Never mind me. How are you?"

"Fine, fine. It's a small price to pay for a good cause." He paused for a moment, then added, "You know Moses, it never ceases to amaze me how some white folks, who think they're so damned superior to us, cannot even recognize a simple bribe when it's staring them in the face." He grinned, then winced from the pain of it, and Moses clapped his friend on the shoulder.

"Gibbs," he said, shaking his head. "You are a fine piece of work!"

They returned to the spot where they had stopped, and called for the Turners. After a few moments the couple came out of the bush, cautiously, as wide-eyed as barn owls. They were aghast when they saw the wound Gibbs had obviously sustained on their behalf, and asked what happened. Gibbs shrugged it off. "It's nothing," he said. "Just part of a game that's well worth the playing, even with lopsided rules."

They carried on at a good pace. There were more tense moments as they passed through Benicia and waited for the ferry to take them across to Port Costa, but they reached the small settlement without incident. A couple of miles down the road they pulled well into the trees to camp for the night. Using the tarp, an auxiliary camp was set up for the Turners, farther back in the trees in case someone came along. Gibbs and Moses took turns standing watch, but even with the extra precaution no one slept a wink.

They were gone at first light, running on pure adrenaline, and by late morning had the Golden Gate in sight. They passed more wagons, but the closer they got to San Francisco the less they had to worry about posses. Nevertheless, the Turners were forced to spend more time underneath the tarp than Gibbs and Moses liked. By the time they had crossed the bay on the ferry, the old couple had been covered for nearly three hours and Moses feared for their welfare. A welcome fog greeted them as they rolled off the ferry and into town. Now they were just two black labourers going home after a hard day's work. Gibbs drove the wagon through the city and turned down the alley behind the Boot Emporium. The two men got out and checked up and down the alley. Finding it deserted, they shifted some boxes to reveal a door, and then told the Turners they could come out now. There was no movement. Moses was alarmed and reluctant to turn the tarp back, fearing that he'd find a couple of corpses. Instead the couple, exhausted from their ordeal, had fallen asleep in the warmth of each other's embrace. When Moses awoke them they had been in the same position for so long they needed to be helped down from the wagon, and into the secret room.

CHAPTER FIVE

T hat was not the last trip that Moses made to Sacramento, but it was the last with Gibbs. Once he knew the route he went by himself, and there was always some tragic story — beyond the tragedy of slavery. One man he brought back was so scarred from being whipped that it made Moses gasp. The man had decided one day that he had had enough, torn the whip from his owner's hands and garrotted him. He was convinced that he'd committed a heinous sin for which he would burn in Hell. Moses told him not to worry about it, that it may have been the first right thing he'd ever done and besides, Hell was so full of slave owners that there probably was no room left for his. He was such a sad case and so poorly educated that he spent longer than most in the secret room, under Gibbs' and Lester's tutelage, but try as they might, they could not get rid of the fugitive look in his eyes. There were posters of him everywhere, so he was smuggled out of town on a Panama-bound ship. It was the worst case of slave treatment Moses had ever seen; afterwards, he went off into the hills and learned how to shoot with the guns.

Meanwhile, the Turners were given forged papers, after Mr. Turner shaved off his beard and Mrs. Turner donned a wig. They were taken on as staff at Mary Ellen Pleasant's boarding house, where they spent most evenings in rockers on the back porch. There were no grandchildren at their feet, however, and both died without seeing their sons again.

The shaving saloon did well. Moses provided good service and the result was a faithful clientele. He was able to expand, and moved to new premises that included a bath house as well as a three-room apartment above, where he lived. Along the way, his first name was either forgotten or ignored and everyone called him Moses. He did not mind, and even introduced himself that way. He only wished that in the same way the other Moses had parted the Red Sea, he could part the sea of racism and lead his people to a better place.

The worst part of his life was the lack of a woman in it. Not a lack of a woman to provide the physical relief that he desired, for there were plenty of those, but the lack of one special woman to share his life and all the good things he was now able to afford. But the sad fact of the matter was that in San Francisco, men outnumbered women six to one. Every time he went to Sacramento he hoped that it might be to bring back a beautiful young woman, who would be so smitten by his valiant efforts to save her that she would gladly give her hand in marriage. But it never turned out that way. Instead, he paid for his female company, beautiful women who would have passed for ladies in good society. They usually came to his apartment and most had more money than he did. Nevertheless, he found their companionship, brief though it was, very comforting indeed, for not only were they well practised in the art of satisfying a man, most were bright, engaging conversationalists. Such moments gave him a glimpse of what a domestic life might be like, and he found them exceedingly enjoyable.

Beyond his personal life, there was San Francisco at large: corrupt, racist and dangerous. Men brought the lawlessness of the mining camps to the city during the winter months and crime flourished. Justice was often crude and swift, sometimes at the hands of the Vigilance Committee. This committee was organized by citizens who were fed up with the volume of crime in the city, as well as the corruption in a legal system that allowed criminals to escape with light sentencing through bribery or simply through being a friend of the judge. In 1856 the committee comprised nearly 8,000 members and had permanent headquarters in Sacramento Street. It openly confronted the authorities if it was not satisfied with a given course of action, and was powerful enough that little could be done to stop it. In some cases, though, the vigilantes were worse than the lawbreakers they vigorously pursued. That things had gotten completely out of hand was made evident in 1856 when there were two public executions.

One of the men executed was Charles Cora, a wealthy gambler. Cora had attended the opening of the American Theatre with his mistress, a local madam. U.S. Marshal William Richardson and his wife were sitting a few rows in front of them and were insulted that a woman of questionable morals was brought into such an elegant place. The next evening, the two men met in the street and an argument ensued. Richardson, who was intoxicated, pulled a gun, but Cora outdrew him. The marshal was killed instantly.

The other case involved a man named James Casey who was angry over some malicious comments made about him by James King, the editor of the *San Francisco Bulletin*. Casey waited outside the newspaper office and when King came out, told him to go for his gun. King did, but Casey got the first round off. The bullet knocked King down, although the wound was not fatal. Later, when doctors were treating him, they apparently left a sponge in the incision, and he died a few days later of complications. It did not matter that malpractice had played a part in his death; the vigilantes wanted blood and went after Casey. On May 14, six months after Richardson was killed, and just a week after King was shot, members of the Vigilance Committee, dissatisfied with the course of due process, went into action. They marched to the jail, took custody of Casey and Cora and hustled them to the committee's meeting room on the upper floor of the building in Sacramento Street. At eight o'clock in the morning of May 22, the two men were sentenced to death by hanging. The execution was to take place after lunch, right outside the windows of the committee room.

Word of the pending executions spread through town like winter fog. Against his better judgment, Moses was drawn to the site. He found the street clogged with soldiers, volunteer supporters of the vigilantes, who carried bayoneted muskets and sabres. Many were on horseback. They formed a semicircle beneath the windows from which the two men would be hung, and their job was to keep those opposed to the executions away. The "gallows" consisted of two temporary beams jutting out from the roof of the building, each above a window; from the beams dangled ropes with nooses. On the sill of each window was a hinged platform supported by ropes from the beams.

At a quarter past one Cora and Casey were brought out to their respective platforms. Their arms were tied behind their backs, and the nooses placed around their necks. Cora stood passively, but Casey requested that his noose be removed while he received absolution from a priest. That done, Casey spoke to all who could hear him: "Gentlemen: I hope this will be engraved on your minds forever and on your hearts: I am no murderer. Let no man call me a murderer or an assassin. Gentlemen, I pardon you as I hope God will forgive you, as I hope He will forgive me, Amen, Oh God, have mercy upon me and my poor mother."[1] Blindfolds were then placed over the two men's eyes. At 1:30 the ropes were cut and the men dropped to their deaths. When the bodies stopped swaying, Cora was completely still, but Casey twitched and went on twitching for what seemed to Moses a very long time. He felt sick to his stomach, and broke out in a sweat. Then he vomited on the shoes of a man standing next to him who, fortunately, was black. Though he had been utterly mesmerized by the scene, it was the grisliest thing he'd ever witnessed. He did not care that they were white men. Those were human lives that had twitched themselves into oblivion, and he was appalled.

Despite the dark side of San Francisco and the racist politics of California, the city provided him with a good life. Good enough, at any rate, that he knew he could never again live on Grand Cayman. Still, he always harboured a desire to return for a visit. He particularly wanted to tell his older brother of his work in the Underground Railroad, and to try to heal the wound in their relationship. Most of all, he wanted his brother to be proud of him. But all of that changed one rainy afternoon. A black man, whose face wore the fatigue of a traveller, entered the saloon and asked for "Wellington Delaney Moses." Moses could tell straight away that he was a Cayman Islander, and was immediately filled with excitement.

"May we have a moment in private?" the man asked.

Moses' excitement swiftly turning to dread, he led the man to a small room that he used as an office. The news from home was not the news he wanted to hear: both of his brothers were dead. The elder one had gone first, from a lingering illness, then the younger one, a few weeks later, had drowned while diving on a shipwreck. They had been dead and buried for six months, but Kensington had managed a letter before he died, with instructions that it be sent out with the first islander bound for San Francisco.

"You must excuse me, sir," Moses said and, after ensuring that the man had lodgings, arranged to meet him for dinner on another day to repay him for his kindness. For now, though, he needed to be alone. After the man left, Moses, scarcely able to control himself, tore open the letter. It was written in a shaky, uneven hand, apparently with great difficulty.

"My Dear Brother,

"It is my prayer that this letter not only finds its way into your hands, but also finds you hale and prosperous. I am not long for this good old world, and as you read these words I might well be long gone. Something gnaws away at my insides that will soon devour me completely. Yet, I have no fear for I have made my peace with my maker. I do, however, have regrets, or at least one, and it concerns you. My dear Wellington, I selfishly sent you away, no doubt riddled with guilt, when I ought to have sent you away with love and good wishes. As family head, your well-being was my responsibility and I failed you in that regard. I should have known that after your return from England this island would be too small to contain you and that you would need to take your chances in the world. Not a day has passed since your departure that I haven't regretted my actions, and I can only pray to God that this letter reaches you so that these thoughts are known and that it eases your burden. I was a fool, and I hope you will forgive me.

"Lancaster is well, and sends his best wishes. I thank God that life fills him to overflowing, even as it slowly spills from my mind and body.

"With great affection, your brother, Kensington."

Tears welled up in Moses' eyes, unstoppable. With the simple entry of a stranger into his saloon, he had lost both of his brothers and was without a family, without blood ties. If he could have turned time backwards for just a few moments, he would have locked the door and never let the man in; lived his life in ignorance of this awful information. His mind whirled and his knees felt weak. He sat down and placed his head in his hands. His shoulders shook uncontrollably. This was not the way things were supposed to turn out. He had always hoped that Kensington would find it in his heart to forgive him, but never dreamed it would be like this. He wished he had gone home to make amends, wished that he had not let his busy life get in the way. Now there were loose ends that would dangle in his heart forever.

He plunged deeper into his work with Gibbs, and other members of the black community, to gain basic rights for Negroes in California. Every time he lifted his head to see how much progress had been made, they were either in the same place or had taken a step backwards. During such moments Moses felt completely frustrated; it seemed to him they were black Sisyphuses, rolling the rock of Negro rights up the mountain, only to have it roll back down on top of them, time and time again. They continued writing and submitting petitions to earn the right to testify in court, but to no avail. Rumour had it that the petitions made the best fire starter the assembly in Sacramento ever had.

And yet, there was some white support for their plight. The argument went that if a man had a faithful family slave and a white thief broke into the man's house while he was away and murdered his wife and child, and the only witness to the crime was the slave, how could the culprit be brought to justice if the slave could not testify? It was a convoluted justification for the same end, but there were enough robberies and murders in California in general, and San Francisco in particular, that many whites took this argument seriously. Even the local paper, in its own inimitable way, jumped on the bandwagon with this article:

> We have no love for the Negro. He is degraded and not wanted in this great state. The Negro's evidence does not carry as much weight as a white man, but it does not follow that their evidence should be excluded entirely. The evidence furnished by a dog may lead to the conviction of a murderer, and although the Negro is below the white man in capabilities, there are exceptions.[2]

If they could accept being compared to dogs, it was a small victory for blacks. So they tried again, and went door to door throughout the state, into places where they were as welcome as pariah dogs, and garnered support for their cause. The assembly voted it down. Six times the organized blacks and white abolitionists submitted petitions, the last one carrying 6,500 signatures, many belonging to whites, and six times the assembly threw them out. Meanwhile, the U.S. Supreme Court made official what blacks already knew: that they could not become citizens.

This decision was the result of the Dred Scott case. Scott was a slave from Missouri who sued his owner on the grounds that temporary residence in a free state made him free. The court ruled that Scott could not sue his owner because he was not a U.S. citizen and as a Negro, never could be. Now, white eyes were looking northward to Oregon where blacks were banned from the territory entirely. They thought that California should pass a similar law, but legislators waffled for a long time. Until young Archy Lee came into the picture.

Archy was a runaway. He had escaped from a man named Charles Stovall, a Mississippian who had come west for his health and settled in California, and who subsequently had Archy arrested as a fugitive slave. The rationale for this went back to the early 1850s when the California legislature enacted the Fugitive Slave Law. It allowed whites who had owned slaves back in the Southern states to reclaim them if they ran away within California's borders. It was not quite legalized slavery, but it was the next thing to it; indeed, many blacks and white abolitionists feared that outright slavery would in fact be the next step. Fortunately the law, which had to be renewed every 12 months, was allowed to lapse in the mid '50s. However, in a state where there was more chaos than order in the legal system, and where much of the white population was racist, the spirit of the law remained. There was however, a glitch in Stovall's plan. Since slaves could not legally be kept, the authorities held Archy for deportation. This upset Stovall because Archy, being young and in good condition, was worth a lot of money: $1,500 to be precise. The only way Archy could be returned to him was if Stovall could prove himself a transient. Incredibly, he was able to convince the authorities that he was, despite owning a ranch with several head of cattle on it, as well as holding a job as a teacher in Sacramento. (He had let Archy work in the community, and taken the young slave's wages.) Based on this "evidence" the commissioner who heard the case ruled that Archy should not be deported, since his owner was transient. Nevertheless, the commissioner did not quite know what to do with Archy and gave the case to the state court to decide.

Meanwhile, the black community rallied behind Archy. Since California was not, at least on paper, a slave state, they wanted Archy freed. The court's decision dumbfounded everyone. It ruled that Stovall was indeed a resident and illegally kept a slave in a free state — the blacks liked that part of the decision — but apparently, the court felt sorry for Stovall because he was ill, thus they were "not disposed to rigidly enforce the rule ... "[3] They gave Archy back to Stovall. He saw the writing on the wall and made plans to leave with his valuable chattel on the next steamer bound for Panama. The blacks, on the other hand, intended to ensure that if he left, it would be without Archy. They applied for and obtained a writ of *habeas corpus* which they tried to serve on Stovall; he eluded them and kept Archy well hidden until the departure date.

On Thursday, March 4, 1858, in a tiny cove near the Golden Gate, Stovall and Archy waited in a small boat for the approach of the steamer *Orizaba*. Stovall knew that the city wharf would be jammed with blacks who would not permit him to board the vessel with his slave, so he had decided to fool them and not show up. Instead, he would intercept the vessel before it passed through the Golden Gate, and board her. No one would be any the wiser, and people would think that he had missed the steamer and was still hiding out in San Francisco. When he saw the *Orizaba* approaching, he shoved off, he pulling on one oar and Archy on the other. Once in position he stood up and waved his oar, and the steamer slowed to a dead stop. A rope ladder was thrown over the side and Stovall and Archy climbed up, Archy first. Some crewmembers assisted them over the rail. Stovall's feet had no sooner hit the deck than he was faced with two burly policemen. One of them held out a warrant and said, "You're under arrest!"

"What's the charge?" Stovall demanded.

"Kidnapping."

Stovall reached for a derringer that he had concealed in his pocket, but the two officers were on him in an instant. After a brief struggle they managed to disarm and subdue him.

"You'll not get away with this," he shouted. "This boy is rightfully mine and I'll be damned if I'll let you take him away from me!"

"That's up to a judge to decide. In the meantime you'll be coming with us," said one of the policemen gruffly.

With the help of some crewmembers, the officers hustled Stovall and Archy back down to the rowboat, and had them row all the way back to the dock from which the *Orizaba* had departed. A happier mood should have prevailed among the blacks waiting there, but word had just come down from Sacramento that the latest petition to allow blacks to testify in court had been thrown out. It meant that Archy would not be allowed to testify against Stovall.

The first thing Monday morning Stovall was in court. His lawyer applied to have the writ of *habeas corpus* dismissed. It was denied. Stymied by the law, Stovall's only recourse was to grant Archy his freedom. The blacks in the balcony were then stunned when Archy was promptly arrested again as a fugitive slave. When he was ordered deported, there was pandemonium in the courtroom. The judge banged his gavel to restore order, but was ignored. The U.S. marshal, whose job it was to take Archy to jail, had to call for reinforcements. The jail was some distance from the courthouse, and the marshal pushed Archy ahead of him with the point of a gun. An angry mob of blacks followed. Several whites who tried to interfere with the blacks were sent sprawling in the street, and a few blacks were later charged with assault and battery. Moses was right in the thick of it and feared for his life. It seemed as if the whole world was teetering on the brink of madness. Someone lobbed a block of wood; it struck one man in the forehead and drew blood, but the mob continued forward like a mindless beast. So volatile was the scene that Moses was certain it would break out in a full-scale riot that would stop only after the last black man was killed. How the marshal got Archy safely into jail, Moses never knew.

The black community gathered to lick its wounds and decide what to do. As things turned out, they did not have to do anything. Fearing a bloodbath, the commissioner ruled that Archy was not a fugitive slave, and granted him his freedom. It was, unquestionably, a victory, but the cost of this progress, both financially and emotionally, was becoming unbearable. The struggle had not eased a bit over the years, and all the signs indicated that things were about to get worse.

There was a bill before the assembly which, if passed, would "prohibit the immigration of free Negroes and other obnoxious persons into this state and to protect and regulate the conduct of such persons now within the state."[4] A second bill not only sought an end to black immigration, but also proposed that blacks who ignored the law and came anyway would either have to pay their own way home or be forced to work for the highest bidder, "for such reasonable time as shall be necessary to pay the costs of the conviction and transportation from this state ... "[5] Further, all blacks currently residing in the state would have to be registered, and would be assessed a hefty fine if they were not. Licences would be required for the right to work, and anyone hiring an unlicensed black would be charged with a misdemeanour and fined. There were other restrictions, equally draconian, all designed to put an end to any black presence in California. The bill had already been passed by the assembly and was now before the senate. Gibbs wrote a letter to the *San Francisco Bulletin*, which said in part:

> Let the bill now before the legislature take
> what turn it may. The colored people in this state
> have no regrets to offer. Our course has been
> manly and law-abiding. To this legislature and
> the press that sustains it, may you have all the
> honor, glory and consequences of prosecuting and
> abusing an industrious, unoffending and
> defenseless people! May God have shame on you!
> May he judge you for your actions! Shame!
> Shame![6]

Moses met with Gibbs, as he often did, in the back of the Boot Emporium after closing time. Over brandies, Gibbs spoke of what was in his heart.

"You may or may not recall, Moses," he said, "the first time we met and I told you that we blacks would not leave California without a fight."

Moses nodded. That night would always be with him. The memory of Lester's beating was seared forever on his mind, for not only was it a brutal introduction to California, it taught him right off, a single, important lesson: that he would always need to be on his guard in his relationships with white people in this country.

"Have we not fought the good fight, my friend," Gibbs asked, "fair and mostly within the limits of the law?"

"Indeed, we have," Moses replied, "and of you, one could not ask more."

Gibbs sighed. His eyes were watery in the lamplight. "I fear we have failed. There are just too few of us and too damned many of them, and they have made it more than plain that they want no part of us. Why do you think that is, Moses? What is inherently wrong with them that they would look upon us as subhuman, fit only to be their slaves? Are we not all men? Are we not all brothers? Good God, even if they don't want to give us equality, why can they not just let us go peaceably about our lives?"

"That's not likely to happen in our lifetime," said Moses. "As to what's inherently wrong with them, you might better ask what is inherently wrong with the human race. If memory serves me correctly, I believe there were more than a few black men who sold their own people into slavery."

"Which only makes me despair even more!"

Gibbs walked over to a small window that overlooked the alley. The last rays of a spring sun slanted down between the backs of the buildings. The alley was cluttered with trash, and wooden crates were piled haphazardly against brick walls. The sunlight only emphasized the neglected look of the place, which was what had made it so suitable for the railroad. Without turning he spoke.

"I thought we might have fared better. In my naiveté I believed that for the first time in our history we actually had a chance to improve our lot. I believed that if we banded together, the strength of our unity and our indisputable intelligence would win them over. I thought that even though a single snowflake is a fragile thing, an accumulation of them can make an avalanche capable of altering anything in its path. How horribly wrong I was in our case. We are melted in the heat of their passion to be rid of us. After all these years of hard work we remain refugees in our own country."

Gibbs reached up and with a thumb and forefinger rubbed at the moisture building in the corner of his eyes. Moses splashed some more brandy into their glasses, and took Gibbs' glass over to him. Placing a hand on his friend's shoulder, he said, "You are a good man, Mifflin, and the history books will show it. But there comes a time when you can no longer climb the barriers thrown up in front of you, and you have to find new roads to travel."

"You echo my thoughts of these past few days," Gibbs said, wearily. "We must stop beating ourselves senseless at what is quite clearly a brick wall. I think we ought to pull up stakes and move north, to the British colony of Vancouver Island. By 'we' I mean every black man, woman and child in San Francisco who is as fed up as we are with the racist policies here.

"I have spoken personally with the captain of the *Commodore*, a steamer on the San Francisco-Victoria run. He came into the store the last time he was in town and I asked him how receptive the community would be to black immigrants. He assured me that we would be made most welcome in the colony, in any number, since the gold rush on the Fraser River has left the town with an acute shortage of labour and businessmen. He was certain that he could get us an official invitation, perhaps even from the governor himself, who, he says, is a mulatto. The *Commodore* is due in two days and I hope to have the answer then, if the man hasn't reneged."

Moses liked the idea of moving to British territory. "This is exciting news, Gibbs," he said, "and an official invitation is just what's needed for those who would not go on speculation alone."

Gibbs went on. "Answer one question for me, though, with the honesty I've come to expect from you. Are we cowards for running?"

Moses thought for a moment, then shrugged. "Cowards for running, or fools for staying, take your pick. We're probably damned whichever course we take, and that, it seems, is the fate of coloured men everywhere."

⌒⌒

Gibbs and Moses soon discovered that they were not the only ones who wanted to leave California to the whites, so a meeting was called in the Zion Methodist Church on the corner of Stockton and Pacific streets. A large crowd had gathered, and they started the evening off singing songs written to celebrate Archy Lee's freedom. At the same time they collected donations of several hundred dollars to cover his legal expenses. Then the discussion turned to the question that was on everyone's minds: where could they go to find the freedom they deserved and would never find here?

Someone suggested Sonora, a state in northern Mexico, but others worried that it might soon become an American state and then where would they be? Someone else mentioned Panama, but many people had come to California via that country and did not have fond memories of it. In the end, Gibbs held the trump card, in the form of Captain Jeremiah Nagle of the steamer *Commodore*, who had come to the meeting well prepared. With maps, Nagle gave his audience a glimpse of Vancouver Island and the colony, and answered a torrent of questions. After he read Governor Douglas' open invitation to the black community, they had all made up their minds. It seemed that if there were a drawback, it was the gold rush taking place on the Fraser River, which was attracting white Americans by the thousands. Nagle assured everyone, however, that British law was quite different from American law and that the flagrant abuse of black people would not be tolerated in Victoria as it was here in San Francisco.

"And how many of us will your vessel accommodate?" someone asked.

"As many as can afford to buy tickets," Nagle smiled, and there was laughter among the businessmen in the crowd.

Before the meeting concluded it was decided that a group of 65 would leave on the *Commodore* when she sailed north in eight days' time. They would be called the "Pioneer Committee," and it would be their job to check out the colony. If it met their expectations, they would stay and pave the way for other blacks to follow.

There was much to be done during the week before departure, particularly by those with businesses and property. They would either have to get them sold in that span of time or find someone they could trust to manage them until a buyer came along. The bath house went quickly, being a sound, profit-making business, but Gibbs and Lester did not like the initial offers for the Boot Emporium, and chose to go with the next group of emigrants. In the end, only 35 of the committee were able to get their affairs in order in time. Nevertheless, it was enough to form a vanguard, which would send back word about the quality of life in Victoria.

The night before the departure, Moses attended a small *bon voyage* party at Gibbs' elegant home, but he felt tense and was not up to being sociable. Pleading his need for a good night's rest he said his goodbyes early and went home. He considered enjoying some female companionship, but decided against it. He wanted most to be alone. So he poured himself two fingers of whiskey, paused, then added a third finger and went downstairs to the saloon where he sat in the dark in one of his velvet shaving chairs. There were three now, and he had had to hire two barbers to help him as well as a man to clean and fill the baths. (They were also bound for Victoria, which gladdened his heart considerably since he had sold the business and premises to a white man who would be taking possession in the morning.) He thought back to when he had first arrived here, less than seven years before. What an extraordinary run of good luck he'd had since then, and how fortunate his chance meeting with Gibbs had been. Gibbs always said that you made your own good luck, which was probably true. He also maintained that a man's fate was determined by his character, but Moses had brought too many men of good character down that long road from Sacramento to fall for that line. There had to be more to it than just character, of that he was certain, but exactly what it was he did not know. Though he attended church fairly regularly, he did so for social reasons; he was not a religious man, yet, admittedly, there were times when he felt a greater power was watching over him.

Now a new road awaited him in the morning and he felt excited and up to the challenges that it was sure to present. He sat for a long time, lost in thought, absent-mindedly sipping his drink. He had no idea how much time had passed, when he suddenly felt weary. He tossed off the dregs of his whiskey and placed the glass on the shelf that had once contained all the shaving paraphernalia now packed away in a trunk. By the faint light from the street, he could just make out a vague image of himself in the mirror above the shelf. Like a ghost, he thought; don't I look just like a ghost. He sighed. It was a fitting image in a city plugged with men who still had trouble seeing him as a human being. He felt his way back up the stairs to his rooms, undressed, put out the lamps and went to bed.

In the morning, after breakfasting at a nearby eatery, he piled his baggage into a carriage, then asked the driver to please wait a moment. Going back inside to his office he got a piece of paper, scribbled some words on it, and pinned it to the sign that read on one side "Open," and the other side "Closed," hanging in the door window. Then he stepped outside, pulled the door shut for the last time and locked it. He climbed into the carriage, utterly satisfied with himself, and signalled the driver to go. He did not once look back.

For those passers-by who bothered to look, the sign in the door read "Gone to Victoria."

Part Three

CHAPTER SIX

Silence fell in the theatre as the lamps were dimmed and the first performer took the stage. He was Emil Sutro, a barrel-chested man with a drooping moustache who, in 1861, was Victoria's best-known violinist. He stood at centre stage with his hands clasped and waited until the audience had become absolutely still.

"Before I begin," he said, "I would ask those improperly seated in the dress circle to please find seats with their own race."

Some of the audience members gasped at Sutro's request. Moses and the others in the dress circle simply glared at him. No one moved.

"I see," the performer said. "Then I refuse to be a party to this flagrant abuse of the proper social order." He quickly did an about turn, and left the stage. Some of the crowd cheered.

Next up to perform was a string ensemble, consisting of a violin, a viola and a cello, which played a movement of a Mozart sonata. Some of the whites hissed at them, and a tomato lobbed onto the stage exploded on the floor in front of the trio. Despite their obvious discomfort, they did not miss a note and finished their number. The artist following them was also hissed at. Moses had heard that several of the performers had been offered $50 by an American auctioneer named James McCrea not to perform, in hopes of having the concert cancelled. Only a few had accepted the bribe, but those who had not were now paying the price.

Suddenly, a score of onions flew in an arc and rained down upon the men and women in the dress circle. Most fell harmlessly to the floor, a few hit people on their backs, shoulders and legs, and one bounced off the top of Moses' head. The onions were an insult, thrown to counteract the odours from what whites called "Ethiopian perspiration" and to induce the blacks to move to seats considered more befitting men and women of colour. A fuse of anger burned inside Moses. He ached to face down the cowards who had thrown them, but held himself in check. A confrontation was what they wanted, and it was best to avoid one. Nevertheless, he and his companions were not about to move. They had every right to be there and unless they were bodily thrown out, they would stay.

The onions stopped and the show resumed. The hissing continued, becoming even more pronounced, and Moses admired the courage of the performers who struggled with their presentations through it. An opera singer stopped in mid-line and before Moses even had a chance to wonder why, a bag of flour landed on Nathan Pointer's head and split open. An eruption of white dust quickly enveloped all those around Pointer who was choking and sputtering as the flour clogged his nostrils and mouth. His daughter cried in horror, "Oh, my father!" There was a collective intake of breath among the audience, punctuated by smatterings of laughter. Moses was set to explode. Shaking with anger and barely in control of himself, he stood to face the perpetrators behind him but before he could do or say anything, Gibbs roared, "Who did that?" Pointer stabbed his finger in the direction of the person he thought was the culprit, a man named Ryckman. Ryckman smirked.

Gibbs leapt at him and punched the smirk off his face. Pointer followed suit and knocked a naval officer to the floor, and Moses went for a man who been rude to him several times before. Others joined the fray. Men cursed while they threw punches and wrestled each other in the aisles. One man had another in a headlock and was holding him down on the floor. Women gasped and screamed, and one fainted dead away in her seat. The stage manager came from behind a curtain and called for calm, but was ignored. Then the police stormed in, wielding sticks, and the sight of them was enough to bring the brawlers partially to their senses. Those on the floor rose to their feet, straightening out their clothes. Instead of fists and curses they now hurled accusations at each other until the police shouted them down and demanded silence. Though it was patently clear that the battle lines were racial, the officer in charge asked, "What's this all about, then."

The flour thrower complained that he had been attacked by Gibbs. "I was watching the show and minding my own business," he added.

Gibbs was flabbergasted. "You lie, sir! If you were any kind of a man you'd admit to your part in this affair!" Turning to the officer, he said, "This man threw a bag of flour that exploded on the head of my colleague … "

The officer interrupted. "It doesn't matter who threw what. We have laws to deal with such matters. In this country we do not take them into our own hands."

More arguing ensued, but the end result was that Gibbs and Pointer brought charges of assault against four of the white men, including Ryckman, who in turn brought charges against the two black men. Not considered an instigator, Moses was not charged. The outbreak ended the concert. Too many bad feelings prevailed and there was a mess to clean up.

Later, Moses joined Lester at Gibbs' spacious, new home in James Bay for a nightcap. The house was indicative of Gibbs' success since arriving in Victoria. It had, however, lacked what Gibbs thought every home needed — children — so he had gone back east to find a wife and returned with Maria, who would soon present him with their first child. Maria had retired for the evening, but an Indian manservant was on duty. He went to a sideboard and poured each of the men double whiskeys. Gibbs paced the floor in front of a dormant fireplace.

"I was a fool," he said. "Of all people, I should have known better. The only way a black man will get anywhere on this continent is through hard work and by making himself indispensable. And also avoiding confrontations like tonight's. Despite harassment, despite all the silly twaddle about Ethiopian perspiration, we've managed to keep to that agenda in this community, but my behaviour tonight may have undermined our efforts completely. It was reprehensible."

"You shoulder too much of the burden," said Lester, flatly. He slouched on a settee. "People of good society will think none the less of us for responding to a pack of ingrate Secessionists who came here because they didn't have the courage to fight for the Confederacy. Had they left their bigotries behind, tonight's brawl might never have happened."

"Exactly," Moses added. "Anybody with a clear head will know who caused it. I shouldn't worry, Gibbs, if I were you."

"But how will it look when a prominent businessman is up before the court for common assault?" Gibbs asked.

"It will look as though the prominent businessman lost his temper, and for good reason," Moses responded.

Lester interrupted. "Regardless, we've made our point that it is our intention to take our rightful place in human society and that we will not be stayed from the course. All you need to do is remind yourself from time to time that your best weapons have always been a keen mind and a sharp tongue — not your fists."

It was not until afterward, when the manservant was driving Moses home in Gibbs' carriage, that he wondered if his friend's outburst of violence was an indication that he was growing tired of the fight. It had been three and a half years since they had left San Francisco, and though most of the Pioneer Committee and those who followed later had prospered in the colony, the years had not been trouble-free. His mind ran back over them as the carriage swayed along Belleville Street in front of the Birdcages, the stylized legislative buildings.

∞∞

He had felt battered when he arrived in the colony. The journey had taken only six days but they had run headlong into one of the worst storms to hit the Oregon coast in years. Passengers were tossed around like driftwood, cramped quarters reeked of vomit, and the decks were crowded with white gold seekers who were not at all pleased to be sharing the ship with 35 black men. But they had arrived none the worse for wear and Moses had been both surprised and pleased with his first glimpse of Victoria. It was little more than a small collection of buildings outside the walls of a Hudson's Bay Company fort, but the day was sunny and warm, the trees were in bloom and, compared to San Francisco, the ground was gloriously flat and level. Truly the new frontier, it was growing fast as men poured in from around the world in hopes of finding gold, so it was perfect for the likes of him, Gibbs and other black men with indefatigable entrepreneurial spirits. Moses and two other men had even had an audience with Governor James Douglas when they arrived and he officially welcomed them to Victoria.

"It won't be easy for you," Douglas had said. "Though you will find most people of British heritage tolerant, and even supportive, of your presence, the town has recently been inundated with American miners who probably won't. Nevertheless, you will enjoy rights here that were not available to you in California. Boundless opportunities await you, gentlemen. It's up to you to take advantage of them!"

The governor had been right in every regard. There were indeed opportunities in Victoria, plenty of them, so Moses dug in and was soon the proud owner of the Pioneer Shaving Saloon and Bath House (Private Entrance for Ladies) on Government Street. He also speculated in land, which was selling for five dollars an acre. If a man could not afford the whole price for a parcel of several acres, he had to come up with a down payment of only 25 percent and pay the rest off over four years. Small lots right in town were selling for $50. Moses was lucky to have been in the vanguard, because when Gibbs arrived two months later, a lot measuring 60 by 120 feet outside the town was selling for $100, and in town anywhere from $1,500 to $5,000. Just after their arrival, someone bought a lot for $5,000 and sold it three days later for $6,200. In fact, there was such a rush on land that the Land Office had to be closed while it caught up with its surveying. Fortunately, Gibbs and Lester had eventually sold the Boot Emporium for an excellent price, and had the foresight to bring with them a mountain of mining supplies purchased cheaply in San Francisco, which they sold at a substantial profit in Victoria. They opened another thriving store, this time selling mining provisions in addition to boots, and Gibbs bought a house and rented half of it out for extra income. When Nathan Pointer arrived a couple of months later, he opened a clothing store.

Just as important for blacks, besides the value of land as an investment, after nine months of being a property owner, a man had earned the right to vote. Casting a ballot was something that most black men had never done before, and they did it proudly and conscientiously. Indeed, they had made more headway here than would have ever been possible in California and the real proof of the pudding happened when an escaped slave arrived in Victoria as a stowaway on a ship from Washington Territory. Upon discovering his non-paying passenger, the captain locked him in a cabin with every intention of returning him to his owner. When Moses and Gibbs got wind of it they obtained a writ of *habeas corpus* and had the slave brought ashore by the sheriff. As soon as he set foot on British soil, he became a free man. He now lived in Victoria and was going to school. Such a feat could not have been duplicated in California, and Moses and Gibbs were proud of it. Yet they soon learned that the town was not without its problems.

They had come to a place that they hoped would be colour-blind, but it was not. On one level, Moses sensed a kind of snobbery on the part of the governing body of the colony, as well as from the professional classes. To be sure, these people sup-ported blacks, but for the most part that support stemmed from a single ulterior motive: a fear of American annexation. They knew that if it came to a vote, the blacks would be against it, so they needed to keep them reasonably content. The superficiality of it made the blacks feel merely tolerated, even used, when they had hoped that their presence would be genuinely embraced.

On a second level, the problem was much more serious. There were now more Americans in Victoria than any other nationality and few had left their bigotries behind. They had little tolerance for "uppity" Negroes trying to integrate themselves completely into the white community, and the unfortunate result was trouble reminiscent of San Francisco.

Paradoxically, it was in church that their troubles began. In their refusal to become cliquey by establishing a black church, Moses and the others attended services at the Anglican church led by the Reverend Edward Cridge. They had only been attending a short time when their presence brought a letter to one of the local newspapers. "The Ethiopians *perspired!*" the writer, an American named Sharpstone, said. "They always do when out of place. Several white gentlemen left their seats vacant, and sought the purer atmosphere outside; others moodily endured the aromatic luxury of their positions, in no very pious frame of mind."[1]

Gibbs had promptly written a response that said, in part, that terms such as "Ethiopian perspiration" and "aromatic luxury" had "long become obsolete even in the United States, and only writers of small calibre and low conceptions resort to it ... It comes with a bad grace from Americans to talk of the horrors of amalgamation when every plantation of the south is more or less a seraglio, and numbers of the most prominent men in the State of California have manifested little heed to color in their choice of companions in an amorous intrigue or a nocturnal debauch."[2]

Soon after that, there arrived in town a breath of fresh air in the person of the Reverend William F. Clarke, a Canadian of the Congregational Union. His church, he told the newspapers, would be open to people of all colours. Furthermore, he was utterly opposed to slavery and let his feelings on the subject be known. The result was that his church was crowded, with a good proportion of the congregation black. Predictably, it was not long before a committee of disgruntled whites approached Clarke and expressed their displeasure with the fact that blacks sat intermingled with whites.

"What would you have me do?" he asked politely.

"Either they are confined to their own corner or we will go, and if we go, your entire congregation will be black."

"I see no undo hardship with that," Clarke replied. "Besides, what you propose is a sin in the eyes of God who makes no distinction between white and black souls. There'll be no 'Negro corner' in my church."

The whites withdrew, and while their prediction did not come entirely true, a major part of Clarke's congregation was indeed black. He was content, though, until a second representative of the Congregational Union arrived in Victoria, this time from Britain. His name was Matthew Macfie; he disagreed with Clarke's stance, and stated so publicly. He even opened his own church, in competition with Clarke. Those whites still attending the latter's services were under so much public pressure that they eventually withdrew, and several blacks, who could not stand the open warfare, returned to the Reverend Cridge's Anglican fold. Eventually Clarke could no longer financially sustain himself or his mission and he had to leave Victoria. It was no small victory for the segregationists.

Then things went from bad to worse. During the summer of 1860 some blacks had tried to attend the Colonial Theatre and were bombarded with rotten eggs. A small fracas that broke out ended up with charges being laid against both blacks and whites. The affair was yet another wedge driven between the two racial groups, and those applying the hammer were still mainly Americans. Though Moses had not been at the theatre at the time, he was deeply affected by the incident. It was precisely the kind of thing that he, Gibbs, and the others had travelled 1,300 miles north to avoid.

⁓

The carriage rattled over the James Bay Bridge. The tide was out and an ungodly smell arose from the flats; the dust in Government Street, often clogged with mud, came as a welcome relief. The light cast from the carriage's lantern caused ghostly shadows to flit along the shop fronts on the street, and here and there lamps glowed behind curtained windows. Otherwise, the overcast night was as black as a coal pit.

In retrospect, they probably should not have gone to the concert tonight, but their reasons for going were honourable. The concert was held to reduce the debt of Victoria's hospital, and many members of the black community had leapt in to help. Since they could afford it, they bought tickets in the dress circle, the best and most expensive seats in the house. It was, after all, for a good cause. But when they heard the rumours circulating around town that there might be trouble, Moses, Gibbs, Lester and Pointer had met to discuss how they should respond and decided that doing nothing was the most prudent course. When they entered the theatre, the air was as taut as a wagon spring. They thought for a moment that they should reconsider their options, but knew that if they did not make a stand there, they would have to do it somewhere else. It was best to get it over with and have it behind them.

It was behind them all right, Moses thought, but what was ahead? There was little doubt that the opposition was relentless, and could throw up walls quicker than men like Gibbs or himself could knock them down, but Moses was not ready to give in. As for Gibbs, Moses knew of no man with a finer sense of justice, nor a better appreciation of what was needed to achieve it, than his friend. He was, and would undoubtedly remain, a formidable champion of Negro rights. Moses was sure that Victoria had not heard the last of him.

The carriage turned right onto Johnson Street and, just beyond Quadra Street, pulled up in front of Moses' house, one of the largest in this part of town. Moses sighed, almost reluctant to get out. Now he had to face the other serious problem of life in Victoria, this one of his own making.

Waiting for him was Sarah, his bride of less than two years. They had met at a soirée at the Gibbses, largely at the instigation of Maria. The Gibbses had met Sarah in Philadelphia where she had sought refuge after working with the Underground Railroad. This was when Gibbs had gone back to east to look for a wife and found Maria. After they were married, the couple went to visit Frederick Douglass in Philadelphia, where the renowned abolitionist had introduced them to Sarah. Douglass spoke of her work and said that some time in the west would undoubtedly be good for her delicate health. The Gibbses were glad to help and offered Sarah work as their housekeeper. She accepted. However, everyone thought her behaviour a little "queer," that she was a "broody sort" and frankly, so did Moses. Yet she was also mysterious, and he had found it very attractive. Unlike most women of the day, she wore her long dresses without a crinoline and while one part of him thought it quite brazen, another thought it exquisitely alluring. When the Gibbses decided that some male company might be good for her, Moses came to mind first. At the party, he had invited her for a walk and she seemed to have to think the proposal over for an eternity before she accepted.

They had stepped out alone, beneath a brilliant August moon, and walked slowly down the gentle slope toward the Birdcages. Though he made his arm available, she had not taken it; indeed, he thought she seemed a little wary, as if she were having some difficulty placing her trust in him. Yet with every step they had taken, side by side, not touching, he wanted her more. His body was charged with sexual tension and he wondered if she could sense it. In his excitement, he prattled like a schoolboy but could not help himself. With great pride he told her of his exploits as a conductor on the Underground Railroad in California. He knew that she had also been a conductor, but when he asked her about it, she said only that it "wasn't much compared to his work." By then he was completely smitten by her. On the way back to the party, she slipped her arm in his and he felt as if he had won the world's best prize. Within two weeks he had asked her to marry him, and almost dropped to the floor when she said yes, without a moment's hesitation. When he found what an excellent cook she was, and that her parents had owned a boarding house, Moses quickly invested in a large house and let her run it. She soon turned it into one of the finest lodgings in town. Even Lady Jane Franklin, widow of the lost Arctic explorer, had stayed with them during a visit to Victoria, and praised the service and how spotless the place was kept.

Spotless it certainly was, thought Moses, almost pathologically so. And that was just one of several things that gave him grave concern about their future. He bade goodnight to the manservant, who stood by so that Moses could see his way by the light of the carriage's lantern. Once he was safely in the front door, the carriage rattled off, the noise fading away in the dark distance.

Sarah was still up, for she did not sleep well, but she seemed wholly uninterested in the evening's events. At least it meant that she did not accuse him of being out with another woman, which she had taken to doing lately, and that was a godsend. Moses had had a headache earlier, from the strain of the evening combined with the smoke and the liquor, but the cool sea air and the jouncing of the carriage over the uneven streets had revived him. By the time they were preparing for bed he was once again charged with the night's excitement. What he wanted most was his wife, intimately, but he did not let on to her that this was the case. He could not stand the thought of being denied his role as a man, which was certain to happen, nor did he feel like getting into a losing argument about it. Not on this night, of all nights, since he had already been denied his rights as a human being. One rejection a day was about all his pride could handle. His heart felt as heavy as granite and it was some time before he fell asleep.

He arose early, even before Sarah awakened to begin preparing breakfast for their boarders, and crept from the house so as not to disturb anyone. It was his custom to take a morning constitutional to clear his head before eating breakfast and opening his barbershop. He instinctively headed down to Wharf Street and the harbour.

Along Johnson Street he passed Nathan Pointer's store, which offered "fancy goods" for gentlemen, where Moses bought most of his clothes. He was wearing a black suit, with a grey vest over a white shirt, and a grey hat with a creased crown and the brim turned slightly up at the sides. A gold watch chain hung from a vest pocket. He looked like a man of means and he was. He smiled easily at those he passed, nodding hello. Most returned his greeting, a few simply turned their heads as if he were not there, proving that, despite his prominence, he could disappear as easily in Victoria as he could in San Francisco. He turned left onto Wharf Street, past the Royal Hotel with its façade of six arches and a balcony that ran the width of the building, then past Haas & Rosenfeld's dry-goods store, where customers could purchase everything from boots to blankets. New brick buildings were springing up here and there, as the city was in the throes of a population and construction boom. Crossing to the west side of Wharf he strode defiantly by McCrea's Auction House. The interior was dark and empty of people, McCrea himself nowhere to be seen, but it did not matter. The gesture was important. Across from the recently built Hudson's Bay Company's warehouse, he turned down the short slope between some sheds that led onto their wharf, one of several along the waterfront that gave the street its name.

He always felt drawn to the harbour. It was a place of movement and a place of transition. These steamers tied up to the wharves, and the handful of small sailing vessels at anchor, were more than just ships. They were lines connecting Victoria to the rest of the world. If a man had the money and the desire to leave, he could go anywhere he pleased: trade fir trees for palms, frigid green water for balmy turquoise lagoons, and temperate weather for tropical. He could even go home. And yet these days Victoria was the destination of choice. Gold, in the creeks of Cariboo, shone so brightly that it was seen in the dreams of men around the world and each ship brought hundreds of them, all marching to the beat of the same drum, and nearly tripping over each other in their impatience to debark. But as was often the case for those who travelled great distances in search of something better, many found little more than a change of climate and more disappointment than they had bargained for.

Moses was not disappointed, however. Besides his successful business ventures, he loved Victoria for the beauty of its setting on a lovely harbour at the tip of an island that he considered to be one of the garden spots of the world. He had even written an open letter to the black newspaper in San Francisco, extolling Victoria's virtues, and stating that it was a God-sent land for coloured people. He hoped that it provided encouragement for other blacks to make the journey northward.

There was no one about, so Moses walked out to the ship tied up at the end of the wharf, enjoying the solitude, the sound of ropes rubbing against wood and the slow creak of the ship's timbers. On the south side of the harbour the masts of moored sailing vessels swayed gently in the light airs that rippled the water. He pulled a pipe and a soft leather pouch from his jacket pocket. Untying the pouch's flap, he removed a plug of tobacco and tamped it into the bowl of the pipe. Then he struck a match and, shielding the flame in his cupped hands, laid it against the tobacco and drew deeply. Other than a comely woman, he found few things more satisfying. He blew a large puff of smoke into the cool sea air and in his mind's eye saw himself stepping down the gangway from the *Commodore* onto a similar dock in Esquimalt. He could not believe how much his life had changed since then, particularly with his marriage to Sarah.

He accepted most of the blame for their present situation. In his desperation for female companionship, he had acted hastily in asking her to be his wife. He had taken advantage of her vulnerability, failing to recognize that she needed more than he was able to provide. He could not define exactly what it was that she needed, but it was not him and that was also part of the problem. Now he would have given anything to be able to push time back to the moment when he first saw her so that they would both be free to walk away without the possibility of anyone getting hurt. He was confused, a state of mind that bothered him greatly, for he had always prided himself on being a clear thinker. He knew that he had to do something; he just did not know what.

His pipe had gone out and he walked to the edge of the pier to knock the dottle into the water. Then he retraced his path along Wharf Street, but turned up Yates instead of Johnson. He passed the Sutro brothers' tobacco shop on the corner and could see one of them inside, getting ready to open for the day. He thought it might be Emil but was not sure because of the reflections in the glass. In any case he knew that Sutro could see him, so Moses glared in his direction momentarily and then sharply turned his head away. After last night, he would not be buying any more tobacco from the Sutros, and other blacks would go elsewhere too. Not that it meant much in terms of hurting the brothers financially; it was more the principle of the thing.

Carts and carriages bumped by and hooves thudded on the hard ground. There were more people on the boardwalks now, adding to the general noise of the town. Passing Ringo's restaurant, Moses decided on the spur of the moment to stop in for breakfast before going to work, knowing full well that he was avoiding Sarah.

Sam Ringo was a giant of a man and as black as it was possible for a black man to be. His hands seemed almost as big as the plates on which he piled his generous servings of food, and his face was scarred by smallpox. He would have been the first to admit that he presented a rather frightening sight for most white men, but behind the ominous exterior was a truly gentle man. He was soft spoken yet exuberant, and few people were as content as Ringo. He had been born a slave, but was given his freedom when, after nursing his smallpox-stricken master back to health, he caught the disease himself. His grateful master promised to free him if he survived. That he was now here in Victoria testified to Ringo's toughness and strength, not to mention his owner's integrity. Now, according to many people, whites included, he served the best food in town, and Ringo was a happy man. He was working in the kitchen and Moses waved hello before sitting down. A sleepy-looking waiter took his order of coffee and Ringo's breakfast specialty: eggs poached in thick cream. Whereas other cooks in town merely seasoned the dish with salt and pepper, Ringo added a secret blend of herbs and spices, then passed a red hot flat iron over the top to brown it. To Moses, it was heaven on a plate.

Just then, voices were raised at a table over by the window. Two white men, arguing about the growing war between the American states, lost their tempers and rose to their feet. One man threw a punch; the other warded it off and landed a blow on his opponent's forehead. The two men stepped back from each other and drew derringers. Moses dove for cover on the floor, and the waiter hid behind a counter. Hearing the altercation, Ringo strode from the kitchen and grasped the two men, one in each of his big arms. Pulling them in tight to his chest so they could not move, he looked down at them and said, "No you don't, gen'lemen. Not in my 'stablishment least ways. You wanna do that sort a thing then do it outside where the rain'll wash away the blood. Meantime, I'm gonna let ya go and you'll put those toys away an' shake hands."

The men looked sheepish, like children caught doing something they should not, and Ringo let them go. The men pocketed their weapons and grudgingly shook hands, though neither would look the other in the eye.

"Now," said Ringo, "why don't you gen'lemen sit down and finish yo' breakfast, an I tell ya what. It's my treat. But just this mornin' only. I don't want you pullin' guns in here tomorrow mornin' just so's you can get another free breakfast."

He let out a hearty laugh at his own joke, and it seemed to break the ice between the combatants.

The two men sat down, the waiter stood up from behind the counter and Moses got back into his chair. As he passed Moses' table, Ringo rolled his eyes and said, "Your eggs in cream is comin' right up, Mr. Moses," and he disappeared back into the domain of his kitchen.

Over his meal and coffee, Moses' mind wandered to Sarah again, but there were no revelations. He finished up, paid for the meal, and gave the waiter a generous tip, a British custom that had been frowned upon in California, but was a matter of course in Victoria. He left for work, waving goodbye to Ringo who was smiling at life in the kitchen.

CHAPTER SEVEN

⚭

I t had been a slow morning as customers dribbled in: a few naval officers, some conciliatory about the previous evening, others silent. The bath house was quiet, but Old John Taylor, the man Moses had hired to run it, was in there, ensuring that it was sparkling clean and there was hot water. After lunch, during a quiet period, Moses sat in one of the customers' chairs and read the *Gazette*. It was too soon for anything about last night's fracas to be in the paper, but he always liked to make sure his advertisements were there and printed properly. He had developed a new product from a mixture of different herbs and oils that he was convinced were beneficial to the scalp when massaged in, and would even grow hair on balding heads. He called it the "Invigorator" and it had proved to be an instant hit, even though he charged $10 a treatment for it. Several men in town with thinning hair swore by it — equating the tingling on their scalp with new hair trying to sprout — and visited the saloon regularly.

Through with the paper, he began to compose a letter to Governor Douglas. His Excellency should know right away how disappointed the black community was in last night's debacle.

"Coming to this colony," he wrote, "to found our homes, and rear our families, we did so advisedly, assured by those in authority that we should meet with no disabilities political or conventional on the ground of color."[1] He read the sentence over a couple of times and decided he liked its accusatory tone without naming names. A more direct approach would only rile the governor and they needed him on their side. He continued, condemning segregation and pointing out that not only were they citizens, and therefore deserving of equality, but as a group that owned more than $200,000 in real estate, they paid a lot of taxes which helped fill government coffers. He thought about that for a moment, wondering if it was a plea for special treatment and decided that it was not. It was merely stating the facts. He went on to praise the virtues of their hard work and its contribution to the overall well-being of the colony, then finished up by saying that they desired to have their "families untrammelled by the perpetuation of a mean and senseless prejudice against color — a prejudice having no foundation that is honorable, and alone supported by the ignorance and brutality of the lowest order of society." He liked that line. "We therefore petition your Excellency to make such recommendations that will guarantee the rights of your petitioners in common with all other men."

He reread the letter, decided it was a good start, then folded it up and put it away, expecting that others of the Pioneer Committee would have thoughts to add to it. Just then the doorbell jangled and a customer came in.

"Good afternoon, Moses."

"Indeed it is, George."

George Blessing climbed into the barber's chair and let out a sigh as Moses threw the cape over him and secured it around his neck. He was a slender man, in his late thirties, with thinning blond hair and a reddish beard, a combination that Moses still found fascinating. Blessing was fastidious about his looks, liked to keep his beard neatly trimmed, and was an Invigorator enthusiast, all of which made him a regular customer. With business as a common ground, and being practically neighbours — he was now a partner in a construction firm just around the corner on Yates Street — they had also become friends over the years. He hailed from Cleveland, and as near as Moses could tell, did not have a prejudiced bone in his body. Blessing seemed a timid man in some ways, not at all the kind of personality to survive in the business world, yet his company was prospering in the economic boom the town was experiencing.

"The usual trim today, George?" Moses asked.

"Please, and then I think I would like to hide in one of your baths for a while. Some days business is a little too good and today is one of them. If anyone comes in asking for me, tell them I've joined the rabble in search of gold."

"You can depend on it. But these are exciting times, are they not? I hear that there isn't an inch of land left on Antler Creek to stake a claim."

"It's probably true," said Blessing. "Otherwise someone would have surely found it by now and banged a stake in it."

Antler Creek was the latest Eldorado in British Columbia. As gold along the Fraser River had petered out, miners, certain there were still riches to be found, had pushed their way north, deeper into the interior. Reasonably good placer deposits had turned up on a small creek flowing into Cariboo Lake and it was not long before there was scarcely room to take a breath, let alone twirl a gold pan. Doc Keithley, the man who had discovered the creek, and three companions decided to move on. They climbed over a nearby plateau to the far side where they found other creeks and followed one as it tumbled away from them. In one place along the bank they came across a large number of antlers, is if it were a place that deer came to die. Farther down, they entered a small canyon and found gold nuggets lying among the stones on both sides of the creek. In no time at all they had gathered $175 worth of the precious metal. This had happened a year ago, in the fall of 1860, and though the men kept it a secret as long as they could, it was like putting up a hand to stop the wind. By this past summer, a small town had grown up on the banks of Antler Creek, complete with a casino and, not far away, a racetrack.

"What about you, Moses? Ever had the desire to sell everything and join the rush?"

"Ten years ago, when I first arrived in California, I was itching to do just that, but a man much wiser than myself steered me in an equally productive direction. What I make as a businessman might not glitter like gold, George, but it's just as spendable."

Blessing chuckled. "I thought you might be reconsidering after that fiasco at the theatre last night."

"You've heard about it?"

"Everyone's heard about it. The word is that your people are to blame for the entire affair, which automatically makes me suspect that just the opposite is true."

"And you'd be right," said Moses, and explained how the incident had unfolded, to which his customer could only mutter and shake his head. After trimming Blessing's beard with scissors, Moses took the straight razor and cleaned up the stubble on his neck. Done, he showed off his work in the mirror, then removed the cape and said, "Old John Taylor's in the bath house and if he isn't sleeping I'm sure he'll be glad to see you." Blessing paid for his haircut, adding extra for the bath and his usual generous tip.

Moses had a few more customers before it was time to call it a day. He said good night to Old John Taylor, who would look after the baths during the evening, for which there was a rear entrance in Langley Street, and went home to see how the day had gone for Sarah.

He worried about his wife. She was an enigma, not the same woman he had fallen madly in love with and married. Something was going on in her mind that was beyond his ken, and beyond, he knew, the ken of modern medicine. On the very first night they had made love she had wept. For him it had been a great release but for her it was something vastly different, in a way that he did not understand. It was as if something flipped over in her mind to show a different personality. He was puzzled and was incapable of figuring it out. Now, more and more, she was retreating from him, turning away at night when he needed her most. He would drape his arm over her shoulder and she would simply not respond, neither by fitting her bottom against him, nor brushing his arm away. It was as if she did not even know he was there.

Some of her daytime behaviour was bothering him too. She had taken to wearing a kerchief about her head in the manner of black female servants and slaves, which he had asked her to remove.

"Women of good society do not wear such articles of clothing," he had said, to which she had answered, "I do," and that was the end of the discussion as far as she was concerned.

He felt that whatever her rationale was, it was probably the same as whatever drove her to wear her dresses without crinolines. That was also how black slave women dressed.

Moses was more and more certain that Sarah's past was a ghost that appeared each day to haunt her. He thought about what he knew of that past and realized it was not much. She had been born Sarah Jane Douglas in Baltimore, free, her parents having been manumitted by a dying master trying to win a place in heaven. Unwilling to move north, they stayed in Baltimore where all their friends were, reckoning that coloured was coloured no matter which state they were in. Sarah's father was a carpenter and her mother ran a boarding house, and together they were able to send their daughter to a school for free blacks that also taught the elements of behaviour in polite society. Sarah worked hard, both with her studies and helping her mother, and as long as she remained servile when she was among whites, things were fine. Yet it was a strange world she lived in, where some blacks were free and others, the majority, were not. Free blacks and slaves even married on rare occasions, with the enslaved person able to spend Saturday nights and Sundays with his or her spouse. Punishment for running away was so severe that few were willing to risk it.

Though she had a subservient role in society, Sarah was always amazed that she walked around free while others did not. She had never given much thought to doing anything about it, however, until the day she met a diminutive black woman named Harriet Tubman.

Harriet had herself been a slave in Bucktown, on the eastern shore of Maryland, until she heard one day that her master was about to sell her to the owner of a cotton plantation deeper in the south. That was when she decided to run. She made her way to the home of Quaker abolitionists, who drove her by covered wagon to the Choptank River, where she set out on foot by herself. Travelling only at night, she followed the river northeast to its source, after which the North Star and moss on the trees guided her the rest of the way to the Pennsylvania border and freedom. Once she was safely among friends in Philadelphia, she decided to devote her life to helping other slaves to escape, and became a conductor on the Underground Railroad. It was while she was back in Baltimore rescuing her niece, a friend of Sarah's, that the two women met.

Mary Ann Brodas, Harriet's niece, had been hired out by her owner to the Douglas' boarding house. Though they hated having to pay her wages to her master, they at least could provide good working conditions, and for many slaves that was a blessing. One day Mary Ann confided to Sarah that she was about to run, that her aunt, a conductor on the Underground Railroad, was coming down from Philadelphia to lead her to freedom. She had to tell someone before she burst, and she trusted Sarah implicitly. She was going to leave on a Saturday night so that she had all day Sunday, when she would not be missed, to run. Sarah knew that her parents would be eager to help and they arranged for Mary Ann to slip back to the boarding house after she had reported in at the plantation — something that was required of hired-out slaves after their day's work — where her aunt could meet her after dark. All the Douglases had to do to protect themselves was report her missing when she did not show up for work on Monday morning.

Sarah did not quite know what she expected a conductor of the Underground Railroad to look like but it was nothing remotely resembling the person who came through the door. Harriet Tubman was short and slender. Her rather plain looks were offset by her poker-straight posture and a scar on her forehead that gave her a warrior-like demeanour. She was an incredibly strong woman, both physically and mentally, and was determined to help on the railroad as long as she was able. When Sarah asked her why she risked the freedom that had been won so hard, she said, "When I stepped over Mason and Dixon's line I looked at my hands to see if I was the same person now that I was free. I saw a glory over everything, the sun shone like gold among the trees and over the fields, and I felt like I was in heaven. I want others to have that same feeling."

Sarah had never before been in the presence of such a charismatic figure and was completely in her thrall. All Harriet had to do was crook her finger and she would have followed her anywhere. Which was why Sarah volunteered to become a conductor herself.

That was the extent of Moses' knowledge about his wife's past, except that she had eventually gone north to Philadelphia for safety reasons and it was there that she had met the Gibbses. She never talked about her experiences with the Underground Railroad and whenever Moses asked, she simply repeated what she had said that night during their walk to the Birdcages: that they were paltry compared to his. But for some time now he had suspected that there was much more, that something terrible had happened to her on one of her runs that she did not want to talk about. That she *could* not talk about.

Sarah was setting the table in the dining room when Moses arrived home. She was again wearing the kerchief, which he so despised, but he said only "Hello, my dear." Her response was simply a nod and to ask him to call their two boarders down for dinner. She did not join in the light conversation around the table and only picked at her food.

Later, in their room at the back of the house, she said, "You were missed at breakfast this morning. But I don't suppose that's of much concern to you."

"I do apologize," he said, "and yes, it very much concerns me. It also concerns me that your behaviour is so mystifying that I would rather enjoy the friendly ugliness of Ringo than endure the rancour here."

"Rancour, you say? You haven't seen the half of it, Wellington! The pain you inflict on me is endless. I know where you disappear to in your absences. I will not be fooled."

"But you *are* fooled, Sarah. You're fooled into thinking I'm involved in some tryst that is only a figment of your imagination. There is no one else, there never has been. I escape *from* you, not *to* someone else. Look Sarah, there's something troubling you and I don't believe that it has anything to do with me. Until you're able to tell me what it is, things will only worsen and you'll have no one to blame but yourself."

Their conversations were always reduced to the common denominators of open or veiled accusations of infidelity, and frustratingly unsuccessful defenses. In her paranoia she truly believed that he had another woman. The good Lord knew that he was tempted more and more with each passing day, but it had not happened. Nevertheless, he was a man and men had needs.

He went to her and tried to take her in his arms, but she turned away and he knew he would get no more from her that night. He hated her rejections and his first response was anger. He wanted to grab her and shake her back to reality but, instead, he left her to her twisted thoughts, stomped out of the room, and went to the parlour. He was thankful that the boarders had gone to their rooms and he was alone. He poured himself a drink, then added more for good measure.

There was a portrait on the wall of the two of them on their wedding day, and even then there was a haunted look in her eyes that he might have noticed had he not been so caught up in his own feelings. How he had loved her then! Now she was slowly driving his love away and he was certain that she did not even realize what she was doing. The world she inhabited was not the same as most people's, Moses knew, and he did not know how to reach into it. It seemed that divorce was the only answer, but the idea disturbed him. Not only was he averse to the thought of deserting her, but it was the sort of thing that was best avoided, especially for a black man of his stature. All it did was make white people even more skeptical of black morals than they already were.

When he arose the following morning Sarah was in the kitchen, dressed in a long gown that accentuated her hips, and a colourful kerchief knotted around her head. It both attracted and repelled him. He went for a walk. After breakfast, he said good-bye to his wife and the boarders and left for the shaving saloon.

Business was steady throughout the morning, and about 11 o'clock a runner arrived with a message from Gibbs, who wrote that he would stop by the saloon at noon in hopes that Moses would join him for lunch at Ringo's. The message boosted Moses' spirits, which had been flagging ever since he got out of bed. Of all the men he had met since leaving the Caymans, he admired Gibbs the most, and having lunch with him would be most welcome.

When Gibbs arrived, his energy permeated the room. "Good afternoon, Mr. Moses," he said, resorting to formalities because a white customer was still in the chair.

"I will be with you in a moment, Mr. Gibbs," Moses replied, wiping the soap from the customer's face. He then removed the cape, brushed the man's shoulders and took payment for his work. When they were alone Gibbs lifted up the newspaper he had been carrying and waved it in front of Moses.

"Have you seen today's *Colonist*?" he asked.

"I've not had the time, but I'll wager there's something in it you'd like me to read."

"Indeed there is, but not here. Ringo's will do just fine."

After locking the shop — Old John Taylor could receive bath house customers at the Langley Street entrance — Moses and Gibbs turned north along the boardwalk on Government Street, stepping out briskly. According to Gibbs, a black man must always show purpose in his walk and should never be seen idling.

The weather was clear and dry, the air unseasonably cold, as if winter was determined to get an early start. Moses buttoned up his jacket and thrust his hands into his pockets. Gibbs was about to speak when he was interrupted by a disturbance in the street. A black drayman with a heavy load was unable to get his horse to move. He had got down from the seat and was cursing the animal, flaying it with a whip along its neck and sides. The horse reared and whinnied in fear and pain. In a flash Gibbs ran into the street and knocked the man to the ground. He pulled the whip from the startled man's hand and grabbing his shirt front, hauled him to a sitting position. He stuck his face into the drayman's and said through clenched teeth, "You are a discredit to our race! Every time someone like you does something like this, the Negro cause is set back a dozen years and the struggle becomes all the harder. Don't ever let me catch you doing anything remotely like this again or I'll have *you* flayed until every inch of your black skin is gone and you can no longer be an embarrassment to our race. Do you understand my words?"

The man nodded sullenly, and Gibbs added, "Now, if I were you I would set about my work responsibly and take some of that load off the wagon. It's far too heavy for that horse."

He let the man go and rejoined Moses on the boardwalk, and the two men continued on to Ringo's, Gibbs breathing heavily, his nostrils flared in anger.

"You never cease to astonish me, Gibbs. Most people of your station would have passed that incident by and complained about it later over tea, myself included. Yet you take it on as if you alone are responsible to make sure such things are not repeated."

"But I am responsible, Moses, and so are you. He had to be set straight by a black man, don't you see? Had it been left to a white man we would not have heard the end of it. We probably still won't but at least it shouldn't be nearly as bad."

At Ringo's, they took a table near the back and ordered the beef stew, which was unlike any other in town. Most restaurateurs cooked theirs in beer, but Ringo cooked his in water, thickened slightly with flour, to which he added vegetables, bits of bacon and a variety of sweet herbs for extra flavour. It was delicious. Gibbs pulled the newspaper from his pocket and unfolded it, then, dampening his thumb, opened it to the inside pages. "Read this," he said, jabbing at a letter to the editor written by Emil Sutro, the performer at the Theatre Royal who had first asked the blacks to vacate the dress circle.

Opening by saying that he wished to state his case about the "Theatre Fracas," Sutro's letter read in part: "When I reached the theatre I learned that several coloured people were occupying prominent seats in the dress circle, which caused considerable dissatisfaction to many English and American residents, preventing numbers from entering ... I refused then to play and left the theatre for home ... In concluding I would remark that I do not believe in any amalgamation of white and coloured people, nor that the latter should socially intermix with the former. No sensible person will object to the coloured population being admitted to any public place of amusement; but let one part of the house, no matter which, be reserved for their particular use — where people will never intrude upon their society."[2]

Moses looked up from the paper. "When he says that it doesn't matter which part of the theatre is reserved for us, I expect he means any part that's outside the dress circle."

"Beyond a doubt."

Moses continued reading. "They form a distinct class, and enjoy their full rights as citizens, but let these 'gentlemen' — *if they claim to be gentlemen* — not force themselves upon white society, where they are not desired, and are furthermore offensive to a majority of the residents of Victoria."

Moses sighed. "The man's a pompous fool," he said.

"Not to mention a damned liar. He's also a Jew and you'd think that he and his own kind had seen enough torment themselves to want to avoid inflicting the same thing on other people. Read on."

Below Sutro's letter was one from Gibbs, who went on at length about the barbarous treatment he and his fellow blacks had received at the theatre, and how precious little was being done by the authorities to stamp out such behaviour. As loyal citizens who paid taxes (he himself had just paid $400) blacks not only deserved the protection of the law, but had also earned it. He finished off by saying, "... in return am I to be told ... that I shall be degraded on public occasions and proscribed to the Box, Parquet, or any other place, to please a few renegade Yankees, who, if they had a spark of patriotism about them, would be fighting their country's battles, and not be laying around here to save their hides and foment strife ... "[3]

Moses nodded his head in agreement with Gibbs' words and said, "Well put, but we should go further than this. We need to take our case to the governor himself. I have drafted a letter, or at least the beginnings of a letter, to Mr. Douglas. It needs work, and I am hoping you and others of the committee will expand on it. It has to be strongly worded, but with tact, so that we will be given an audience."

He handed the letter to Gibbs who read it. "Excellent!" he said. "I'll attend to it straight away. I have no doubt that the governor will hear us out. I despair only that a hearing is necessary."

Just then, the waiter intervened with their food and placed the steaming bowls on the table with a flourish.

"Ah," said Gibbs. "Ringo has at last dispensed his happiness from the kitchen. Eat up, my friend. Nothing of which we speak will ever be as palatable as this!"

CHAPTER EIGHT

The following morning Gibbs and Pointer were in police court in Bastion Square, facing the assault charges from the theatre incident. Moses sat in the gallery with Lester. The presiding magistrate was Augustus Pemberton, a Dublin-born Anglo-Irishman, who himself had given work to some of the blacks when they first arrived in the community, and was thought to be supportive. He called the first case, a man charged with being drunk and disorderly who was fined $10 for his sins. Then he called the assault cases.

First up were several witnesses who testified that Ryckman did not throw the flour. When asked if he himself threw it, one witness refused to answer, even though he did not have any reason to believe that it might incriminate him. Pemberton could have found the man in contempt of court, but for reasons of his own did not, and excused him. One of Sam Ringo's waiters was the only black who had actually witnessed the incident to come forward. He told the court that Ryckman had put pressure on him not to testify, but he had no corroborative evidence. Ringo himself took the stand, and when asked if he had been the recipient of any pressure, he said that even though he had lost a lot of business over the past week because his employee was going to testify, he had not been asked directly by Ryckman, or anyone else, to fire the man.

Since Gibbs freely admitted to his part in the affair, there was no need to call witnesses in that regard. Insofar as Pointer was concerned, only one witness could recall the extent of his involvement and that was the naval officer he had punched.

When the proceedings were done, Pemberton chastised all of the men for their behaviour, saying their conduct was unbecoming to men of their station. He then acquitted the four whites and Pointer for lack of evidence but, as Gibbs had pled guilty, he fined him $15.

Later, over brandies in the back room of Gibbs and Lester's store, Moses asked his friend if he thought that he had been ill-treated by the law.

"Since I confessed to my part in the incident," said Gibbs, "Judge Pemberton had no alternative but to fine me. I broke the law and that's the truth of the matter. But we were up against a pack of cowards today, Moses. That bag of flour didn't launch itself into the air. One of those men did it but hadn't the courage to stand up and admit it. Unfortunately, people like that can obstruct the law with bare-faced lies, and did so in this case. But there is a greater court in which they will one day be judged and their lies will be of no use to them there."

"True," said Moses. "And regardless of the outcome, I suppose there is some victory for us in the fact that black men were in a court of law, offering testimony."

"You're right. It is a victory, and no small one. But look at the distance we've had to travel and the exotic port to which we've had to sail to acquire such a basic right. And we still have to be on our guard that the court doesn't fall asleep whenever it is hearing black men."

Another week passed and October sat on the fence, undecided as to whether it should be fall or winter. One morning Gibbs came striding up the street, clutching a letter and breathing clouds of condensation in the chilly air. Moses' shop was filled with miners who were flooding the city for the winter, and he was busier than he'd ever been. Gibbs took one look at the crowd and waved the letter.

"When you've got a moment, Mr. Moses," he said, "we should meet." Then he was gone.

Moses reckoned it must be a letter from the governor saying the committee would get an audience. Gibbs looked too buoyant for it to be otherwise.

A week later, Moses and Gibbs were in a carriage on their way to the Birdcages. Though it was within easy walking distance from their shops, this was too important an occasion for them to be seen on foot, so Gibbs had had his manservant pick them up. As they clattered across the James Bay Bridge, the horse at a smart trot, the main building of the legislature stood out on the far side like something blown in from foreign soil. Architecturally unclassifiable, it was part brick, part wood, painted in several shades of red, and had been variously described as Elizabethan, "something between a Dutch Toy and a Chinese Pagoda," and a sheep corral.[1] It had been outrageously expensive to build, but its cost was borne partly by the Hudson's Bay Company and partly by the sale of lots in town. That none of it had come directly out of the taxpayer's pocket was a blessed relief to everyone. Even if it had, though, neither Moses nor Gibbs would have complained much because to them, the building symbolized the possibility that any man could govern in this land — any man from any walk of life, as long as he worked hard.

A low fence of brick pillars connected by wrought-iron pickets fronted the site. Behind the fence was a newly landscaped area of grass and shrubs and a semi-circular driveway that led from the east gate to the steps of the legislature, then around to the west gate and out to the road again. The gate was open and the carriage moved briskly up the incline to the building, an effect that Moses liked: all business, a visit from men to be reckoned with.

They were met within the building by an army sergeant who ushered them upstairs and into the governor's office, then retreated outside the door to stand guard. The room was large and impressive, the walls lined with floor-to-ceiling oak shelves filled with leather-bound books, the windows framed by red velvet drapes, while the rich wood floor was partially covered by a colourful Oriental carpet. Most impressive was James Douglas himself, who came from behind a massive oak desk and shook hands with them.

"Welcome, gentlemen, do sit down," he said, indicating the two chairs that had been placed in front of the desk. He was a big man, sturdily built but portly now as he neared his sixtieth year. Burnt-toast eyes that drilled right through ordinary mortals looked out from beneath bushy eyebrows, and his mulatto heritage was quite apparent in his dusky complexion. He had muttonchops, and thick strands of grey hair were combed straight across a balding pate in order, Moses thought, to hide it. Although his clothes were grand, (it was said that he ordered them from London) they were ill-fitting, and were it not for his position and commanding presence he might have seemed a caricature of a British nobleman. His manner when speaking to subordinates, which to him was everyone else in Victoria, was also aristocratic, aloof and cool. His voice was sonorous and he was known never to use a simple word when a more difficult one would do or, for that matter, a single word in place of several.

"So, gentlemen, I have here your epistle dated October 1st in the Year of Our Lord 1861, in which you have clearly stated your complaint. First, I must apologize for any inconvenience that may have come your way as a result of the unfortunate incident on September 20th last. Let me assure you that I have no sympathy with those who would make creed or colour a barrier to any of Her Majesty's subjects attaining and occupying any social position to which their character and capacity may entitle them. However, I regret to say that I am unable to remove the invidious distinction that exists between classes of Her Majesty's subjects. Nevertheless, I would not wish you to leave this office thinking that I have somehow not fulfilled promises I made to you upon your arrival in this colony. To recapitulate, gentleman, I believe that my only assurances were opportunity and enfranchisement, and as near as I am able to ascertain, you have turned opportunity into glowing success and that all of you, at least those who have met the specified waiting-period requirements, enjoy enfranchisement."

Douglas paused for a moment. He had to be careful where he trod here. He was facing retirement and did not want anything to jeopardize a positive ending to his his career. He also did not want to offend his visitors, for he needed them on his side until the awful possibility of American annexation was no longer a concern. Fortunately, the Americans were at war with each other now and their focus had shifted away from the north. But once the war ended, he was certain that they'd be at it again, especially if the rumours about their buying Alaska from the Russians were true. With British Columbia and Vancouver Island they could own the entire west coast from Mexico to the Bering Sea. Not if he could help it. It was British sweat and blood that had opened this land and by God British sweat and blood would keep it!

"So, I have but one solution to offer, gentlemen: time. Time to let the tide of change flow in and drown those who would prevent you from taking your proper place in society; time for the gold creeks in this country to yield only gravel, as they most assuredly will one day; and time for a war to end so that the United States can become a palatable place to which her less than creditable citizens can return. Time, gentlemen. It is on your side if only you'll cultivate the patience to let it do its work."

"We have been patient, Your Excellency," said Gibbs. "But our patience has been worn to a nub, else we would not be taking up *your* time."

Douglas nodded but looked directly at Moses. "I believe I warned you, Mr. Moses, did I not, that settling here, though rewarding, would be arduous and challenging."

"Yes sir, I do recall that," said Moses, clearing his throat. "However ... " He was going to say that blacks like himself, Gibbs and other businessmen in the community had earned the right to sit in any theatre's dress circle and should not be relegated to the gallery where the lowest orders sat, but Douglas interrupted. The man projected such a powerful presence that Moses felt intimidated and unable to assert himself.

"The Americans are by far the largest segment of the population at present," the governor continued, "and therefore wield considerable influence in the legislature. That has to be reckoned with for now, but it will not always be the case. So you must let time work its magic as it is wont to do. Now gentlemen, I must conclude our business and wish you good day."

He stood up, a charismatic figure of authority, signalling the end of the meeting. He shook their hands and ushered them to the door. "Time and patience, gentlemen. Time and patience, and the world will be yours."

On their way back to town it was Gibbs who summed up the reactions of both men. "I feel as if I've just been lectured to by an uncle I never liked, who always frightened me."

Moses gave a small laugh. "You did seem at a loss for words back there, Gibbs, but then again the governor does have a reputation for preferring monologues to dialogues, particularly when they are rolling off his own tongue."

"Well, regardless of his homilies, time only works when you make it work. We must not sit idly by. We must continue working hard for our rights. We must keep pressing. *Vulnerat omnes, ultima necat.*"

"Which means?"

"Each hour injures, the last one slays."

"Hmmm. I'm not sure I feel quite that desperate."

"You're coloured," said Gibbs. "You ought to."

⌘

Cold air spilled out from the interior of British Columbia and pushed October into an early winter. Over the last couple of weeks every steamer between New Westminster and Victoria had been crammed with miners vacating the goldfields with the intent of wintering on the island. The streets were crowded with men, as were the hotels, while the edges of the town were expanded with tents and shanties. In the span of a month the population almost doubled. Larger ships, up from the south, anchored in Esquimalt harbour and brought in more gold seekers wanting to be on hand at the first sign of next year's spring thaw. Some vessels brought in livestock, mostly packhorses, and the Esquimalt road was churned up like a corral as the animals were herded toward town and beyond, to some of the outlying farms for winter grazing. Meanwhile, construction was still going on at a feverish pitch and wood or brick buildings were springing up everywhere. The local industries and businesses were able to absorb some of the men who needed work, as plasterers, carpenters, labourers, clerks, waiters and anything else that would help them eat through the coming winter, but the competition was fierce and for many, the coming months would be lean.

The town was now completely surveyed and subdivided into 60- by 120-foot lots that were being bought up fast, and the roads leaving town to the north and east were lined with cottages. The bridge that joined Victoria with Songhees, on the west side of the harbour, was taken down so that ships could make better use of the area, and two new bridges were built as replacements, one at Rock Bay and another at Point Ellice. A gas works was under construction, the first priority of which would be to light the streets. These were good times for merchants and many could not keep enough supplies on hand to meet the increase in demand. In the Birdcages, there was a proposal to incorporate Victoria as a city, as well as an attempt to give it a local government with teeth. The town's finest citizens flaunted their prosperity by hosting lavish soirées in their lovely James Bay homes, while along the boardwalks of Government and Yates streets, pinched-face miners in threadbare clothes, who could not find work and had run out of money, went begging among the same citizens for enough to buy a decent meal. On the northwest side of town, among the shanties and tents of wintering miners, men's sexual needs were met by local Indian women, some brought by their husbands who negotiated with the miners for their wives' services.

The thermometer dropped even further and the Fraser River froze so hard that all shipping from New Westminster to Yale was stopped. The mainland was snowed in, and Victoria also took on a thick mantle of snow, with ice in the inner harbour, though it was not thick enough to prevent supply ships from the south from docking. The snow continued to fall and settled in for the long haul. In Saanich, it was several feet deep and in town it was blown into sweeping drifts along the streets and boardwalks. It molded eaves and gables, softening their stark angularity so that most of the buildings looked quite beautiful. Occasionally a horse-drawn sleigh, of which the town had only a few, could be seen on the streets, some with bells that announced the Christmas season. Old timers shook their heads in amazement. "This much snow is so unusual in Victoria," they said.

The influx of more Americans brought more cases of overt discrimination. Blacks were crowned with snowballs and, in one instance, a fight that broke out between a white and a black man was allowed to continue, simply because the town had been so quiet and dull with all the snow that the spectators welcomed the excitement. A black man was caned in a saloon for no reason other than that a white man was offended by his presence. Blacks were barred from most saloons owned by Americans and overcharged in others. Lawsuits were brought against the owners, to no avail. Despite such incidents, however, Victoria was no San Francisco.

Over the winter Gibbs used his spare time to read English common law under the tutelage of a local barrister, and Moses was kept busy at the saloon and bath house. The latter was extremely popular and it was all he and Old John Taylor could do to keep enough water coming in from Spring Ridge, and enough wood stocked for the fire to heat it. It was an expensive endeavour, but something for which his customers gladly doled out their money. Since most returned on a regular basis, he got to know some of them quite well, and one of his favourites was an enterprising young man named Bob Stevenson.

Stevenson was just 24 years old, but he had packed a lot of experience into those years. He hailed from Glengarry County in Upper Canada, although Moses thought he had the entrepreneurial spirit of a Yankee. He said he'd been one of the first men to cross the Cascade Mountains, west to east, by horseback. In 1860, he and a small party of men had made their way from Seattle to the Similkameen country to look for gold, and had run into Indian trouble along the Columbia River. They were surrounded, he said, but managed to get away with their scalps when the Indians sobered up and rode off. He did not find much gold and eventually became a customs officer at Osoyoos, but when word of the gold strike at Antler Creek reached him, he decided upon a new venture. He bought 100 horses that he drove up to Lillooet and sold for a $10,000 profit, then went on to Antler Creek where he bought a warehouse. He was shrewd enough to know that the real gold was in the pockets of would-be miners, and he intended to fill that warehouse with supplies and provisions come spring. Stevenson was wintering in Victoria, at the Royal Hotel, which spoke volumes to Moses about the man's cash flow. He also had a bottomless cache of stories and Moses always looked forward to his visits just to hear another one.

Meanwhile, there was Sarah to contend with. Their relationship continued to founder, though some days were better than others. Her paranoia was in check on the good days, but on the bad ones she was absolutely certain that Moses was seeing other women behind her back. One night they went to the Gibbses for a small get-together with some business acquaintances and though most of those who did not know her would have thought her quirky, to Moses she seemed almost normal. However, later at home she accused him of flirting with one of the other men's wives and no matter how much he denied it, she would not be appeased.

She struck out at him, but he caught her wrist in time, then the other wrist when she tried to hit him with that hand. He held on to her and was alarmed by her tremendous strength. It was as if some other being inhabited her body, and he was barely able to keep her in his grip. Then suddenly she fainted and sagged and would have fallen to the floor if he had not been holding on to her. He carried her to the bed and was covering her with a comforter, with every intention of going for the doctor, when she woke up. "No!" she gasped as she pummeled him with her fists. In the half-light of the lamp, he could see terror in her eyes, and once more he restrained her. "Sarah! Sarah! You are all right. It's me, Wellington!" When she realized where she was, she moaned and turned away, sobbing. There was nothing he could do to console her.

The dreary winter months served only to darken her mood even further, and though he was reluctant to do so, he finally confided in Gibbs. He asked his old friend what, if anything, he or Maria knew of Sarah's past. Something had happened to her that she was not able to talk about. Could they enlighten him?

"I know nothing," said Gibbs, "except that she suffered some form of trauma. She seemed to have little trust in men, even in the likes of me, and some even terrified her. Maria and I were pleasantly surprised when she took to you, for we thought it was what she needed. Indeed, she seemed to change for the better, so we were even more pleased when you married. But a blind man could see that all is not well between the two of you, and Maria has wondered if Sarah had lapsed into her old self. I tell you, Moses, women are not easy creatures to live with, for they are not persons of the highest order as men are. Indeed, they'll drive a man to distraction with their monthlies and their vapours, and spend all his hard-earned cash in between. But I digress, dear fellow. It's not women in general that are your concern, it's Sarah. I will ask Maria if she and Sarah have had any tête-á-têtes. Since they are women, it seems unlikely that they wouldn't have."

But they had not, so Moses remained in the dark and tried to cope.

CHAPTER NINE

There was great excitement in the air during March as Victoria shed one of the coldest winters in memory. The snow had gone, wildflowers were beginning to show their colours, and the ice on the Fraser River was breaking up rapidly. The real harbinger of spring, though, was the arrival of the steamer *Brother Jonathan* in Esquimalt harbour, bringing with it the first load of optimists from the south. There was still deep snow in the interior, but miners were champing at the bit to get moving, and the town boiled with activity as they bought clothing, supplies and pack animals. Bob Stevenson had come into the saloon as excited as any man. He had been looking for a reliable partner all winter, to no avail, but had just teamed up with a fellow Glengarrian named John Cameron, who had come in on the *Brother Jonathan* with his wife and daughter. The two men were in the process of buying up stock for Stevenson's store in Antler. Stevenson would go first to prepare the store while Cameron would follow later with the supplies when the roads were in better condition. The young Glengarrian was determined to be on the first boat out to Yale and the first into Antler, and Moses would have bet on him had a wager been available.

A few days later, the partners were in mourning. Cameron's 14-month-old daughter had died from a fever she had picked up in the tropics, and now the parents had to do what parents everywhere fear most — bury their child.

It was a windy, wet day as the funeral cortege splashed its way through the mud, on its way to the cemetery on Church Hill. Moses went out to the boardwalk and stood with his head bowed as it passed by. Other townsfolk on the street stopped, and men doffed their hats. He felt great sympathy for the parents, for he understood the anguish and pain of losing one's own flesh and blood. Stevenson rode in the wagon with the Camerons, and it would be a year before Moses saw him again. By then the young man would have a story to tell that would never be topped in his lifetime.

Soon after the Camerons arrived, smallpox also came to Victoria. It found a good home among the Indian community and systematically began to wipe them out. Though some 500 natives were vaccinated, by April the encampments at Ogden Point and Songhees smelled of the dead. Indians were ordered to move far away from the town, and their encampments were burned to the ground to enforce the order. Natives visiting in town were rounded up and sent back to their villages along the coast. The disease went with them.

April turned into May and spring turned toward summer, when word came down from Cariboo that a number of its creeks were rife with gold, the latest being Williams Creek, named after Bill Dietz, the first man to discover gold in it. The news added fuel to a flame already burning brightly from the Fraser River and Antler strikes, and when Billy Barker hit pay dirt in August, gold fever was pandemic. Victoria's streets were jammed with people of all nationalities, horses, mules and oxen, and an equal variety of vehicles. As boatloads of miners arrived from the south, boatloads departed for New Westminster and connections to Yale and Port Douglas. Stores hummed with activity and it was said that the clink of money could be heard as far south as Seattle. Gaslights were springing up along Government Street, and the town officially became an incorporated city with a mayor and council. Gibbs had run for a seat, but lost by four votes. He was disappointed, but just having the opportunity to run was deemed a giant step forward.

Moses was caught up in the day-to-day routine of cutting hair, shaving faces and saving men from baldness. His saloon was always full and so was the boarding house. Despite Sarah's bizarre behaviour, she could still cook and offered some of the best meals anywhere in town. Nevertheless, she seemed to be walking a thin edge most of the time. She frequently got severe headaches, for which the doctor had prescribed a potent medicine containing opium and alcohol. While it made the pain bearable, its after-effects pushed her deeper into prolonged black moods from which she had difficulty emerging. Moses worried that she might be driven to take her own life and begged her to seek help. She steadfastly refused. Over time, she withdrew even more and became so lackadaisical in her routine and so difficult to cope with that eventually, her boarders sought other lodgings.

Moses felt frustrated. He was at a crossroad with Sarah and knew that whichever direction he took was bound to be unpleasant. One night, after several drinks in a saloon he normally would not patronize, he thought, why not do what Sarah had been accusing him of all along? If she believed he was seeing another woman anyway, what would it matter? He needed the physical intimacy with a woman so much that he was determined to have it, even if it meant paying for it. He sat for the longest time trying to make up his mind, then tossed his drink back, had one more for courage and left the saloon. He knew of a woman who lived down on lower Broughton Street, who was considered one of the city's more exclusive prostitutes. He would go see her.

Along Government Street, the new gas lamps on the corners cast bright pools of light that made him feel conspicuous. It was the same way he had felt back in Bragman's Bluff many years ago. He pulled his collar up and his hat brim down, though a small part of him knew he was fooling nobody but himself; he was known too well around town to go unrecognized. It helped being slightly drunk, except that he had to concentrate in order to walk a straight line. He turned right onto Broughton Street, to a two-storey brick house with a large front door of oak and an impressive brass knocker made to look like a gold nugget. He lifted it up and let it drop with a thud. A tall blond woman answered.

"Yes?" Her face looked hard and she eyed Moses up and down, trying to get some measure of him.

He removed his hat. "Good evening, ma'am," he said, glad that he did not slur the words. He felt acutely on display, and not knowing the right thing to say, let slip the first words that popped into his mind. "I am in desperate need of your company." He instantly felt like a fool despite the stark truth of the statement.

Her face softened, and she nodded. "Come in," she said, and stood back to let Moses enter. She introduced herself as Constance and led him into a beautifully furnished parlour where, after discussing the options available to him, they settled on a price. He followed her upstairs to a perfumed room rich in green velvet with a canopied bed. In the lamplight and his loneliness she looked the loveliest of creatures. He undressed her, and she him, then she took his passion and molded it into something so exquisite he thought he might weep.

He spent longer than he should have and might have stayed the night had Constance not urged him to go home. When he left, he was at loose ends. The liquor was wearing off and his defiant spirit was beginning to flag. Guilt was asserting itself, as was anger, at both himself and Sarah, and with the circumstances that had driven him to a prostitute in the first place. He took a long route home, mostly down unlit streets, trying to sort out his thoughts, but he was no further ahead as he walked up the stairs to his front door.

Though it was late, Sarah was still up. She glared icily at him and said, "Up to your usual perverted antics, I suppose."

"Not usual," he said, "but perverted nonetheless." He did not feel like hiding his indiscretion.

She seemed slightly taken aback by his answer. "And what do you mean by that?" she asked.

"I mean that I've been with another woman. For the first time. A woman I paid to do what you won't. If you come close you can smell her on me." He instantly regretted adding that last part. It was uncalled-for and cruel.

"How dare you come into my home and tell me that!"

"How dare you call this a home! Sarah, *please*. I can no longer handle your antics, your silly suspicions and your unwillingness to fulfill your marital duties. I only did what you drove me to do."

Her shoulders began to shake and then heave. "Get out!" she sobbed. "You're no different from every other man. I knew you could not be trusted. Get out of this house and don't come back!"

"You seem to forget that this is my house, bought and paid for with my money."

"Get out!" she said again, her voice rising in hysteria, "before I do something I'll regret for the rest of my miserable life."

There was now such a wild look in her eyes that he had no doubt that she was capable of doing something terrible. He put a few toiletries, plus a bottle of whiskey, into a carpetbag and left. Fortunately, there was a room available at the Oriental Hotel on Yates Street. The clerk knew him but was sensitive enough not to ask any questions other than how long Moses would be staying.

"That hasn't as yet been decided," he said. He paid for one night and went upstairs to his room. He stretched out on the bed fully clothed and drank his way through the barriers of the night, until the last one fell away and he was able to sleep.

He awoke late the next morning with a colossal hangover, his clothes rumpled. At first, he had no idea where he was, but then the events of the night before came flooding back, and he was utterly disgusted with himself. He looked in the mirror and felt even worse. The image looking back at him had all the earmarks of a tramp. He filled the ceramic bowl on the sideboard with water from its companion pitcher and splashed his face and head and the back of his neck. The water was cool and revived him slightly. There was a gnawing in his stomach that seemed to need food, but the thought of eating made him nauseous. His head was in an awful turmoil and he was in desperate need of his own bath house. He had to grip the banister as he descended the stairs to the lobby for fear that he'd tumble to the bottom.

The bath house was across the street and around the corner from the hotel and he shakily made his way there, hoping he would not run into someone he knew. He saw George Blessing coming up the street and waved, but quickly let himself in through the saloon door and relocked it, not bothering to remove the "Closed" sign. He did not want to talk to anybody, least of all a customer as valuable as Blessing. He hurried into the back and had Old John Taylor fill a bath for him, then got a bottle of brandy that he kept in a storage room for medicinal purposes and poured a drink. It burned his throat, but sent a surge of good feeling through his gut and chest and perked him up a bit. He sank into the hot water, languished in its comfort and must have dozed off for the next thing he knew Old John was shaking his shoulder. Standing next to him was a police constable.

"You'd best get home right quick, Mr. Moses." His tone was hard and unsympathetic, as if he was displeased about something Moses had done. "They've pulled your missus out of James Bay."

Oh my God, thought Moses, what have I done? "What happened? Is she all right?"

"She jumped off the bridge, but other than getting a good dunking and swallowing more of that water than is good for a body, she's fine," said the constable gruffly. "Luckily someone saw her and went in after her. But she was extremely distraught, and claimed she did it because you ran off with another woman."

Moses moaned. "I'll be along right away. Thank you, constable." he said.

Upon reaching home, Moses found Dr. John Helmcken in the parlour. He was a distinguished-looking man of about 40, with neatly trimmed hair and a beard flecked with grey. He was quite popular in the community, although some attributed it to his marriage to one of James Douglas' daughters. He spoke with the confidence of a man who is accustomed to having others hang on his every word.

"Ah, Mr. Moses," he said. "Mrs. Moses is resting comfortably. I have given her a sedative that should let her sleep for several hours, and although I can't be sure, I doubt that it will have any effect on her behaviour once she awakens. I expect I don't need to tell you that her mental instability borders on lunacy. Unfortunately, there is little we can do for her here. The only lunatic asylum in Victoria is in the jail and, thank goodness, it's for men only. Indeed, there is a lamentable lack of medical facilities here for women at all, so they are usually sent back to the east or to England, depending on where they're from.[1] Meanwhile, I can have a nurse sent over with the proper medication, to provide care for her until we know whether or not it's necessary to arrange for her transportation."

Moses paid the doctor, thanked him for his services, and saw him to the door. His hangover had returned so he had another brandy, then went upstairs to see Sarah. Though she was in a deep sleep she did not look at all tranquil and the darkness under her eyes spoke disquietingly of her troubles. He stroked her temple lightly, and whispered, "My poor Sarah." He opened a crocheted coverlet that was folded at the foot of the bed and placed it over her upper body, brushed his lips against her forehead, and went back downstairs. Once the nurse arrived there were many things that would have to be attended to, but most of all he needed the company of his old friend Gibbs.

The nurse was a matronly woman who took charge of the house and Sarah straight away. Moses went immediately to Gibbs' store and was relieved that his friend was not critical of his behaviour. Gibbs' advice was succinct: "You must stick by her, Moses, at all costs. The eyes of the community will be on you."

Moses was dismayed that Sarah's attempted suicide had made the newspapers, along with her reason for doing it: bitten by the "green-eyed lobster," it had read. Since it was something over which he had no control, he did not respond to the article, kept his head up and maintained his dignity in public. He also took Gibbs' advice to heart and devoted most of his attention to Sarah.

He wished that her illness were physical rather than mental, because he might have known how to deal with her. As it was, there were times when her condition frightened him, not only because he did not understand it, but because he did not know how close his own mind was, or anyone else's for that matter, to slipping into a similar abyss. And no one knew what to do when a mind shifted onto a different plane, not even the medical profession and least of all Moses.

A week passed and Sarah's condition did not improve. She suffered extreme paranoia and anxiety when she was awake and without medication, and headaches still plagued her. Dr. Helmcken recommended that Moses not delay any longer in getting her back east where there were institutions that might be able to help her. Through Gibbs, he located a woman who wanted to return to her home in Philadelphia, but could not afford the fare. If Moses paid it, she would escort Sarah to Baltimore so that her parents could see she was properly cared for. Along the way, she would ensure that the medicine prescribed by Dr. Helmcken was administered. Her name was Jessie, but to Moses it might have been Florence Nightingale. He bought two tickets on the next ship out.

On the morning of Sarah's and Jessie's departure, Moses, Gibbs and Maria gathered at the wharf to see them off. The weather was sombre, which seemed to match everyone's mood. Before Sarah went up the gangway, Moses took her hands in his and looked into her vacant eyes. "I regret having to send you on such a journey," he said, "but the best care available awaits you in Baltimore. You must listen to the doctors so that you'll get well. You must listen to Jessie when she tells you it's time for your medicine. She knows what's best in that regard. I have also given her a letter to your parents along with a banknote for your return fare when this illness is behind you." He pulled her to him and wrapped his arms around her, and she felt limp and pliable, as if the drugs had stolen her soul. Whispering in her ear so that no one could hear, he said, "Goodbye, Sarah. Come back to me." She did not respond.

Jessie assisted Sarah onto the ship and the last Moses saw of his wife was her back disappearing through the companionway leading to the staterooms. He was filled with the dread that he would never see her again. The gangway was removed, the lines cast off and the ship slipped away from the wharf with a blast of its whistle, then turned for Juan de Fuca Strait and the ocean beyond. Moses stood there until the vessel rounded Laurel Point and disappeared from view. He accepted Gibbs' invitation to return to his house for a drink. Part of him felt as empty as a used whiskey barrel. Another part felt relief.

∞∞

Moses lost himself in work and brandy, although not necessarily in that order, and refrained from visiting Constance. Gibbs and Maria had him over for dinner from time to time and the visits were a welcome respite. Their conversations were almost always political, for that was Gibbs' nature. He was still not happy with the conditions for blacks in Victoria, particularly for black women. The problems men had to contend with were bad enough, but women were completely ostracized from the white community. It upset Maria deeply. A graduate of Oberlin College in Ohio, she was well educated and sophisticated, and saw herself as being equal to any woman regardless of colour, so she could not fathom their intolerance. If the situation did not change by the time the war was over, she said, she was taking the children and going back to Ohio.

This was a surprising piece of news to Moses, but he could not blame her. No doubt Sarah had felt ostracized as well. Even Moses, with his genial disposition, sometimes felt he was on the outside looking in. Men like George Blessing, with whom he frequently had a drink, were few and far between. Perhaps, he thought, it was time to consider moving on.

Meanwhile, he strongly believed that blacks needed representation in the military community, so he joined the Victoria

Pioneer Rifles. This was a black militia unit set up to protect the colony after the regular militia, comprised mostly of expatriate Americans, prohibited blacks from joining its ranks. Moses loved the resplendent uniforms and always looked forward to the meetings when he could wear his. Some of the men even wore plumes on their caps but Moses thought that too pretentious and wore his plain.

In March, Bob Stevenson and his partner, John Cameron, arrived in town with the strangest of cargoes. Apparently, Cameron's wife had died the previous October and had requested that her husband not bury her in Cariboo, but take her home to Glengarry County. So they had brought her down, some 600 miles, on a sled. Cameron was going to bury her in Victoria until he could afford the boat trip home. That would not be long, for they had struck it rich on Williams Creek — even richer than Billy Barker — and had only to wait until the weather improved to get the gold out of the ground.

News of the strike spread around town in surprisingly little time and it was soon the topic of conversation on everyone's lips. There was much envy among the miners wintering in Victoria, and it made them even more impatient for the spring thaw. And since most people were in awe of a rich man, Mrs. Cameron's funeral was the largest the town had ever seen, with thousands of people lining Yates and Government streets to view the procession. If Moses' memory served him correctly, it was exactly one year and a day since he had watched the procession for Cameron's daughter. His heart went out to the man. Despite Cameron's new-found wealth, Moses thought him much the poorer for it.

The next day Stevenson came in for a shave and a haircut. "Good to see you, Moses," he said as he hung his hat on a peg.

"Bob! Welcome back! My condolences to both you and Mr. Cameron. This town has never seen the likes of such a procession, and may never again."

The shop was empty of customers so he waved Stevenson to the barber's chair. He noticed a difference between the young man who now sat in the chair and the one who had occupied it a year ago. This man had a full beard and looked much older, as if the year had aged him twice its length, and he looked tired. Moses congratulated Stevenson on his good luck.

"I tell you, Moses, the night before we made our discovery I had never felt such despair. It was costing us a small fortune every month to run that claim, and if the truth were told, we didn't know how much longer we could last. Then when Mrs. Cameron died, it was difficult to set our minds to the task at hand. But it's phenomenal, is it not, how one's fortunes can change with the turn of a shovel? Rest assured, there's nothing like finding a pay streak a yard wide to lift a man's spirits!"

Stevenson rambled on with details of the discovery, digressing only long enough to say "leave me a moustache." Moses cut his beard short with scissors, then took a beaver-hair brush, worked up a good lather in a soap mug and slathered it over Stevenson's cheeks, chin and throat. He deftly stropped his straight razor with rhythmic strokes and began removing Stevenson's beard. Moses was happy for the young man, who was now anxious to get back to Cariboo and start working the mine. "The next time you see us, Moses, you'll need to shield your eyes from the glint of the gold we'll be carrying. You could very well be blinded!"

Moses laughed. "I'll be cautious," he said.

Stevenson's visit had put Moses in a good mood, and ignited a spark of optimism that he had not felt for some time. He thought even more about leaving Victoria. Perhaps Cariboo would be a good place to put down some roots. Maybe he could invest in a mine and be as lucky as Stevenson. It certainly deserved some serious thought.

Yet he waffled for a long time and May was half gone before two events galvanized him into action. The first came in the form of a letter, the other was the public execution of some Indians.

It was on a Friday that the letter arrived, a blustery day with white clouds racing across the sky and people chasing after their hats if they failed to hang on to them. Business was slow, so

Moses decided to close early and go around the corner to the Adelphi Saloon for a drink before carrying on to Ringo's for supper. It occurred to him that George Blessing might like to join him, so he headed in the direction of Blessing's office to inquire. On the way he could make a detour past the new post office on Wharf Street to see if he had any mail.

He had been checking the post office regularly, hoping that there might be news about Sarah, but to date he had received nothing. Most of his mail was from acquaintances and businesses in San Francisco, and even at that there was not a lot, so he was pleasantly surprised when he was handed a thick envelope. His name was scrawled on it in handwriting he did not recognize, and the postmark, at first glance, was illegible. When he examined it closely he saw that it was Baltimore. But instead of being filled with excitement, he was flooded with an awful sense of foreboding.

CHAPTER TEN

Moses did not feel hungry any more, nor did he want to go to the saloon, so he hurried home, reluctant to open the letter before he got there. He was afraid that it contained the worst of news. He avoided Yates Street so he would not have to pass Gibbs' store without stopping in or waving hello. He did not want to see anybody. Whatever was in that letter had to be important and he did not want it revealed to him until he was alone so that he could prepare himself to deal with it publicly. He tapped his jacket pocket a dozen times before he got home, to make sure it had not fallen out on the street.

In his parlour he poured himself a brandy and noticed there was a slight tremor in his hand. He took a long draught, sat down at the table and tore away the wax seal on the envelope. Inside was a sheaf of papers fronted by a brief letter from Sarah's father in Baltimore.

"My Dear Mr. Moses," it began, in shaky handwriting that was difficult to read, "it is with great sorrow that I tell you of our dear Sarah's passing. Though she was under the watchful eye of a doctor she managed, nevertheless, to take her own life. I will not upset you with the details.

"From what we were able to ascertain from your letter, you had no inkling of the circumstances which led to the tragic turn in her life. However, Mrs. Douglas and I feel it is something you ought to know lest you think ill of our daughter. To that end I have enclosed her account of her last trip as a conductor on the Underground Railroad, after which she was never the Sarah we had known and loved. She wrote it down soon after her escape, but would never speak of it afterward.

"Once again, I am so sorry to be the bearer of such bad news. Please visit us if you are ever in the Baltimore area. This war must end some time.

"Yours respectfully, John T. Douglas."

Moses closed his eyes. Tears should have come, but they did not. Instead, he felt a great weight bearing down on his heart, as if it were about to sink into his abdomen. He put the papers down, went to the sideboard and topped off his glass with more brandy. At least, he thought, if her condition was not curable she had found peace with God and there was some solace in that. With great apprehension, he picked up the papers and turned to the first page. He recognized Sarah's handwriting but the syntax was awkward and difficult to read. Nevertheless, Moses was able to follow it.

∞∞

Apparently, Sarah had been making her third trip when she ran into problems. It was in late October, under a full moon, and she was leading some passengers, a family of three, north to freedom.[1]

Usually, runaway slaves from the west side of Chesapeake Bay were channelled by their conductors through Baltimore. Met on the outskirts of town by some form of transportation, they were taken to a safe house where a new conductor would lead them to Philadelphia. It had always been dangerous work but it became even more so with the passage in 1850 of a new Fugitive Slave Act, which stated that runaway slaves, even if they had made it to free soil, could be captured and returned to their owners. It also made it possible for any black anywhere in the United States to be accused of being a runaway slave and taken south into captivity. Since blacks could not testify or give evidence in court, this section of the act held terrifying ramifications for every free black.

∞∞

The parents had decided to flee when their pre-teen daughter was about to be sold away from them. Sarah always tried to vary her route between the safe houses, and the more water she could find, preferably streams, the safer she felt. Harriet Tubman had said that running water never told tales, and the last thing any conductor wanted was to leave a trail that dogs could easily pick up. No matter which route she took though, there was always the Susquehanna River to cross. There was a bridge, but it was usually guarded, so the Underground Railroad had a skiff hidden in some overhanging bushes along the river's edge. They would use it to row across, and later, someone would return it to its hiding place. This was the most dangerous part of the journey because the same area was used so often. Overused, Sarah thought, but the river was too wide and the current too strong to swim. It was at the Susquehanna that her life changed utterly.

They were not long away from a safe house, making for the river over frosty ground, when they heard the hounds. She guessed that the house had been under suspicion and was being watched. She grabbed the girl's hand and said to her parents, "We must hurry!" They broke into a run, aided by a full moon on the sparkling rime, and reached the tiny cove from which the skiff was usually launched.

"Wait here!" she said to her passengers and waded into the frigid water, where she ducked under a concealing bush. Moments later she reappeared pulling the skiff by a rope. "Get in!" she ordered the family, and steadied the boat as the father helped his wife and daughter in before clambering in himself. Then, pushing the boat toward the current she tried to leap in herself but slipped on a stone and fell, banging her head and scraping her face on the gunwale. In the few moments that it took to collect herself, the boat had drifted into the current with the father fighting to use the oars. But a thing as simple as a rowboat was beyond his experience and by the time he had figured out what to do with the oars, the skiff was too far out and downstream to turn back. "Go!" she yelled at them even though she knew they had little choice in the matter. She splashed from the water and ran northwest along an old river trail, knowing the dogs would pick up her scent and concentrate on her instead. How far was it to the Pennsylvania border, she wondered? Ten miles? Fifteen miles? Whatever the distance, she knew it was too far.

The baying of the hounds somewhere behind filled her with overwhelming fear. She had heard that kind of baying before but she had never been the quarry. She had several layers of clothes on, worn purposely to protect her from dog bites in case she was ever caught, but they were soaked from the water and were working against her. Every time she lifted a leg she felt as if she were pulling it from quicksand. She tripped over a root and went down with a thud that knocked the wind from her. Staggering to her feet she pulled out the knife she always carried and cut away the outer layers of clothing. It was the only chance she had of outdistancing the dogs, who were so close now she thought she could hear them panting; then she realized that what she was hearing was herself trying to catch a breath.

The moonlight was in her favour and she ran on, each footstep leaving a feast of scent for the dogs. She had to increase the gap because she knew that if the slavecatchers caught a glimpse of her, they would unleash the dogs and let them take her down. They were trained to make it a horrific experience for their prey, and some slaves had had an ear or a nose bitten off. She was more terrified than she had ever imagined possible and her heart raced so fast she thought it would explode. She felt like an animal, although an animal could have at least clawed its way up a tree, out of the dogs' reach. Branches tore at her clothing as she ran, half stumbling, until she realized that her legs would not carry her any farther. There was only one choice now and that was to take to the river, even though she did not know how to swim. The dogs would know where she went in, but if she was lucky she could drift downstream, past them, then head back to the safe house and hope it was still safe. Without further thought, she splashed into the shallows and dove into deeper water.

It was so cold it almost stole what little breath she had left. She let the current take her and then drifted to the surface, desperately needing a deep breath, yet unable to fill her lungs. She saw an overhanging branch and grabbed hold of it, realizing that the water was shallow enough to stand up in. The bottom was rocky and slippery and it was difficult to get her footing, and now she had to fight the cold. Her body shivered uncontrollably and her teeth chattered so loudly that if the dogs had not been yelping she was certain they would have heard her. They passed her, which meant that they would soon come to the place where she had entered the river. She knew that after searching the area the hounds would return downstream, but hoped she could hang on until they gave up. She found a bit more breath and started drifting again, along the shore. Fear alone kept her afloat. Farther out the water was swifter, and she dared not chance going there. The dogs were somewhere very near on the trail, and they sounded even more determined to find their quarry. She began to feel sluggish from the cold. Her limbs seemed as stiff and heavy as ironwood and her feet were becoming useless. Seconds were like years and a minute was for ever, still she waited. But her pursuers were not giving up. They knew that she either had to come out or die in the river. And so did she. It would have been so easy just to let the river take her to her death, yet she fought it. She did not want to die. Though she knew that with any one of these slavecatchers, her life would probably be a living hell, it was at least life and she chose it.

She reeled from the river, sheer willpower taking her to the trail where she collapsed. The dogs heard her and went wild, but the owners hung on to them. They knew that they had her. Someone had lit a torch, and one of the men said, "It's a goddamned wench! Keep those dogs away!" With every ounce of her strength and all the defiance she could muster, she struggled to stand and face her pursuers. The man with the torch approached her and she saw his fist coming toward her face but could do nothing to avoid it. Like a mallet it crashed into her mouth. Her head flew back, perhaps right off her shoulders was her last thought, yet there was no pain, only blackness as her mind tumbled into oblivion and her body crashed to the earth.

When she woke up, she felt nothing for a moment, then a dull ache in her jaw and a splitting headache seeped into her awareness. Her muscles were stiff and sore and when she tried to move she could not. For a moment she thought she was tied up. When her mind grasped that she was not, she began moving her fingers and toes until she could feel the blood flowing through her limbs. She tried to take in her surroundings in the dim light of a lamp burning on a nearby table. The slope of the ceiling told her that she was probably in an attic, and she thought it might still be night because she could see no other light. Other than that pitifully small bit of information, she had no idea where she was or how much time had passed since her capture. She knew only that her life would probably never be the same again. She heard a key scratching in a lock and then a door squealing open. A shaft of light shone like a beacon out of what looked like a stairwell. She heard footsteps on creaky stairs, and tried to sit up but her body would not co-operate. Her head ached so badly she thought she might vomit. A man, tall and angular, arose out of the stairwell and came to her side. He looked to be in his fifties, and his grey-streaked hair was slicked back, as though fresh from a wash. He was clean-shaven, his white skin moist in the lamplight. He grinned, showing a gap between his front teeth that Sarah instantly recognized. It was the man who had punched her. Her heart stumbled in her chest.

"You're awake, girlie," he said. "You gave us quite a chase, but your slave-running days are over. You're mine now, and what a lovely catch you are." He laughed, a low sinister laugh, as though he were the devil himself.

He took her then, and though she found a new reservoir of strength to resist, she was no match for him in her weakened condition. When he entered her body, it felt like a knife had cut her and she screamed in pain. He reared back and slapped her and a bright light exploded in her head. He grunted over her like a rutting bull, and after the shock of his penetration, she let her mind escape into another world, beyond the awful shame of what was happening. When he was done and had removed himself, his snarl brought her back to the nightmare.

"You'll need to do better than that, girlie," he said, "but you're young and you'll learn. At least you'd better." He did himself up and then he was gone.

After that, he took her whenever he felt the urge. If he was drunk and she was unresponsive, he would beat her, so she learned to make the noises he seemed to want to hear, that somehow defined his masculinity. Even so, some part of her body always had a bruise on it. At first she dreaded the sound of his key in the lock and his footsteps coming up the stairs, but after a while she resigned herself to her fate. She thanked God daily that there appeared to be something wrong with his seed, or with her, for she never got pregnant. If she had it would most certainly have been a devil's child.

He kept her locked up in the attic at night, from which there was no escape. During the day, he allowed her downstairs where she kept the house spotless, did his washing, mended his clothes, cooked for him, and performed whatever other menial chores he could find. He even let her outside to tend a garden that was surrounded by a deer fence; beyond it were his two dogs, which paced and watched her relentlessly. Whenever he went out and had to take the dogs, he locked her away, as he did at night, so that he could sleep without fear of reprisal. One day he showed her what he would do if he caught her trying to escape. He made her strip naked and then bound her wrists together with twine. He ordered her to squat with her arms outside her knees and her hands resting on the floor. Then he took a broom handle and stuck the end inside the crook of her right arm and behind her knees until it came out inside the crook of her left arm. He removed his belt and, wrapping the buckle end around his hand, whipped her with it, two hard lashes across her back. She did not want to cry out in pain but could not help herself. He left her like that, unable to do anything but squat, until she fainted and fell over.

She measured the passing of the days and weeks by the intensity of her hatred for him. So much filled her being that she hoped that she could use it to kill him before it killed her. He felt the intensity of her animosity and was always wary, keeping his guns locked up and only allowing her to use one knife for cutting up meat and vegetables. Then he made sure it was put back in its proper place, high in a cupboard where it could be reached only by bringing a chair from the dining room to stand on. Nevertheless, she managed small acts of revenge that made her feel fleetingly triumphant. Cooking meals provided the best time for these. She would spit in his tea and coffee and blow her nose into his stew. She would save little bits of her stool and incorporate it into his food, hoping that it would make him sick, but it never did. If she could have found a tasteless poison, she would have gladly served it to him in proportions large enough to fell an ox.

There were times when she thought of taking her own life, especially when her head ached, but she could not, and felt weak and worthless because of it. She would have run, had it been an option, but the two dogs roamed freely outside the house; they knew her smell and would have torn her apart. As the weeks and months passed she perceived a change in herself. Ever so slowly the hatred that had marked her early days began to slip away into some secret part of her; she began to accept her lot and sometimes even thought she deserved it. She found herself acting more and more like a slave, saying "Marse" this and "Marse" that, without having to be told to, being obsequious, her eyes always cast down to the floor when he was around. She was devoid of all feeling, except for her headaches. And fear. There was never any shortage of that.

It was in her second summer with him that she noticed he was not after her as much any more. When he came home drunk and stumbled up the stairs, he sometimes just sat on the edge of her bed and moaned about how much he missed his wife, who had apparently died from the fever. If he did not get a sympathetic response from Sarah, he would vent his anger on her. Sexually he had grown tired of her, but instead of feeling grateful she was filled with an even greater dread. How long would it be before she was sold to a slave trader? And what form of despicable subhuman life would she end up with then?

She had also noticed that he was dropping his guard occasionally, not locking her up when he went out, probably assuming that she was fully under his and the dogs' control. Nor did he seem to worry about knives any more. But it did not matter. Sarah was too afraid of him to attempt anything.

Then one afternoon he brought home a new girl, barely into her teens. He was drunk and looked at Sarah with pure contempt as he dragged his new prize by the arm up the stairs to the attic. He never even bothered to shut the door, not caring if Sarah followed and watched or not. She did. Watched in horror as he tore the girl's clothes off, and threw her on the bed. As he forced himself on her, the scene was suddenly transformed in Sarah's mind. What she saw was herself, under him, herself being ravaged by this vile creature, and something exploded in her brain, blasting it open so that a light as bright as the sun illuminated all the hatred that had been repressed for so long. She turned away, ran down the stairs to the kitchen and got a knife from the drawer where they were now kept. He was too gorged with lust to notice her entering the bedroom, and as he grunted over the young girl, she plunged the knife deep into his back, right where his heart would be if he'd had one. He let out an ungodly groan as life left him and he went slack. She grabbed his shirt and pulled him off the girl onto the floor. Though he was a big man, he felt light as a feather, such was the strength that coursed through her body. The girl was sobbing and sitting up on the bed so Sarah sat beside her and pulled her frail body close, and held her, soothing her with cooing sounds as she would a baby. She wanted to stay strong for this child but then she, too, began to cry, filled with such an overwhelming sense of relief and sorrow that she thought her entire being would collapse in on itself. They sat there in each others' arms, rocking back and forth, the dead body at Sarah's feet, until there were no more tears left to shed.

The girl's name was Mindy and the man had bought her at an auction in Baltimore, which she reckoned was about 25 miles away. Baltimore! That would account for the smoky haze Sarah had seen periodically to the east. After Mindy had collected herself, they began preparing for their escape. Sarah was close to being paralyzed with fear, but mustered the determination to carry on. The first thing they had to do was deal with the dogs. They would have to be shot, but to do that Sarah needed access to the man's guns and for that she would need an axe. The axe, though, was out by the woodpile around which the dogs roamed freely. Somehow, they would have to be distracted, and since they knew Sarah's smell, she was the logical choice to do that.

She got a large chunk of venison from the larder and rubbed her hands all over it so that it was full of her smell. Then she went to a side window and, throwing it open, called to the dogs. They came growling and bounding toward her and leapt up the side of the house trying to get at her but the window was too high. She threw out the meat, and the two animals tore at it in a frenzy. Meanwhile, Mindy flew out to the woodpile and got the axe. Sarah grabbed it, smashed open the locker and took out a rifle. She had seen the man load it many times before, so she knew how to do it. When it was ready, she returned to the window. The dogs were still tearing at the meat and she shot one of them. The wind blew the powder back in her face and she almost gagged from the stench. By the time she had gathered herself and reloaded the gun, the other dog had run off. Never mind. She would deal with it outside. They put some food together in a blanket, picked up the gun and left. The other dog approached them, snarling, its teeth bared. Sarah waited until it was so close she knew she could not miss and shot it. Even though the animals had been like prison guards to her, she felt worse about killing them than she had their owner.

They headed east, walking through the remainder of the day and through the night, past farm houses set far back off the road. Dogs barked at their passing but did not bother them. In the grey light of morning, they reached the outskirts of Baltimore and hid in a copse of trees to wait for a wagon on its way to town, preferably one driven by a solitary black man.

The second one to come along was exactly what they were looking for. Sarah took the gun and strode into the middle of the road before the fear she felt made her change her mind. Seeing the gun, the driver pulled up.

"I mean you no harm, brother," she said, unable to control the tremor in her voice and her shaking hands, "but we are in desperate need of help." Though she thought she recognized the man, her fear of what she might have to do if he did not co-operate terrified her.

"Lawd, sister, but you've come to the right place!" the man exclaimed, looking as if he'd seen a ghost. "If this ain't the rail-road you be lookin' fo', and if you ain't Sarah Douglas, why I'll eat these hosses, tack 'n all. Folks had all but given you up fo' dead! Now don't you worry, Miss Douglas, I know 'xactly where you wanna go, an' I reckon yo' mammy and daddy will be right glad to see you. All you gotta do is climb aboard, and do it quick fo' someone comes along!"

Sarah's legs almost buckled from relief. They had stumbled upon an ally, a friend, and they were only a few miles from the safety of her parents' boarding house. Mindy came out of the woods and the man's eyes grew even wider.

"Good Lawd, why yo' jest a child!" Turning to Sarah, he smiled and said, "How many mo' you got hidin' in them woods, Miss Douglas? Fo' you know it, I'll be needin' a bigger wagon!"

Sarah managed a feeble smile as she helped Mindy onto the wagon before climbing on herself. They concealed themselves beneath some burlap sacks. The wagon lurched forward and each revolution of the wheels seemed to take an hour hand. Around them the city was clamouring to life, and as the wheels began to grate over flagstone roads she knew that they had not far to go. When the wagon finally stopped and the driver said that they could come out, she was afraid to look, afraid that she had been taken back into slavery. But no, there was her house — her home — looking just as it had when she had left more than a year and a half before. It seemed like a miracle when she was finally in her mother's arms, her face nuzzled into that familiar hair, absorbing the wonderful smell of her, the two of them sobbing, her mother stroking her hair, saying, "Oh, my child, my child. We thought you were lost to us forever."

∽◌∾

And Moses wept too, because now she was lost to him forever. The tears that he never thought were in him found release; they flowed in streams down his cheeks and splashed onto the table. Sarah had teetered on the brink of insanity for so long and instead of reaching out a hand to pull her back, he helped push her over. He could not remember a decent thing that he had ever said to her. All that ran over and over in his mind were these words: "You'll have no one to blame but yourself." He grabbed the edge of the table in both hands, shot to his feet and heaved it over. The papers scattered across the floor; the glass flew and smashed against the wall in glittering shards. Brandy dribbled in streaks to the floor. A primal sound issued from his mouth that he could not identify as his own. He fell to his knees, covering his face in his hands because there was still a part of him that was embarrassed by his tears, then, finally, he slumped to the floor, his head on his arms and stayed there until the lamp dimmed and the fire died and the room went cold.

In the morning, he did not bother to light a fire. Instead, after his morning ablutions, he dressed hurriedly and went into town. Gibbs should be at work now and he wanted to tell him the news.

"I'm so sorry Moses," Gibbs said. "One always hopes for the best and when the worst happens, it's devastating in the extreme."

Moses handed him Sarah's story to read. Gibbs never once looked up or paused in his reading and when he was finished, the blood had drained from his face. "The poor woman," he said, shaking his head, "the poor, poor woman. Neither Maria nor I had imagined anything as horrible as this. That she even lived through the experience is testimony to her courage."

"She may have lived through it, but she didn't survive it."

Gibbs nodded. "It's no wonder she couldn't tell anybody. Even you."

"Least of all, me," said Moses, with such sadness that his friend gripped his shoulder with great compassion. Gibbs looked as if he was about to say something more but he just shook his head, his eyes glistening with tears.

For a long while after receiving John Douglas' letter Moses passed the time in a daze. It was all he could do to keep from crying whenever he thought of Sarah. He had difficulty concentrating on his work for it seemed to have lost all meaning for him. He drank more, which only worsened the situation. Life and the town were turning him sour. He saw its ugly side more easily now, especially the way the black population was treated, and if anything, it was getting worse instead of better. Sometimes he was so filled with hatred for the white race it was all he could do to be civil to his white customers. During such moments, he fantasized about slitting the throats of those he never liked in the first place. It would have been so easy.

May dragged itself to June and June to July, and the passage of time did nothing to improve his mood. He wished the damned war would end, at least, and relieve the town of its American bigots. When he said this to Gibbs, his friend responded stoically, "Well, at least you know where they stand. Not like some of those two-faced Britishers who say one thing and do another."

Gibbs was also unhappy with the atmosphere in Victoria, but he was determined to stick it out for a while yet, even though Maria was still talking about returning to the east.

∞·∞

The second event, which further deepened Moses' depression, was the public execution of four Indians in July. All were guilty of the murders they were charged with; nevertheless, the hangings seemed to Moses more like revenge against a minority than true justice.

The murderers had struck in the Gulf Islands, their leader a Lamalchi Indian named Ah-Chee-Wun who claimed to be a centenarian with, according to some, supernatural powers. He purportedly had the body of a more youthful man and had been seen walking through solid rock. It was said that he could disappear in front of people's eyes and cause torrential thunderstorms simply by raising his arms. He also hated non-Indians with a passion and was determined to rid his land of them even if it meant doing it one by one. He was thought to have been directly or indirectly involved in at least 11 or 12 killings. His last victims had been a man named Frederick Marks, and his 15-year-old married daughter, Caroline Harvey. They were on Saturna Island when Marks was shot in the back while Harvey was chased down and stabbed to death. The outcome of the trial of Ah-Chee-Wun and his cohorts was their sentence to be hanged.

Of course, not every black felt the same way as Moses did. Before Ah-Chee-Wun dropped to his death, one of Moses' customers, a black man named Howard Estes, who farmed up in Saanich, had said, "We'll all rest easier when that madman is put away."[2] His daughter and son-in-law homesteaded on Saltspring Island and he had been worried about them.

"Have you ever seen a hanging, Mr. Estes?" Moses asked.

"I haven't, but I look forward to Ah-Chee-Wun's with much anticipation. We have as much right to that land as they do, so if it'll make other Indians think twice before trying to drive any of us off, it'll have served a good purpose."

Moses doubted that. He recalled the double hangings of Cora and Casey in San Francisco and the thought of it still made his stomach heave. "It's not an easy thing to watch," he said and refrained from further comment. Estes was, after all, a customer.

On the day of the executions, Moses could hear the wailing
of the Indian families as they watched their loved ones drop into
eternity and it soured him against Victoria even more.

∞∞

Three months later, during the fall, Bob Stevenson and John
Cameron arrived from Cariboo with their hoard of gold, and the
townsfolk showered them with the respect usually reserved for
royalty. Cameron exhumed the bodies of his wife and daughter
and he and Stevenson took them home, just as he had promised.
The act touched Moses deeply and proved to be the only really
positive event of the year.

Winter passed as slowly as a funeral cortege into the summer of 1864 and on his morning constitutional down to the
docks, when the rising sun was offering up one of those glorious summer days that made Victoria the lovely place that it
was, Moses knew it was time to make some changes in his life.
He had turned 48 in the spring but felt like an old man. He
had been spending most of his spare time in saloons, sometimes drinking himself into enough of a stupor that someone
would have to escort him home. His hangovers were horren-
dous, and at work he found himself making frequent trips to
the storage room where he kept a supply of brandy. Occasionally, the liquor made him belligerent and he reckoned that one
day it was going to get him in trouble. If he flew into the same
mindless rage that he once had in Georgetown, and left some
white man dead, he would be certain to follow in the footsteps
of Ah-Chee-Wun. Not only that, even his best friend had chastised him. Gibbs had told him bluntly that his behavior was
pathetic. "It's one thing for a common labourer to act as you
are," he said, "but for a prominent business man it's unaccept-
able." Moses was chagrined. The first thing he had to do,
then, was cut back on his drinking. He had also been visiting
Constance far too often, which would have to stop as well,
before his reputation was in complete tatters. The third order
of business was to sell out and leave town.

When he told Gibbs of his plans, his friend offered only encouragement despite the fact that he was losing a strong ally in his constant struggle against racial injustice. He said, "I heartily approve, Moses. A fresh start is just what you need to put your life back in order. In a way, I envy you. I sometimes wish I could pack up everything and leave but there's too much at stake right now. It goes without saying, though, my friend, that I'll miss you."

Within a month Moses had sold the shaving saloon and bath house, with the proviso that Old John Taylor be kept on as attendant if he so desired. He sold his home and all of its contents just as easily. The only things he kept from both transactions, besides a few personal belongings, were his professional barbering equipment, his supply of Invigorator and the ingredients he used to make it, all of which Gibbs would ship to him if he needed them. The last thing to be carefully packed was the picture of himself and Sarah on their wedding day.

❧ Part Four ❧

CHAPTER ELEVEN

T he file of horses, some carrying packs, others riders, came around the side of the hill and entered the town of Richfield. The road was lined on both sides with shops, saloons and hotels, all of them wood buildings with pitched, shingled roofs. The town quickly petered out as the road ran precariously along the hillside above the creek bed, past cabins and working claims. It was nothing like what Moses had imagined. To begin with, there was no Williams Creek, at least not in the valley in which the miners worked and lived. It had been diverted by flumes that seemed to go every which way with no apparent rhyme or reason. The creek bed itself was nothing but a series of small piles of gravelly debris, which made it look like the home of giant moles. The once heavily forested hillsides were now vast areas of stumps, a scene of devastation that was repeated down the entire length of the valley, at least as near as Moses could tell.

Following the narrow, badly rutted road, the horses descended through the valley. Farther along was Middletown, which people were now calling Barkerville, and below that was Cameronton; the last settlement was a small collection of buildings on the flats called Marysville. There were no lines separating these last three communities, which ran alongside the creek bed as a single town. Here, as in Richfield, buildings lined both sides of the road. Fronting them on the upper side of the road was what appeared to be a raised boardwalk, but it was little more than a series of connected porches of varying heights. On the creek side, the road was parallelled in places by a shallow drainage ditch, spanned by plank footbridges that allowed access to the buildings there. Barkerville was not a pretty place — it was, after all, the frontier — but it was vibrant and exciting. The valley rang with the noise of industry, a sound that pulsated with hope, and people in constant motion thronged the main street. The gutted carcasses of two deer hung on the porch of one building. Halfway through the town the saddle train stopped in front of the Occidental Hotel which, except for the sign, was scarcely different from the buildings on either side of it.

Moses dismounted, stiff and sore after nearly three days in the saddle, and retrieved his bags from one of the pack animals. Luckily, he was able to get a room, although it was not much more than a cubbyhole with a bed and a washstand. Nevertheless, it was considerably better than his lodgings the previous two nights on the trail. The proprietor was friendly, too.

He freshened up and then went across the street to the New England Bakery to satisfy a craving for something sweet. He bought a large piece of pound cake and ate it as he walked down through Cameronton, trying to work the stiffness out of his muscles. Many of the people he encountered along the boardwalk nodded, even smiled and said hello, and seemed blind to Moses' colour. Already he liked the town. He recognized a few faces from Victoria and was pleased to run into Bob Stevenson. The young man had returned from the east last spring and had been on the first scheduled stage out of Yale for the creeks.

"Hello, Moses!" he said. "Welcome to Eldorado. It'll be a good thing for the town if you're here to set up shop. For you, too. There's more hair per acre here than possibly anywhere else in the world."

Moses laughed and they shook hands. "Thank you. It's certainly my intention to investigate the possibility. How was your trip to the east?"

"It turned out not to my liking. There were some issues that Cameron and I couldn't see eye to eye on and we parted ways without resolving them. But that's another story."

"I understand," said Moses. "I presume you're back in the thick of a new treasure hunt?"

"Yes. So far not anywhere near as productive as last year, of course, but we're making ends meet. Come to the claim and have a look for yourself, once you get settled in. It's right over there." He pointed to a group of lean-tos, log-and-plank buildings, and flumes where a number of men could be seen working.

The two men chatted for a bit, then Stevenson took his leave, but not before directing Moses to a place where he might find the owner of a building that he thought was for sale. It turned out to be right next door to the Occidental.

He was able to purchase the building, although he cringed inwardly when he heard the price. It was expensive, but the next best thing to a productive claim on the creek was a piece of real estate in town. Besides, he could afford it. He had made a good profit on the sale of his home and saloon in Victoria and still had more than enough money left to tide him over the winter, even if he did not get any business. And that was hardly likely.

The building was perfect for him. He set up shop in the front half and used the back half for his living quarters. The only item he had to purchase was new bedding; everything else was included in the sale. He did not have a barber's chair, of course, but had already arranged to have one brought up from the coast the following spring. Meanwhile, he had found a comfortable chair for his customers to sit in. And since the last thing he wanted to do was cook his own food, he sampled meals at the various restaurants in town and eventually settled on the Cosmopolitan. It was the farthest from his shop but it was the best and he paid the owner $20 a week for board.

Fall turned toward winter and the town became less noisy and less hectic as many miners left for the milder climate of the coast. Nevertheless, a sizeable population stayed behind, because the new wagon road to Soda Creek allowed supplies to be brought in more frequently over the summer and stockpiled. When the first snow came, it began quietly, without a wind, in huge, silent flakes that covered the ground and stump-riddled hillsides astonishingly fast. It fell so thickly that it filled the street, covered the boardwalks and piled up on the steeply pitched rooftops. Visibility up and down the street was limited to no more than a half dozen buildings. There would come a time over the course of the long winter when people would grow tired of all the snow, but the first snowfall, especially one as beautiful at this, was greeted as a welcome signal that much of the backbreaking work of the summer had at last ended and there would be more leisure time.

After a couple of days, the snow stopped and the sky cleared. Even with the sun, the temperature was well below zero and the air was so cold that it sliced into Moses' lungs like razor blades. But he found it invigorating, totally unlike the sweltering heat of Grand Cayman that sapped a man's strength so quickly.

The thing about Barkerville that struck Moses most was its egalitarian nature, and it seemed that it was not so much the gold as the *possibility* of gold that was the great equalizer. That neighbour you looked down on today might be a wealthy man tomorrow, so it was always best to be careful. But there was more to it than that. There was recognition on the part of most people that they all had common goals and that in order to achieve them, they could not expect to maintain whatever pretensions to good society they may have had before they arrived. Hard work was the order of the day and few people let anybody or anything get in the way of it. Which is not to say that there were not social divisions. There were.

The professional classes tended to be somewhat cliquey, and there was obvious separation between whites, Chinese and Indians. None of these three groups understood the others and they generally avoided association beyond a business level. On the other hand, the handful of blacks in town mingled quite freely with whites, eating, getting drunk and even living with one another. In short, there was no perceptible colour barrier for blacks in Barkerville, and that was why Moses decided to stay.

Word got around town about the "amiable black barber" and Moses' business grew. People he had seen many times on the street came into his shop so he met them formally. They hailed from every walk of life and most of them had a story to tell. Some were even instructive.

Dr. Siddall, one of several physicians to hang out a shingle in Barkerville, came in one day and Moses asked him about typhoid. Two years earlier the disease had been endemic on the creek; indeed, Sophia Cameron had succumbed to it. Now it had all but disappeared, and Moses asked the doctor why. Siddall said that he and a colleague, Dr. Chipp, who worked out of the Williams Creek Hospital, had also wondered why and had been studying the question. Previously, the disease was thought to be the result of an unhealthy climate, hence its other name, "mountain fever." But the doctors had developed a different theory. They now believed that decaying vegetation caused typhoid; that rotting leaves from the trees which lined the smaller creeks flowing into Williams Creek formed a poisonous miasma that seeped into the drinking water. Over the past two years, much of that timber had been cleared away, eliminating the poison and effectively banishing typhoid from the area. It made so much sense and seemed so obvious now that the doctors wondered why they had not thought of it sooner. They were going to report their findings so that other communities could avoid a similar tragedy.[1]

Moses devoured such information and it instantly became fodder for other customers, for if there was one place in any town that was a natural centre for gossip and storytelling among men, other than a saloon, it had to be a barbershop. This was one of the great rewards of the profession and Moses loved it. He never ceased to be enthralled by the incredible tales some of the men had to tell. If they were not describing a terrifying sea journey around Cape Horn, they were talking about crossing the malarial Isthmus of Panama, or fending off marauding Indians in the American west. Several of the men had come overland from Canada and told breathtaking stories of danger and loss of life on their perilous journey. He learned the most harrowing of these indirectly, through Bob Stevenson.

One day Moses was giving a haircut to a sour-faced miner named Bill Rennie. Rennie had a haunted look in his eyes and did not talk much and when he did, it was usually in monosyllables. His hair was thinning, which prompted Moses to tell him about the hair restorer that would be here in the spring but Rennie seemed thoroughly uninterested. Indeed, Moses got the feeling that it was probably best to give the man the shave and haircut he wanted so he could go. Just as Rennie was leaving, Stevenson came in, stamping the snow off his boots on the boardwalk. Because of his fame Stevenson seemed to know just about everyone in town, and he greeted Rennie with a smile and a hello. Rennie returned the greeting tersely and left. Stevenson took his place in the chair and sighed as Moses threw the cape over him.

"Now there goes a sad tale, Moses," he said. "Just when you think you've heard the worst of them, along comes a man like Rennie to show you just how wrong you were."

"I thought there might be something in his past that haunted him, but he's a hard man to get a word out of," replied Moses.

"What happened to him isn't something a man can easily talk about, unless he's primed himself with liquor. He told it to me one night over drinks at Cunio's saloon. It isn't for the faint of heart."

The Rennie brothers, Bill, Gilbert and Thomas, and their two companions, John Helstone and John Wright, came from London in Canada West. They left late in the spring of 1862 for Cariboo and took four and a half months to reach the Fraser at Tête Jaune Cache. There, they lashed two dugout canoes together for stability and on October 17, set out for Fort George, expecting to be there in two weeks. On October 29 they ran into trouble on the Giscome Rapids, about 47 miles above Fort George.

The bulky canoes slid onto a submerged rock in the middle of the river and stuck fast. After five days of freezing and trying to move the vessels, the men set out for Fort George but did not get far. Ice plugged the river and could not be portaged around. Someone had to go for help and the only ones up to the task were Bill and Gilbert.

On November 4, the two brothers departed for Fort George, believing that it would take only five days to get there and five more to return with help. Accordingly, they left a 10-day supply of food with their companions, and took the scanty remains for themselves. Six days later, they had covered only half the distance to their destination. Their food supply ran out. They shot the occasional mink, squirrel and bird but it was never enough to get rid of the hunger, and barely enough to keep them going. They struggled on, through the snow and over the rugged terrain, finally reaching the Nechako River on December 1. Instead of five days, it had taken 28.

The fort was in plain sight across the river, but they were unable attract anyone's attention. They spent another interminable night exposed to the elements. In the morning, the agent's wife spotted them and sent over a canoe. By this time, Bill's feet were so badly frostbitten Gilbert had to support him. The Rennies were two months at the fort recovering from their ordeal. Meanwhile, the snow was too deep and the river not frozen hard enough to send a rescue party for their companions. Eventually, they gave them up for dead.

By late January of 1863, the brothers were well enough to move on to Quesnelle Mouth, and that spring heard the fate of Thomas Rennie, Wright and Helstone. Apparently, Indians had passed by the camp and found two crazed men eating the third. Only the legs were left. Probably fearing that the Indians would kill them, the survivors pulled out their guns and drove off their last hope of survival. Incredibly, this was just as the Rennies were departing for Quesnelle Mouth. Two weeks later the Indians decided to return to the campsite to kill the cannibals, whom they greatly feared, and found only one still alive, feeding on the remains of the other. He scrambled to get away, but the Indians easily ran him down.

A trapper named John Giscome, who knew the Indians and passed by the campsite himself, verified the story. He found the bones of one man stacked neatly in the corner of the shelter. The skull looked like that of a youth, which he presumed was Thomas Rennie, although Wright was not much older. He also found Rennie's coat with nine knife-holes in it. The skeleton of another man lay close by, showing several ax blows to the head. The naked body of the last survivor was 350 yards away, evidently hacked to death by the Indians.

"Good God!" said Moses. "It's no wonder the poor soul looks haunted." So engrossed were both men in the story that Moses realized he had hardly touched a hair on Stevenson's head. "So what happened to Gilbert?"

"Gilbert worked on the wagon road for a while, till he earned enough money to go home. I'd bet that he's as angry with himself as Bill is for letting themselves be talked into giving the others up for dead. I expect losing a younger brother is hard on a man, especially if you feel you're responsible."[2]

"I know exactly how hard it is, even when you're not responsible," Moses said. He told Stevenson about losing his own brothers. "You might as well lop an arm or a leg off, because it's just like losing a part of yourself."

∞ ∞

The weeks passed, rather quickly Moses thought, as he spent much of his free time playing cards in Cunio's. Sometimes the game was whist, sometimes poker, but there was always money on the table. He was a cautious gambler and neither won nor lost much. It was mostly the convivial atmosphere he was there for anyway, despite the fact that some men were sore losers. Some nights there were arguments that ended in fights if there was too much liquor flowing, but at least no one carried a six-shooter like the gamblers in San Francisco. Fortunately, there was a good police force in town if things ever got out of hand. Moses himself tried not to drink too much and sometimes made a shot glass of brandy or whiskey last the entire evening. But he slipped occasionally, usually when he was thinking of Sarah. An anger would rise in him then, commensurate with the level of whiskey in his belly; anger at himself and at the kind of world that spawned men like the one Sarah had had the misfortune to run into. Sometimes the anger became hatred for white men everywhere, even those he sat with. One night he felt close to doing something regrettable, but before he did, he swept his money from the table and lurched from the building, leaving a bunch of bewildered men in his wake.

Bob Stevenson took him down into one of the shafts on the Cameron claim and he could not wait to get back out. He sat in a bucket and a windlass lowered him 35 feet into the mine. The shoring that kept the shaft from collapsing was soaked and looked far too fragile for Moses' liking. At the mucky bottom, the lamp light was meagre and there was water dripping everywhere. A horizontal tunnel had been started on one side of the shaft and Stevenson pointed out rock with traces of gold in it, but Moses felt that no payoff would be big enough to entice him to work in these conditions. He was glad to return to the surface and appreciated his barbershop more than he ever had before.

At Christmas Moses gave gifts of free shaves to those he had come to know well. The snow piled up deeper, and more than once he had to go up and clear it from the roof. Sometimes the wind blew up the valley in swirling eddies of granular snow, and other times it moaned so hard a man had to go inside to hear himself think. But there was always plenty of firewood on hand and nobody needed to be outside unless it was to get to a restaurant or a saloon, or to obtain more wood. Then gradually, the weather began to warm up and soon the snow was melting from the roofs and hanging in thick icicles from the eaves. There were still big patches on the ground when the first miners began trickling in from the lower country.

They brought with them both good news and bad. The American Civil War had finally ended; Robert E. Lee had surrendered to federal forces at Appomattox in Virginia, but the ink was hardly dry on the paper when Abraham Lincoln was assassinated. It was this news that was the most stunning and had the greatest effect on the Americans up and down the creek. People had expected that the war would end sometime, but no one could have foreseen Lincoln's violent death. Regardless, the end of the war was bound to change the complexion of Barkerville and Victoria, for it meant that many Americans would be returning to their homeland. Abolition of slavery had been won for blacks and many of them would be returning as well. Moses wondered if Gibbs was thinking of leaving, so he sent a letter off to him in the first mail.

A few weeks later, an answer was handed to him personally by none other than Gibbs' younger brother, Isaiah, who had arrived with his wife, Rebecca, and his mother, Maria Gibbs. They had come because Moses had spoken so highly of the place. Not only had they brought a letter, they also delivered a supply of Invigorator, plus the ingredients to make more, and a parcel of handbills advertising it. Moses had asked Gibbs to have them printed up and sent along with the Invigorator.

According to his letter, Gibbs was doing well. He had severed his partnership with Peter Lester, got out of the retail business, and was now speculating in real estate. Not only had he turned over several sizeable properties for dazzling profits, he had also made lucrative investments in a few businesses around town, one of them being George Blessing's construction firm. Houses were still going up at a steady rate, although orders for them seemed to be dwindling now that the war had ended. The positive side of the ledger was that, as many Americans began pulling up stakes, the racial situation in Victoria began to improve, though he still was not entirely happy with it. Last year he had campaigned for a seat on the city council and had been defeated by only a narrow margin. He was more determined than ever to run again in '66. With the Americans gone, he felt certain that he would win a seat. Gibbs ended his letter on a sad note. His latest child, a son, had died not long after Maria had delivered him. She was speaking even more earnestly now of going home.

Moses missed his old friend and quickly sent off a note of condolence.

Now that summer had arrived, Barkerville was in full swing again. The population of the area had increased tenfold, and though many people worked on outlying creeks, the town was constantly crowded. Profits soared for all businessmen and Moses was no exception. His hair restorer was selling extremely well and was a very lucrative part of his business. His advertising had proved very effective. The handbill proclaimed that the Invigorator would "... prevent baldness, restore hair that has fallen off or become thin, and to cure effectually Scurf and Dandruff. It will also relieve the Headache, and give the hair a darker and glossy color, and the free use of it will keep both the skin and the hair in a healthy state." And just so women wouldn't think that his product was for men only, he added "Ladies will find the Invigorator a great addition to toilet, both in consideration of the agreeable and delicate perfume, and the great facility it affords in dressing the hair."[3] But the ad that he considered to be his shrewdest was not really thought to be an ad at all. He paid three labourers, who were leaving the creeks for good, to sign a testimonial as to the efficacy of the Invigorator. The three men signed, as authors, a letter that Moses himself had written to the editor of the *Cariboo Sentinel*. It read, "This is to certify that from some cause or complaint of the head our hair commenced falling out so rapidly that we feared we should lose the whole. In this condition we went to W.D. Moses and strange to relate in THREE applications of his wonderful Hair Restorative our hair became as strong as ever and is now soft and lively."[4]

The Invigorator also took customers away from Moses' main competition in town, another black barber whose name was Isaac Dickson, or "Dixie" as most people called him. This was good for two reasons. Moses believed that the spoils of enterprise should always go to the best man, plus; he disliked Dixie. For one thing, Dixie had cut Lord Milton's hair when the British nobleman had visited Williams Creek in 1863 with his companion and doctor, Walter Cheadle, and he never let Moses forget it. He went on *ad nauseum* about what a privilege and honour it was, and how impressed the lord had been with his tonsorial skills. This always irritated Moses who would counter with the fact that he had rubbed shoulders with nobility many times while living in England. It annoyed him even further that it was quite apparent Dixie did not believe him.

But the worst thing about the man, by far, was that he was the kind of black that Mifflin Gibbs would have taken by the scruff of the neck, like an errant schoolboy, and given a good tongue-lashing about setting back, rather than advancing, the cause of black people everywhere. Dixie was an educated man who liked to write letters to the editor of the *Cariboo Sentinel* in the dialect of an illiterate Negro. In welcoming the newspaper to the creek during its first month in business, he wrote: "To De Editer of De 'Cariboo Sental:' It gibs me much pleasure indee to see genelman ob your cloth on Wiliams Crek dis air season, an hope, sar, de indefatable entarprice an de talen I sees 'splayed in de columbs ob yer valuable jernel will meet wid its juss rewad, dat is, dat de paper will pay big … "[5]

Even though Moses recognized that the letters were cleverly put together and sometimes contained paraphrased lines from Robbie Burns and Shakespeare, such gobbledygook irritated him no end and he told Dixie so.

"It's a joke, Moses," Dixie said. "It's just me playing a joke on those gullible white folks. Don't take it so seriously, for God's sake!"

"But I do take it seriously, because it's a joke that most of them don't get. That makes it more harmful than funny. Every letter you write is a hammer blow on the wedge between black people and white people. Why do you want to drive it deeper?"

But that was not the way Dixie saw it and he continued writing his letters.

When Moses spent time in black company, it was usually with the Gibbses. He was pleased that they had come. He helped them get established up in Richfield, where they bought a small house to which they were adding an extra room. Maria and Rebecca had started a laundry business and were nearly overwhelmed with work. Isaiah bought into a claim that included a few other black miners and encouraged Moses to invest in it too. The ground had been studied thoroughly by those who knew about such things, he insisted, and it was deemed that the possibilities of its paying huge dividends were excellent. The investors called themselves the Davis Company, after Wilbur Davis, a miner with great expertise, and it was the only company on the creek co-owned by blacks and whites. Since his own business was flourishing, Moses bought in, reasoning that if it happened, and they struck it rich, he could probably handle being an extremely wealthy man. Besides, he liked Isaiah, who had the same shrewdness as his older brother, but was quieter and did not mind getting his hands dirty.

Moses' admiration for Rebecca grew daily. His first impression of her was that she was rather plain, but there were many things about her that he found very attractive. She had a penchant for literature and could quote the great poets of the day. Indeed, she aspired to write poetry herself. Her compassion for the underdog was always apparent, and of all the poems of her own that she showed to Moses, his favourite was "The Old Red Shirt."

> A miner came to my cabin door,
>   His clothes were covered with dirt;
> He held out a piece he desired me to wash,
>   Which I found was an old red shirt.
>
> His cheeks were thin, and furrow'd his brow,
>   His eyes were sunk in his head;
> He said that he had got work to do,
>   And be able to earn his bread.
>
> He said that the "old red shirt" was torn,
>   And asked me to give it a stitch;

But it was threadbare, and sorely worn,
  Which showed he was far from rich.

O! Miners with good paying claims,
  O! traders who wish to do good;
Have pity on men who earn your wealth,
  Grudge not the poor miner his food.

Far from these mountains a poor mother mourns
  The darling that hung by her skirt,
When contentment and plenty surrounded the home
  Of the miner that brought me the shirt.[6]

Rebecca possessed the "fine madness" that separates writers of rhyme from the rest of humankind, and was therefore considered eccentric by people up and down the creek. Moses, however, was charmed by her eccentricity and delighted in how it elevated her above the mundane. He enjoyed being with her, enjoyed her intelligence and generous heart. She was easy to talk to and in some ways reminded him of Sarah, and what she might have been like had her life not taken such a cruel turn. He had never thought it possible that a woman could be a friend, but he could think of no other term for his relationship with Rebecca other than what it plainly was — a friendship. Yet even on that level, it felt good being around a woman again.

Deeper into summer the barber's chair that Moses had ordered arrived and it was difficult to tell who was more pleased, Moses or his customers. He was kept busy, but then the entire valley was busy, particularly the miners who were trying to accomplish an entire year's work in only a season or two. Most of the mines were in operation 24 hours a day and a handful were producing gold; not fortunes, but enough to sustain the hunt. Some miners ran out of money and claims changed hands, sold to other optimists who laboured under the belief that they would be the lucky ones to find the mother lode. Other than during Sunday-morning services, the valley echoed with the noise of industry.

Cornish waterwheels groaned, operating pumps that sucked water from the pits to keep them dry. Picks and shovels clanked and hammers banged as miners dug dangerous shafts down to bedrock and shored up the walls to prevent cave-ins. They hollowed out the ground bucket by bucket and sent the fruits of their toil up to the surface by squeaking windlasses. Then the gravel was dumped unceremoniously into sluice boxes and washed, with hopes that there would be heavier gold particles to drop through and be caught in the bottom baffles. Each shovelful of earth turned over in the pit held the chance of revealing the mother lode, and each bucket winched to the surface and washed contained the possibility of better days to come.

It was backbreaking work, heartbreaking for some, but it went on relentlessly. The Davis claim was no different, except that white men worked alongside black men, sharing the same dreams. Then in late summer the Davis men stepped out of the ranks and proved that they were different in other respects as well. They hit pay dirt.

CHAPTER TWELVE

I t was not the mother lode, but it was a good streak and would put substantial sums of money into the principals' pockets. Moses and the others were the talk of the town and for a while he basked in it. Yet, surprisingly, it worried him in some ways. He really had not expected much to come from his investment, which was more of a lark than anything else, and was not sure that he needed it now that his life seemed to be rolling along so smoothly. He spoke to Rebecca about his ambivalent feelings, since the strike would affect her as well, and she was calm about the possibility of being wealthy.

"I don't know what you're looking for, Moses," she said. "Only you know that, or at least you ought to, a man your age. All I've ever wanted from money is enough to meet my needs, with some left over to satisfy my wishes. And there's not much I wish for other than good friends, good books of poetry, and a pen and some paper so I can write my own. But what do you wish for? It doesn't matter, you know. It can be as ordinary as a piece of pie or as extraordinary as a mansion on a hill, high above the unwashed masses. It's up to each of us to decide. And as long as our income can satisfy our wishes, there's a good chance we'll live relatively happy lives."

It was a sensible perspective, Moses acknowledged. His most basic wish had been fulfilled just by being accepted as a legitimate member of the human race, and not spurned as some sub-species inferior to the white race. That, at least, was the case here in Barkerville. He also cherished his friends, but neither his friends nor his equality depended on whether he had money. As it turned out, he need not have fretted so much. Before any of the gold could be taken from the ground, the Aurora Company, who owned the adjoining claim, insisted that the Davis claim was legally theirs. They filed suit against the Davis Company and the matter was turned over to the gold commissioner, Judge William G. Cox.

Cox was an imposing man. Everything about him seemed oversized, including his girth. His face was wide, his forehead high, and a great, drooping moustache bent around his mouth, in the manner of German aristocracy, that lent him a rather gruff appearance. But his looks belied his demeanour, which was gentlemanly and polite. He listened to the claims of the Aurora men who said that they had staked the land and that the Davis men were claim jumpers. The Davis men argued that there were no stakes, and that even if there had been, Aurora had let their title lapse by not working the land in the time specified. After hearing both arguments, Cox decided in favour of the Davis Company.

Moses hoped that it would end there, but it did not. The Aurora Company ignored Cox's ruling and began sinking a shaft on the Davis claim. Rebecca just laughed when Moses told her and said, "The meek might inherit the earth, my dear, but there won't be any gold left when they do."

The worst part of it was that ill feelings were running high between the two factions, and spreading out among the community. People were beginning to choose sides and some even felt the affair was taking on racial overtones. The Davis men went back to Cox who once more ruled in their favour; the Aurora men were incensed and went around the commissioner by appealing directly to Judge Matthew Baillie Begbie. What the outcome of that would be, no one could predict. Begbie had a reputation for being fair, but some thought him a despot with his own views of how the world should run. Meanwhile, all work halted in the valley as winter came down like a heavenly arbiter to still the arguments. Men packed up and left for the coast where the weather was more hospitable. Moses decided that he would follow suit.

Some time in Victoria would not only do him good, it would allow him to deal directly with a few business transactions, mostly concerning the Invigorator, which had hitherto been handled by an agent in Victoria. He would no doubt spend the money he had saved, and then some, on living expenses while he was there, but the change of scenery would be worth it, particularly the opportunity to see Gibbs. He took with him letters from Rebecca, Isaiah and Maria and left with Bob Stevenson in late October.

The two men snowshoed out to Quesnelle Mouth and caught the *Enterprise* on her second-to-last run downriver to Soda Creek. As yet, there was not much snow on the wagon road south of the creek, but it was enough to prevent the coaches from running, so they bought horses for the journey to Port Douglas. It was a trip that Moses would not have made without the company of a man like Stevenson. He was knowledgeable and fearless, with a good head on his shoulders and an unerring sense of direction, even when the road was obscured. At Port Douglas, they sold the animals for nearly as much as they paid for them and were on the next steamer to the coast, arriving in Victoria on November 4. When the ship rounded Laurel Point and slid alongside the Hudson's Bay Company wharf, Moses felt more like a visitor arriving than someone coming home.

☞☜

"Believe me, Moses, this government is a sham and it is run by imbeciles." Gibbs was on one of his tirades. "I thought Douglas was a poor administrator because all he wanted to do was perpetuate the *status quo*. Any mention of the word 'progress' would set him to trembling. When Kennedy took over last year, after Douglas retired, I hoped there might be a change for the better, but how wrong I was![1] All the man knows how to do is party and spend money, and his associates are a bunch of old fogies who haven't any inkling about good old Yankee enterprise! They're going to drive this colony right to the poorhouse if they're not careful. They don't seem to understand that the gold rush is all but over. Victoria has only half the population it had when you were here, Moses, and the stores are crammed with items that won't sell. It's why I got out of the retail business. A blind man could have read the writing on the wall. It's a sorry state, my friend, and leads me to believe that what this country needs most is responsible government, of the people — by the people and for the people."

"Good Lord, Gibbs, that sounds suspiciously American. You wouldn't be proposing annexation now, would you?"

"The alternative appears to be a confederation with the Canadas, which might very well prove to be a nightmare if the men who run it are as inept and self-serving as those who run this colony. Not to mention the drunkard who's now in charge of British Columbia.[2] A large number of Americans went home once the war ended but there still seems to be a small core of support here for annexation, and I'm exasperated enough to want to join them. To hell with the Americans' racist attitudes. At least I know where I stand with them. As much as I admire the British for their fairness, this land should belong to people who can use it most efficiently and develop it best. If that happens to be the Americans, then I'm all for it."

Moses could scarcely believe his ears, and he did not much like what Gibbs was saying. Talk of confederation had also reached Williams Creek, and Moses fully supported the move. The Americans had wreaked enough havoc among the blacks and the Indians in their own country, and it was best to contain them south of the international boundary. To let them take over the north was pure folly. Better British ineptitude than American ruthlessness.

Despite their lack of agreement on such fundamental issues Moses enjoyed these talks with Gibbs and always looked forward to them. So did Gibbs, who was pleasantly surprised that his old friend was back in town even if it was just for the winter. "We have an extra room," he had said when Moses showed up at his James Bay residence, "and I insist that you save your money and make our home yours for the duration. Maria will be pleased to have another man around to harangue."

Moses took Gibbs up on the generous offer and was glad he did. The Gibbses' home was the finest in James Bay, which was fast becoming one of the most exclusive areas in Victoria. The house was located on the southwest corner of Menzies and Simcoe streets on five acres of beautifully wooded land. It had three storeys, with a porch and balcony that ran along the front and both sides. Moses' room was on the top floor, and because the house sat on a small rise he had a magnificent view of the harbour, spoiled only by the backside of the Birdcages. It was wonderful to be in a home filled with the smells of cooking and the sounds of children, and for a while Moses was envious. By Christmas, however, he had decided that much as he liked children, he would be content if they always belonged to someone else. Still, the children loved him and called him "Uncle Moses," an honorific of which he was proud, and he lavished gifts upon them in return.

One evening, under the pretext that he was going to take a "turn around the town," Moses stopped to see Constance. She would not let him in the door. She was leaving town, she said, going back to San Francisco. As far as she was concerned Victoria had become as constipated as an old man's bowel. From what he could see of the house in behind her, it was in disarray.

"I'm sorry you're leaving," Moses said, and then smiled. "Perhaps just a drink then."

"It's never 'just a drink,' Moses. We both know that."

"But I had always thought I was more a friend than a customer."

"Then you were sadly mistaken. Good night." She shut the door in his face.

His face and the back of his neck felt hot as he walked down Broughton Street and turned onto Wharf Street. He'd never been given the brushoff by a prostitute before and he felt utterly humiliated. There are moments in one's life, he thought, when a corner to crawl into seems entirely appropriate. He walked over to Ringo's, noticing that there were now gas lights along Wharf, which should have been a sign of a burgeoning city but, according to Gibbs' sharp eye and Constance's astute comprehension of economics, it apparently was not. In the front of an empty lot a curiosity struck his eye. A miniature gallows had been built, hardly big enough to hang a small dog, but completely workable. Moses wondered what on earth its purpose could be and decided that he must ask Gibbs.

"Moses!" Ringo cried from the kitchen when he saw the barber enter. The big man came rushing out. "I heard you were back in town fo' a while. How come it takes so long fo' you to come by and visit an ol' friend?" His coal-black face was split wide by a grin that showed crooked, yellowing teeth.

"Truth to tell, Sam," Moses said, "there is someone in town who cooks better than you. Indeed, I'm going to send Mrs. Gibbs over here to personally give you lessons. Meanwhile, let me see if your plum pudding still stands up to close scrutiny."

Ringo laughed heartily. "Sit down, Moses. 'Low me to take your hat."

"Not on your life, Sam. I haven't forgotten your reputation."

Moses was referring to the odd occasion when Ringo, not liking a customer's attitude, would break a half-dozen eggs into his hat. It gave the big man no end of delight to watch the result.

Moses had no sooner sat down than George Blessing walked in, accompanied by a younger version of himself. He waved the two men over.

"Good to see you again, Moses!"

"Good to see you as well, George," Moses replied.

The two men sat down and Blessing introduced his companion. "This is my brother Charlie. Charlie, meet Moses, an artist when it comes to shaping a beard and a genius when it comes to restoring hair. Like me, you'll need the likes of him one day!"

Moses laughed and shook Charlie's hand; he seemed every bit as easygoing as his older brother. George asked, "How goes life in the goldfields? Are you filthy rich yet?"

Moses reserved his answer until the waiter had taken the Blessings' order for a slice of squash pie each, then explained that he might be on the verge of being better off. He outlined the problems between the Davis and Aurora companies, adding, "Apparently everyone here is convinced that the gold rush is all but finished, but our discovery proves them wrong. There's still gold in those creeks."

"Hmmm. Just the words I think Charlie wanted to hear."

Charlie nodded and said that he had not had much luck with investments in San Francisco and laughed sheepishly, pointing to a stickpin in his cravat that was a small gold nugget in the shape of an angel. "This is about the extent of my profits," he said, "and that's why I came here. But according to George, Victoria is running out of opportunities. In fact, he reckons that not more than a handful of buildings have gone up during the past year and it's becoming harder and harder to get work."

Moses said, "Why don't you come up to Barkerville and see what's there? I don't think you'll be disappointed. I'm returning in a few weeks and we could travel together. Besides, I understand the trip up through the canyon is quite breathtaking, and worth the effort alone." Moses' previous trips to and from Williams Creek had been via the Port Douglas-Lillooet route and he was eager to try the alternate road up that followed the Fraser and Thompson rivers.

"Thanks for the offer," said Charlie. "I'll give it some thought."

Since the Blessings were Americans, Moses switched topics and asked George his thoughts on annexation.

"Something big certainly needs to happen or else Victoria risks becoming a ghost town. But I don't think annexation has a snowflake's chance in hell. Certainly, there will be a few outspoken types around pushing the idea, and it will be picked up by the papers, but if it ever comes down to a vote ... " He paused for a moment, "Well ... there's just too much British sentiment in this town to overcome. We've also been promised a railroad that would connect us to the east. On top of that old John Butts has another name for annexationists, and he makes more news than anybody."

"How so?" Moses knew John Butts well, as did everyone in town. He was a strange bird who had shown up in Victoria during the Fraser River gold rush and put his stamp on the town straight off. His stentorian voice got him a job as town crier and in addition to doing advertisements for theatres and auctions, and announcing the arrivals and departures of ships in the harbour, he read aloud government proclamations and orders. Later, he was given a contract to clean up the mud on Government Street, and did, but he got rid of the mud by dumping it on Yates Street. He then negotiated a contract to clean up Yates. His chicanery was legendary and, unable to change his ways, he was sentenced to three months on the chain gang, cleaning Victoria's streets. But John Butts hated physical work and fell down one day, claiming his legs had gone lame. He was hospitalized and poked with needles to see if he was feigning his illness. Though he never once cried out in pain, the doctor was skeptical. One day Butts was seen to move one of his legs, so the doctor surprised him with a bucket of cold water over his head. Butts stood up, in shock. Another couple of buckets sent him running off into town. The last that Moses heard of him, he had been arrested for spiking the temperance meeting's tea with whiskey.

"What is Butts up to now?" he asked George.

"Right now he's trying to put the fear of God into every annexationist. Have you seen the small gallows on Wharf Street?"

Moses nodded. "I passed it on my way here."

"Well, Butts built it, and twice a day — once in the morning and again in the afternoon — he stands there and loudly announces the name of every annexationist in town. With every name, he shouts 'Traitor!' and trips the trapdoor. It's no wonder that enthusiasm for the cause seems to be waning. Thank God my name isn't among them!"

Moses laughed. "I thought for certain old Butts would have been run out of town by now."

"I believe Judge Pemberton is trying his damnedest to do just that!"[3]

Moses finished his plum pudding and the Blessings their pie and, shaking hands goodbye, they agreed to meet at some later date for a drink.

Left to his own devices, Moses walked up Johnson Street, to his old house. It was apparent that the new owners were not as careful as Sarah had been in keeping the place up. The flower garden in the front yard was grown over in weeds, and all of the windows were in need of a good wash. He did not want to be seen staring at the place so he walked down the street a short distance to where he could stand at look at it unobtrusively. He lit a pipe.

Barely two years had passed since the house belonged to him; it seemed both a lifetime ago and only yesterday. The part that really hurt about the memories it evoked was that while the house had been his, Sarah had never been. He was still frustrated over his inability to deal with her and her problems. He knew he should have handled it better, but he did not know exactly how. Certainly that night with Constance was one of the most thick-headed things he'd ever done. He had come to a fork in the road that night and had blindly taken the wrong one. He had no idea where the other would have led, but if it had been to Sarah alive and reasonably contented, it would have been worth the trouble. What a fool he was. He felt tears welling up inside him, at the loss of Sarah and his own stupidity, and left before he made an even greater fool of himself in public.

Having tried Victoria on for size again Moses found that it no longer fit as well as it used to. Even so, he was glad he had come, if only for the time he had had to spend with Gibbs, who was now working harder than ever toward becoming the town's first black councilman. Yet when he thought about it, the best thing about this trip was that he now knew just how much he appreciated Barkerville. He missed the town, the people and the camaraderie, and he missed Rebecca. He was beginning to think of the return trip as "going home." It was ironic in a way because Barkerville was an island just as surely as Grand Cayman was, only instead of ocean, it was surrounded by thousands of square miles of wilderness. In a sense, he had only traded one island for another, yet he was at peace with the knowledge.

Charlie Blessing had decided to investigate the possibilities of Williams Creek, which was good news for Moses. He and Blessing met for drinks occasionally and Moses found him to be a remarkably agreeable young man who would make a good travelling companion. On a fine May morning that held the promise of summer, the two men boarded the steamship *Enterprise* and sailed away as the sun reflected off the snowy peaks of the Olympic Mountains, rising like a rampart across the strait.

CHAPTER THIRTEEN

aro Strait gleamed beneath the morning sun as the *Enterprise* steamed northward through the broad channel. To starboard, between the ship and San Juan Island, a pod of killer whales broke the surface in unison, their dorsal fins and backs sleek and black. It was the first time Moses had seen these animals, and their grace and beauty quickened his heart. On the port side, D'arcy Island slid by, placidly awaiting its future as a Chinese leper colony, while overhead, the blue sky was streaked with wisps of cirrus clouds. On shore, the sun would have been hot but on the water it was tempered by the breeze of the ship making headway.

Moses leaned against the ship's rail and enjoyed the scenery. For the first time in a long while, he felt a reasonable contentment and he was thankful for it. Forward, along the rail, two white men were having a conversation. By the cut of their clothes, Moses presumed they were labourers, perhaps on their way to the mainland to find work. Every now and then one of them would spit a dark gob of tobacco juice over the side. Though Moses could not hear everything they were saying, he was able to pick up a phrase or two, carried to him on the breeze that sent the tobacco juice sailing by below him. It seemed to be about the lack of work in Victoria at first, but then they turned their attention to him as a topic for discussion. He heard one of them say, "... that don't make any sense."

"Course it does," said the other, a little louder so that Moses could not fail to hear. "They ain't got souls like you and me, like real people. Niggers just are, that's all."

My God, Moses thought. How often had he heard those kinds of remarks before, or something equally asinine? They usually came from white men who felt diminished by well-dressed, successful-looking blacks who appeared to have achieved something greater than they ever could. In order to elevate their own status they invariably resorted to what Gibbs called "twaddle." Moses pushed off the rail and walked up to the two men. Looking the man who had made the offensive statement hard in the eye he said, "Pardon me, but do you have the time?"

The man fumbled for his watch, embarrassed by the unexpected encounter with a man he had just dismissed as being non-human, and unsure of what he should do.

"Er, uh, yes," he said, his face flushing red. "It's … "

Moses interrupted. "Then if you devote a good measure of it to trying to determine why you're the damned fool that you are, it will not have been wasted."

He strode away without looking back, thinking that the moment was one that would have brought Gibbs supreme enjoyment.

Returning to the first-class stateroom that he shared with Charlie, he found it empty. Blessing must have gone to the lounge for a drink. Moses resumed reading Charles Dickens' *American Notes*, which Maria Gibbs had given him as a going-away present. The book chronicled the author's travels through the United States, and in a chapter on slavery he wrote with such passion against the institution that Moses was deeply moved: "Shall we whimper over legends of the tortures practiced on each other by the Pagan Indians, and smile on the cruelties of Christian men? Shall we, so long as these things last, exult above the scattered remnants of that race, triumph in the white enjoyment of their possessions? Rather for me, restore the forest and the Indian village; in lieu of the stars and stripes, let some poor feather flutter in the breeze; replace the streets and squares by wigwams, and though the death-song of a hundred haughty warriors fill the air, it will be music to the shriek of one unhappy slave."[1]

Such passages consumed him, even as the *Enterprise* steamed through the narrow arteries separating the small islands in the Fraser River delta, and made her way up the muddy waterway to New Westminster.

Moses and Charlie took rooms in a clapboard hotel, then filled the evening playing billiards and sipping brandy. Charlie had some skill at the game, but the cue was like a club in Moses' hands and he had no feel for it. Regardless, he enjoyed Charlie's company for he was an affable, articulate man who appeared comfortable with his niche in life. Given the look of his hands, which were smooth and uncalloused, he was a stranger to physical work.

When Moses commented on this, Charlie grinned and said, "I hate work. I'm incorrigibly lazy, even though George will tell you that when I work, I work hard. But to be brutally honest, I only work hard to get it over with so I can be lazy again. As a child, when I had to bring in wood for the stove, I usually brought in more than I could carry and would leave a trail of pieces behind me. My father always called it a 'lazy man's load' because I was too lazy to make two trips. He knew his son, that's for sure."

He went on to say that he and his brother George had chosen their parents well. Their father had become a prominent contractor in Cleveland and they could always fall back on him if they needed money. George was like their father with his business acumen, but Charlie much preferred the life of a vagabond. True, he had made some reasonable investments in California, but nothing that would impress his father. Perhaps Williams Creek would be the place to write home about. In the meantime, he was enjoying life and was as carefree as any man who never had to worry about where the next dollar was coming from.

The following morning they were on the steamer for Yale, a hundred miles up the Fraser. The *Lillooet* left at seven o'clock precisely. She was a sternwheeler, one of the newest ships on the river and considered one of the fastest. A rack of deer antlers graced her pilot house as a symbol of her swiftness. She noisily pushed her way against the current into the broad Fraser Valley, the steam screeching from her stacks and the paddles slapping endlessly on the water. She steamed past the Hudson's Bay Company's Fort Langley and about 20 miles below Fort Hope she entered the mountains, where the valley narrowed between peaks more than a mile in height. The river was running high, and hid the myriad gravel bars that were usually exposed near its banks in drier seasons. They stopped at Fort Hope to offload supplies for the small community beside the abandoned HBC post, then continued on up the river and into the Fraser Canyon. With only about an hour of daylight left, the mountains loomed dark and foreboding above them. In some places, they plunged straight into the river, which narrowed and swirled past the *Lillooet* with a mighty surge that caused the vessel to labour hard. Soon Yale appeared on the west bank; the engine slowed and the ship's whistle sounded. People on shore came streaming down to the landing as the *Lillooet* tied up.

A sense of déjà vu reminded Moses that Yale was not unlike the unassuming port towns he had seen along the Mosquito Coast. The skin colour of the people and the building materials might be different, and it was edged by a different kind of jungle and treacherous stretch of water, but otherwise it was just another port of call on a distant shore. Sometimes those days seemed long ago, deeply imbedded in the past, but at times like this, he felt as if he could reach out and touch them.

Yale was the head of navigation on the lower Fraser River. Its single street, lined with false-fronted and gable-roofed businesses, houses and hotels, many of them new and all facing the river, was duly called Front Street. Throngs of people milled along the dusty road and boardwalk despite the fact that there were not many places to go. Up at the north end of town was Barnard's Express Company or "B.X." for short, where the stage to Soda Creek would leave the following morning at 3:00 A.M. The coach carried mail and had to keep to a schedule so it always left promptly, whether paying passengers were on board or not. At $130 a ticket, few people missed it.

Yale was crowded and the best beds that Moses and Charlie could find were two billiard tables in a back room of one of the hotels. It did not matter much; they had to be up at 2:00 a.m. anyway. The two men managed a couple of hours of restless sleep before the clerk was shaking Moses by the shoulder, saying if they wanted breakfast before the stage left they should get a move on. After a quick meal of leftovers from the previous night, he and Charlie went out into the darkness.

The town was quiet as the men walked up Front Street to the B.X. office. A team of four horses, three raven black and one milk white, had just been hitched to the stage. In the lamplight shining from the office windows, Moses could see that the carriage was painted red, and had open windows on both sides that could be covered with drop-down tarps. Waiting to board were five passengers besides Moses and Charlie, all male: three would-be miners, a doctor and a salesman of medical supplies. None of them, including himself, felt very talkative at this time of the morning. Baggage and other items were stowed in the rear boot of the stage and on the roof, mailbags were tucked away in the front boot beneath the driver's seat, and the passengers climbed aboard, one of the miners taking a seat beside the driver. With a click of his tongue, the driver shook the reins and the coach departed precisely on time, rattling into the canyon, beneath a star-filled sky that ran like a glittering stream between the lofty mountain peaks. Less than a month from the longest day of the year there was enough ambient light to see the road and since there had been no rain for the past few days, it was hard and dry.

Any thoughts that Moses may have had about resuming his interrupted sleep promptly vanished when the coach started moving. It swayed and bumped over rocks in the road so that anything beyond a catnap was impossible. He was glad that he sat on the outside of the bench seat where there was a hand grip. Charlie, who was in the middle, had to grab onto Moses whenever the road got particularly rough. Over smooth sections, of which there were few, the swaying motion was similar to that of a ship at sea and one of the passengers complained of feeling ill. The scheduled time to Soda Creek, 300 miles to the north, was 52 hours, provided there were no delays. There would be two stopovers at roadhouses along the way, one at Hat Creek, the other at 150 Mile House, as long as the stage was able to stick to its schedule. If it fell behind because of breakdowns, road conditions, weather or some other unforeseeable reason, the driver would make up time by reducing the length of the stopovers. Better that the passengers have a hurried meal or lose sleep than that the mail be late.

Even in the darkness the canyon was awesome. The road had been blasted out of solid rock, literally carved into the cliff, and was mostly as narrow as a ribbon. In some places, it was supported by cribbing; in others, crude bridges spanned small gullies cut by gushing streams. It rose and fell as it twisted along the canyon wall, sometimes close enough to the river to hear its roar, other times so high above that it was dizzying. There were no railings and often the big wheels of the coach seemed only inches away from tumbling horses and passengers to their death on the rocks or in the river below.

Just beyond Spuzzum, 12 miles up the road, they descended to the brand-new Alexandra suspension bridge and thundered across it, stopping for a moment to pay the toll. They reached Boston Bar, about halfway through the canyon, in broad day-light. Some of the passengers wished it was still dark, for the precarious road was frightening. They climbed mountains to vertiginous heights, sometimes at speeds so slow Moses could have walked as fast, then descended almost as slowly on the other side, the horses straining to hold the load back. Through it all, Charlie seemed to be enjoying himself immensely.

At Lytton they stopped to eat lunch, then turned northeast into the Thompson River canyon, which proved to be every bit as spectacular. Turbulent green water crashed into foamy shards on huge boulders, which in one place jutted up like worn peaks at midstream, the water surging around them at terrifying speeds. The mountainsides were generally pine-clad but in some places looked as barren and dry as a desert. They crossed the river at Cook's Ferry and began the long climb to 88 Mile Bluff, a spectacular gash through the rock so high above the Thompson that Moses felt detached from reality.[2] He could never have imagined anything like this in a thousand years. So many things could go wrong that his heart was in his mouth most of the way. A rockslide could come roaring down from above and obliterate them, or the coach could lose a wheel, or the horses might bolt, and the entire contraption would disappear over the side in a confusion of animal and human screams. He was able to breathe again when, beyond the bluff, the road left the river and the landscape of arid hills and sagebrush was wonderfully dull and safe.

It was hot in the coach, and as the sun dropped and shone directly inside, it grew even hotter. Conversation, difficult at the best of times, had ceased altogether. Eventually, at Charlie's suggestion, two of the passengers reached outside and undid the ties that held the rolled-up canvas cover and let it drop, which brought some relief from the heat. Sitting on the opposite side, by the uncovered windows, Moses stared out at the desolate landscape while dust rose in billowing clouds beside and behind the stage, marking its passage as surely as a wake follows a ship. Over time the dust seeped inside, through the windows and the floorboards, to cover everyone in a thin film. The coach rumbled and swayed down the road and every time a wheel hit something other than the rut it was supposed to be in, it sent a jolt clear up through Moses' spine. To add to his discomfort, his head felt clogged, and every breath added another layer of dust in his sinuses, closing them off even more. He shifted into another world where he could ignore his misery and, judging by the vacant looks on the other passengers' faces, they had done the same. All except one of the miners, who had hardly ceased complaining since the stage left Yale.

Charlie came out of his hibernation long enough to comment on how much the country reminded him of the gold-bearing hills of California. Then the road descended in a long, sweeping turn and ran past Cache Creek, and alongside the Bonaparte River which, to Moses' mind, was far too modest to warrant the capacious valley it ran through. At top speed, the stage rolled up to Hat Creek House, the stopover point for the night. Moses was so cramped that he could hardly get the bend out of his back, and alighted from the coach like an old man. Even Charlie, who was 20 years younger, had difficulty getting the kinks out. "If you feel half as bad as you look and I look half as bad as I feel, we're both in serious trouble," he said to Moses. Then as an afterthought, he added, "Don't ask me to repeat that."

Hat Creek House sat near the junction of the trail that ran east to Kamloops and west through Marble Canyon to Lillooet. It was a long, low, log house with several outbuildings, and what it lacked in decorum it made up for in the quality of its food, served up by a smiling Chinese cook named Kum Lee. After a dinner of beefsteak and parsnips, Moses and Charlie joined the doctor and the salesman in the saloon for a nightcap. The miners followed, but sat by themselves. The drinks seemed to revive the others, but the two friends were so tired they could hardly keep their eyes open. They excused themselves and went to bed. The doctor and salesman left shortly after, but the miners looked as if they might be there for the night.

Their sleeping quarters were austere, but not as bad as they could have been on the road to the mines. Sometimes the roadhouses were so crowded that every inch of floor space was taken up by weary travellers, but here they had the luxury of a dormitory room and their choice of several bunks lined with straw mattresses. It was by no stretch of the imagination the most comfortable bed he had ever had, but Moses was asleep the moment his head hit the duck-down pillow. And as on other nights, Sarah drifted in and out of his dreams.

They were away early the following morning, on schedule, and minus a passenger. One of the miners had got so drunk the night before that he refused to rise from his bed and was determined to stay there rather than spend two days in a row in that "goddamned torture chamber on wheels." He would wait for another to come along, when his body could take the punishment, or buy a horse if he had to. Without a word, the driver threw the man's belongings onto the ground in front of the roadhouse, and the stage was off in ghostly streams of dust.

They left the desert landscape behind and began the long, gradual climb, full of dips and sweeping turns, to the plateau that is the heart of Cariboo and consists of rolling, thickly forested hills, numerous lakes and spruce bogs. They passed a splendid chasm, a singular, great gouge out of the earth that seemed to have no reason for being there. Much later, they trundled along the shore of Lac La Hache, the road badly rutted and pocked with mud puddles because of the recent rain in the area. This slowed the stage somewhat, but the driver made up for lost time by shortening their luncheon stopover.

Considering that for hundreds of miles on either side of the road there was nothing but wilderness, it was a busy thoroughfare, with most of the traffic heading north at a much slower pace than the stagecoach. Besides local traffic near the many roadhouses along the way, they had passed several miners with pack animals, a couple of pack trains and two freight wagons in tandem pulled by a 10-yoke span of oxen, all bound for the goldfields. Moses commented on the size of the wagons and one of the passengers said that the bull punchers used one ox per ton of cargo, which meant that this one was taking as much as 20 tons of freight up to the mines. The passenger added that the animals only averaged about eight miles a day, so it was a slow round trip from Yale or Lillooet.

After another hard day's travel they pulled up to the inn at 150 Mile House in a cloud of dust that obscured everything. Moses noticed that the driver always approached and departed these populated places at high speeds, and reasoned that it was done to impress the locals.

It was an easy journey up past Williams Lake to Soda Creek the following day. When Moses and Charlie left the stagecoach and boarded the steamer to Quesnelle Mouth, Moses commented on the relative comfort. Charlie snorted good-naturedly and said, "I have travelled on the steamboats on the Mississippi River and *that* is comfort. *This* is transportation."

The *Enterprise*, under the command of Captain J. W. Doane, a man as renowned for his tippling as he was for his seamanship, departed the creek at 4:00 the next morning for her 10-hour run north. All of her wooden parts were built of hand-sawn lumber from the surrounding area, while her metal and glass components had been packed in by mules. Unlike her namesake, which plied the waters between Victoria and New Westminster, there was not a thing about her that could be called "refined." Nevertheless, even with the noise, Moses saw her as a welcome relief after nearly three days in a stage coach, regardless of how Charlie felt.

The river was wide, the current slow, and the motion of the vessel negligible, which was the part most appreciated by the two men as they sat in the saloon sipping brandies. Moses was enjoying the trip immensely as was Charlie, who was impressed by the countryside. "This is magnificent, Moses," he said, "and so unlike the Mississippi that it is astonishing they are both called 'rivers.'"

Charlie was the first man Moses had met who had actually been on that famed river, and he was curious. "How are they different?" he asked.

"This river is straight as a die compared to the Mississippi. It twists and turns all the way to the gulf. Did you know that the river is not in the same place as it was when La Salle sailed down it nearly 200 years ago? There are inland towns that used to be river towns until the river cut away from them. Some of them are 30 miles from the water now. That's because the land is so soft the river can go anywhere it wants. The Fraser can't, though. The mountains force it to cut a deep trench that's relatively straight and narrow compared to the Mississippi. It's at least a mile wide over most of its length."

The sound of the engines and the tremor they sent through the vessel suddenly ceased, and the *Enterprise* began drifting backwards and toward shore until she ground to a halt along a gravel bar and word circulated that there were minor engine problems that would be fixed in short order. It was five hours before they were under way again.

"Besides money," Charlie said, "the only other thing a traveller really needs is patience. Things like this don't bother me a bit. I think I was born to travel. Some folks are born to be doctors or farmers or some other grand calling, but if my life so far is any indication, I was born to be footloose. I'm 30 years old, Moses, and haven't had a thought about settling down." He smiled. "I haven't met anyone beautiful enough to induce me to do that."

He told Moses about travelling through the slave states because he had wanted to see what they were like, and how outraged he was by the experience. He had heard stories similar to Sarah's several times over, and others equally horrific. "I met a man in New Orleans, a prosperous man, who said that he made his money by selling slaves over and over again. What he'd do was entice a slave to run away by saying that he would resell him somewhere else, give him part of the money, then assist him in getting to a free state. But instead of keeping his word, he'd sell the slave again and again, telling him that he wouldn't get his money unless he co-operated. Then, when the slave's face became too well known because of the posters that invariably circulated, the man would shoot him. Imagine it, Moses! He boasted to me about this with impunity! I tell you, I was sickened. As far as I'm concerned, any war that brings an end to such atrocities is fully justified." He paused, and looked at Moses. "I can't for a moment conceive of what it must be like to be a black man on this continent."

Moses thought for a moment, and said, "I can tell you what it's like, Charlie. Do you recall those big rocks in the Thompson, with the river surging around them, giving everything they've got to resist a torrent that's doing its best to sweep them away? That's pretty much what it's like being a black man."

Quesnelle Mouth, like Yale, was a long row of buildings that faced the river, built largely to accommodate people who were passing through. The town was busy but Moses and Charlie managed to find decent lodgings at the Occidental, a two-storey hotel with protruding balconies that looked slightly ostentatious among the more modest frame buildings lining the main street. After they were settled in and had had dinner, the two men meandered over to Brown & Gillis' saloon. Just as they were about to enter, Moses heard his name being called. He turned, and saw coming toward them a man he recognized as James Barry, an irregular customer of the Pioneer Shaving Saloon back in Victoria.

Barry was a burly man of medium height who wore a black goatee, a style of beard that was unusual, which Moses had never liked. Not only did he think it unnatural for a man to shave his face in such a manner, it made him look like a devil. Barry called himself a "professional gambler" which to Moses meant that he probably made his living by nefarious means. He found the man manipulative, and there was something else about him that he could not quite put his finger on. Maybe it was his eyes, which were too small for his face and too close together. Even worse, there was never much to see in those eyes, beyond the surface green. It was as if they hid something dark, although Moses was willing to concede that it might just be his imagination.

"Good to see you again, Moses," Barry said, extending his hand.

Moses took it, but said only, "Yes."

Barry ignored the barber's complete lack of enthusiasm and laughed. "How about buying a drink for a poor gambler down on his luck?" Without waiting for an answer he herded the two friends into the saloon. Despite having picked up on Moses' lack of interest in Barry, Charlie bought three drinks from the bar, paying for them with a $20 Bank of British Columbia note.

"I suppose you gentlemen are going to Barkerville. Would you mind if I joined you?" Barry asked as they sat down.

"I'll be staying in town a couple of days," Moses said. "I have some business that I need to take care of." It was nothing urgent and would not take long, but he was thankful that he had an excuse that he could use without lying. He hoped Charlie would stay behind as well.

But Charlie did not want to. Barry seemed all right to him, and just because Moses obviously did not like the man was no reason to treat him like a leper. "Well," he said, "there isn't much to keep a body entertained here so perhaps I should get on up to the mines."

"Then we can travel together!" Barry said as if it were already decided.

Later, after the men had parted company, and Barry and Charlie had arranged to meet the following morning, Charlie asked, "What do you think of that arrangement, Moses?"

"Well, frankly, I've never liked Barry, though I have nothing to base that on. There's just something about him that bothers me. I heard that he spent some time on the chain gang in Victoria, but then so have a lot of honest men. But anything can happen on the road to the creek, and if you don't want to stay behind with me, you're better off travelling with someone than alone. Whether that 'someone' should be a man like Barry, is hard to say. I suppose it depends on how anxious you are to get up to the mines."

Charlie grinned. "The gold is up on Williams Creek and not here in Quesnelle Mouth, so I'd best get there before it's all gone. I'll see you there." He added, half-jokingly, "But don't forget my name, Moses, if anything should happen to me in this country."

"You'll be all right, Charlie, but he's smooth, so don't gamble with him, or turn your back on him for that matter. He might have your wallet if you do, or at the very least that gold stickpin you always wear. Tell you what. I'll meet you in Van Winkle instead. It's about 15 miles this side of Barkerville. There might be some good investments there that would be worth your while investigating till I catch up with you."

So the two men promised to meet in Van Winkle. In the morning Moses saw Charlie and Barry off, and went about his business. By lunch time he had worked out arrangements with the local druggist and barber to stock his hair restorer and collected some money owed him. Afterward, he spent the remainder of the day finishing off *American Notes*. There was a passage about whites brought up in slave states that he reread two or three times because it bothered him and made him think of Barry. Dickens was adamant that the cruel nature of slavery fostered brutal men. They were cowards, mainly, but brutal nonetheless, who carried cowards' weapons hidden in their breasts and would shoot men down or stab them in a quarrel. Moses knew that Barry was from Alabama. He also knew that the man carried a gun. He had seen it when the gambler leaned over to pick up a coin that Charlie had dropped on the floor, and his coat had fallen open. Other men sometimes carried weapons so that was not unusual, but he regretted not having encouraged Charlie to stay behind with him.

The road to the mines was suitable for coaches only as far as Cottonwood House, some 26 miles from Quesnelle Mouth. From there, a person had the choice of walking the remaining 40 miles to the mines, buying a horse, or joining other travellers in a train of rented saddle and pack horses. Moses chose the latter, since it would offer company.

Now that he was outdoors, the weather changed and chose to rain. This was a fine country under blue skies streaked with wispy mare's-tails, but beneath dark, sombre clouds that hid the hilltops and let loose torrents of rain, it was a miserable place indeed. The train plodded along a twisting, muddy trail that did not know the meaning of level, and by the end of the day Moses felt far worse than he had after a full day in the stagecoach. They spent the night at "Bloody" Edwards' roadhouse on Lightning Creek. Edwards was a Cockney whose vocabulary included but one adjective: "bloody." Everything was "bloody" this and "bloody" that, to the point that when he spoke it was the only word most people heard. Unlike other roadhouses, which usually served sumptuous meals, Edwards only served beans, bacon, bread and tea and charged his customers a whopping $2.50 for the privilege of trying to digest it. Breakfast was the same, but instead of tea there was coffee as vile as swamp water.

Moses asked Edwards if he had seen Blessing and Barry, and described both men. The Cockney remembered Barry but not Blessing. "No bloody red-'aired man 'as stopped 'ere," he said. "Not bloody recently, anyway."

In Van Winkle, a small collection of log buildings hemmed in on all sides by timbered and stump-ridden hills, Moses made further inquiries. People there had seen Barry, but no one could remember Blessing. Maybe they had had a row, Moses thought, and Charlie, unwilling to travel with Barry any more, had struck out on his own to get away from him. It was possible that he had gone into one of the creeks off the main road at someone else's invitation. Moses hoped that this was the case but a part of him refused to believe it for a minute. He was afraid that something awful had happened to his young friend. Nevertheless, he sent his bags on to Barkerville with the saddle train and stayed behind an extra day, just in case Charlie showed up. He never came.

Moses set out the next morning in the rain, on foot, but by the time he reached Barkerville the sky had cleared. It felt good to be home again, good to be made welcome by nearly everyone he passed in the street. The first thing he did, after collecting his bags and unpacking them, even before he hung his "Open" sign in the door, was go looking for Charlie. He had a hunch this would prove fruitless and he was right; he came away none the wiser for his efforts. Charlie was nowhere around and no one had seen him. Barry had not arrived either. Moses was at a loss to know what to make of it, but he did not have a very good taste in his mouth.

He went immediately to see Rebecca, whose mere presence restored some of his flagging faith in the world about him.

CHAPTER FOURTEEN

Several days later, on a balmy June morning, Moses had only just opened his shop when James Barry came in. He looked decidedly more prosperous than he had back in Quesnelle Mouth.

"Where's Charlie?" Moses demanded, without even saying hello.

Barry looked the barber right in the eye and said, "I left him on the road the other side of Beaver Pass. He said his feet were too sore to continue walking."

You're a damned liar, Moses thought, but did not voice it. "You'd best find someone else to cut your hair. I'm busy," was all he said. Barry shrugged and left without an argument, which made Moses all the more suspicious. A man with nothing to fear would have at least asked Moses why he was so angry.

Moses ran into the gambler two or three times over the next few days and each time he asked him what had happened to Blessing. Each time he got the same answer. Moses persisted until finally Barry got angry. A savage look flashed across his face that caught Moses off guard. Barry muttered something that sounded like a threat and stomped off. It alarmed Moses enough that he made his mind up to go to the police.

John H. Sullivan was Williams Creek's law enforcer and kept an office up in Richfield. Moses hitched a ride on a wagon heading up that way and found the officer going over some papers at a table that doubled as a desk. Sullivan was long, lean and lithe, and moved as deftly as a cat. His face was shaped like an inverted triangle and his narrow chin was beardless, although a sparse moustache lined his upper lip. His eyes were direct and unflinching and when he listened to someone talk he gave his undivided attention. Waving Moses to a chair opposite him, he said, "You look troubled, Moses."

Moses described his and Blessing's meeting with Barry and the subsequent mysterious events. He finished up with, "Barry was flat broke in Quesnelle Mouth, but seems to have no shortage of money here."

"We can't arrest him just because of that, Moses," the policeman said. "You know as well as I do that fortunes change here by the minute. If you think harm has come to Mr. Blessing, you'll need more substantial evidence than your feelings on the matter. As things stand, there's not much I can do to help."

Moses did not know what else to do except go back to Quesnelle Mouth and check along the trail for a body. But it was a big country out there, with plenty of ways to cover up a crime, and a search would probably prove futile. He thanked Sullivan for his time, and left.

The buffer between the frustration Moses felt and wanting to do something nasty to Barry, was Rebecca. It was her good sense that kept him reined in, kept him from doing things he might later regret. She always seemed to dispense good advice and when Moses asked her about this, she laughed and said, "I simply try to figure out what a person's probably going to do anyway, and then advise them to do it."

June galloped down the trail to high summer and though Moses had not forgotten about his friend, he was distracted by the Aurora Company's lawsuit against the Davis Company and the arrival of Judge Matthew Baillie Begbie on the creek.

It was always an occasion when Begbie rode into town. His courthouse and lodgings were in Richfield, but news of his presence always spilled quickly down the creek. And the truth of the matter was, he loved it. He knew the effect he had on people and played it the way a consummate stage actor plays an audience. His size alone — he stood 6' 4" — was intimidating enough, never mind his handsome features and keen intellect. He was fluent in at least two languages and conversant in others, but there were four words that were most important to him, that provided the direction in his life regardless of the language in which they were spoken: Queen, duty, law and order. Beyond that, he was the closest thing to a Renaissance man that British Columbia had to offer. If the country had been his to run, more than a few miners thought that he would have been a despot. Benevolent perhaps, but a despot nonetheless.

On June 16, the lawsuit came before Begbie and a seven-man jury, as both civil and criminal cases were tried by judge and jury. Two groups of men arguing in court over a valuable piece of land was one of the most exciting things to happen on Williams Creek since John Cameron had struck it rich, so the courthouse was jammed with spectators, and all ears up and down the valley were turned toward Richfield. Counsel on both sides presented their arguments which, when all the rhetoric was peeled away, revealed the same core: each company insisted that it had staked the claim first and each accused the other of "non-representation," by which was meant that the claim had not been worked in the time allotted after filing.

Begbie listened to the arguments, but when a witness from the Davis Company insisted that upon his arrival on the scene there were no stakes in the ground, the judge interrupted. "I beg your pardon, sir, but I have been down to the claim and have seen the stakes for myself." Then addressing the jury he added, "When men go to jump ground they do not see their enemy's stakes." When the jury finally retired, it needed only a short time to reach a verdict: since both companies had worked the ground, they were both entitled to its produce, which should be shared equally.

Begbie was not at all satisfied with this verdict. "Inasmuch as I admire your diplomacy," he told the members of the jury, "your verdict is not legally sustainable. Your responsibility was to decide which of these litigants was a claim jumper based on the evidence presented, which you have clearly not done. While

I am a firm believer in the jury system, as a judge I cannot accept a verdict that cannot be legally supported. Therefore I would suggest to the litigants that rather than repeat these proceedings, I will settle the case, with their permission, of course, but as an arbiter rather than a judge."

After some discussion between counsel and their clients, it was agreed, albeit with some trepidation, that Begbie be appointed to decide the issue, and on June 19, they met to hear his decision. Like the jury, he had split the claim up, but not equally. He gave the Aurora Company most of the land, three-quarters of it, in fact, and it happened to be the portion with the gold.

There was pandemonium in the courthouse and outside as Begbie's decision reverberated down the valley. On June 25, several hundred concerned miners met in Richfield to protest, not so much the decision, but the means by which it had been reached. "The grand bulwark of the British Government," said one speaker, "besides free speech and free press, is trial by jury, but when such institutions are disregarded and treated with contempt by a supreme judge, what is one to expect?" A resolution was then passed "that in the opinion of this meeting the administration of the Mining laws by Mr. Justice Begbie in the Supreme Court is partial, dictatorial, and arbitrary in setting aside the verdict of juries."[1] At this point, someone shouted, "Three groans for Begbie!" and the crowd raised its voice in a chorus of groans that could be heard clear down to Marysville. Beyond that, in the corridors of power in Victoria, it fell on deaf ears.[2]

Moses was extremely upset by the decision and it had nothing to do with the money he had lost. He had enough to satisfy his wishes. However, he was concerned that Begbie's decision had racist overtones. After all, many of the Davis Company men were black. When he expressed this feeling to Rebecca, she said, "I think it's just bureaucracy rearing its unreasonable head. I doubt that Begbie's a racist. He just thinks that he's superior to most mortals, and from what I've seen of him, he probably is."

Moses picked up a copy of the *Cariboo Sentinel* from the table and said, "An article in here quotes an interesting remark Begbie made about Indians. He said that they had 'far more natural intelligence, honesty, and good manners than the lowest class — say the agricultural and mining population of any European country he ever visited, England included.'"[3] Moses tapped the newspaper. "The judge's racism is just a little more subtle, that's all."

"Perhaps so," said Rebecca. "But I still think his actions have less to do with racism and more to do with the lofty view he has of himself."

Summer wore on in Barkerville. As the furor over the Davis and Aurora companies subsided and miners got back to the business of mining, Moses found himself spending more of his free time at the library, which had been established the previous year by John Bowron, one of the Overlanders. There was a reading room where badly outdated newspapers from around the country, England and the United States were available, as well as a lending library of a hundred titles. Moses appreciated the lending library more than anything, and contributed his copy of *American Notes* to its inventory. Indeed, the library had several of Dickens' works and Moses was still an avid fan of the author. As far as he was concerned, no writer understood the plight of the working man and the underclasses as well as Dickens. When he said this to Rebecca, she remarked, "That may be so, but he wouldn't recognize a real woman if she up and bit him on the end of his nose."

Despite its location deep in the wilderness, Barkerville was quite a cosmopolitan place. It was very different in that respect from Grand Cayman, which was one of the reasons why Moses enjoyed it so much. There were people from all levels of society and of high and low culture, from the privileged classes to the lowest classes and from skilled professionals to common labourers, and all contributed to the character of the town. It was a large city in microcosm, with the added benefit that a man's identity was not lost among the masses. Moses had just turned 50 and had decided that all he really needed could be found right here. Evenings of reading and discussions with Rebecca and other well-informed people nicely balanced out nights in the saloon playing cards with friends or in the theatre enjoying some of the entertainers who came through town. There was also an occasional visit to Fanny Bendixon's "private saloon" where young, attractive women accommodated the needs of single men.

One cold day in late September, Moses came out of the Cosmopolitan after lunch and, before returning to the shop, crossed the street to Wa Lee's laundry to pick up a couple of shirts that the Chinese had washed and ironed for him. They were a funny people, the Chinamen, Moses thought. They'd been on the creek for a couple of years and still kept pretty much to themselves. The whites found them enigmatic and culturally distasteful, and only associated with them on a business level. Nevertheless, had the Chinese pulled up stakes, the services they provided would have been sorely missed. Not only were there laundries like Wa Lee's, but some Chinese had farms near Quesnelle Mouth and provided a substantial amount of the fresh produce consumed on the creeks each year. A local Chinese also sold vegetables that he grew in a terraced garden on the hillside behind Barkerville. Another was a tailor, and yet another was a pimp down in Marysville, running a house of six white women, all as hard as bedrock. Even so, some of the miners would have said that this was their favourite Oriental enterprise.

Moses recrossed the street, stepping up to the boardwalk on a large wooden box put there for the purpose. Horses stood idle, tied to posts, and people moved up and down the street. He was just passing the drugstore when he nearly bumped into a Hurdy Gurdy girl coming out of it. The Hurdies were dancing girls who had been brought over from Europe at the beginning of the summer by an entrepreneur who reasoned, correctly, that mining communities such as those along Williams Creek suffered from a dire shortage of female companionship, and that there was money to be made from it. The women all dressed the same, in red dresses with black, silver-buckled belts pulled in tightly to accentuate their waistlines. The one coming out of the drugstore was no exception, but a glint from her bodice caught Moses' eye and stopped him in his tracks. It was unmistakably Charlie Blessing's stickpin. He grabbed the woman's arm. "Where did you get that?" he demanded, pointing to the pin.

The suddenness of the encounter startled the woman and she reared back in alarm. Others on the street stopped to see what was going on. Moses let go of her arm. "I'm sorry," he said, "but I need to know where you got that pin."

The Hurdy's English was rudimentary, but Moses understood enough. She got it from a man named Barry, who had bragged to her that his father was a wealthy cotton plantation owner in the American south. She had not doubted him for he seemed to have lots of money. He had had many dances with her, which Moses knew cost a dollar each time. Not only that, Barry had bought her drinks as well, but best of all, he had given her this valuable stickpin.

"You hang onto it at all costs, madam. What you have there is more valuable than you might think. It's evidence that might bring a murderer to justice!"

Moses left the Hurdy with an astonished look on her face and hied up the creek to Richfield to see John Sullivan. He was stunned at how the simple act of going to Wa Lee's before going home had altered the mystery of Charlie's disappearance. Had he not bumped into the Hurdy their paths might never have crossed and he would never have seen the pin. He could not believe his good fortune. It was only a mile from the Cosmopolitan to the government buildings at Richfield, but it seemed to take forever to get there, and he swore that every person in the valley purposely set out to obstruct him. By the time he reached the constable's office, he was breathless. As he walked through the door, Sullivan, who was talking to Judge Cox, was clearly shocked to see him.

"I was just on my way down to see *you*, Moses. I'm sorry to say that a body has been found by a grouse hunter just the other side of Bloody Edwards' place. It might be your friend,

Blessing. It's pretty badly decomposed, but there's a bullet hole through the back of the skull, so it looks like murder. You might recognize these items that were found beside it." From a small leather bag, he produced a gold pen and silver pencil set that Moses instantly recognized as belonging to Charlie. But the real clincher was a wallet; it was badly weathered, yet still visible on it were the embossed letters: C.M.B.

Moses' head swam, and he had to sit down. Charlie was dead, for sure. This evidence removed all doubt, and Moses was certain that Barry was the murderer. He told Sullivan about the Hurdy in Barkerville, that Barry had given her Charlie's stickpin and had spent a lot of money on her, for dancing and who knows what other favours.

"I think Mr. Barry bears investigating," said Sullivan. "But first, you and I ought to go for a ride. I need you to positively identify the body. In the meantime, my assistant will see if he can locate our man. I haven't seen him around lately so he might have left town."

Moses got a ride back to his shop and, as quickly as he could, threw some extra clothes, a rain cape and some hardtack into a pack and obtained a horse from Jacob Mundorf's livery stable. He and Sullivan were on the trail within 90 minutes of their meeting,

The two men urged their horses to a canter along the road as it left the creek and skirted Richfield Mountain. Despite the low, threatening clouds, there was no rain and the ground was dry and hard-packed. Moses noted that Sullivan sat his horse well and looked sublimely at ease in the saddle. But then he ought to since he spent a lot of time in it, handling complaints in outlying mining camps. Though he would never talk of it, the policeman still bore knife scars from trying to prevent the escape from the Quesnelle Mouth jail of a Nicomen Indian named Nikel Palsk. Palsk was accused of murdering a miner near Soda Creek and though he got away, his freedom did not last long. He was captured down in Osoyoos, brought back, and was now awaiting trial. Sullivan had ridden all the way down to get him, so sitting on a horse for long hours was all part of a day's work. To Moses, however, it was still a foreign, uncomfortable means of transportation and he would have much preferred a buggy beneath his posterior.

The two riders quickly passed through Van Winkle and by nightfall had reached Bloody Edwards' place. Edwards was aghast that a "bloody" murder had taken place so close to his "bloody" house, and insisted that Sullivan and Moses be his guests for the night, without charge.

"By the way," he said to Moses, "that bloody chappie you were asking about the last time you were 'ere"?

"Barry?"

"Aye. 'E rode through 'ere just yesterday bloody morning. Said 'e was going 'ome to the bloody States."

Moses looked at Sullivan, who winced at the news. "He's got a good head start," the lawman said, "but since he doesn't know he's been found out, he shouldn't be in a hurry."

At first light the following morning, the two men set out for the crime scene with the hunter who had found the body. William Fitzgerald was a stocky, muscular man with a black moustache and few words. He barely spoke as he led Moses and Sullivan a short distance west of the roadhouse. There was nothing remarkable about the spot at which they stopped, nothing to indicate that a murder had taken place not long ago. There was a faint trail that led off into the bush, but that was not unusual; most people stopped and camped when they felt tired, so there were all kinds of faint trails branching off from the road. The men ground-tethered their horses to allow them to graze and Sullivan and Moses followed Fitzgerald into the bush. About 30 feet in, they came to a small clearing with a circle of stones that had once enclosed a campfire.

"Behind there," Fitzgerald said, pointing to a small hummock. "I'll wait here. I've seen all I want to see of it."

Moses had to steel himself to look at the body. At first glance there was nothing about it that even hinted of Charlie. It was in an advanced state of decay, and had been gnawed at by animals. Even so, Moses recognized the clothes, particularly the hat, as those that Charlie was wearing the last time he saw him. Though badly torn, they were easily identifiable. The skull was about 15 feet away from the body, and Sullivan reckoned that it had been carried there by an animal. He bent down to examine it and could see a few small tufts of red hair on the pate. There was also a sizeable bullet hole through the back of it. When the constable pointed this out, Moses was infuriated.

"My God! What kind of man shoots another from behind?"

"A bloody coward is the kind," said Sullivan.

Moses was near tears. "I only knew Charlie for a short time, but from what I knew of him, he was a good man." If Moses' memory served him correctly, Charlie had had only about $50 or $60 in his wallet, and for that paltry sum Barry had ended the young man's life. Moses shook with rage, and more than anything else in the world he wanted revenge. If he could just get his hands around Barry's throat, he would squeeze the life out him and spit in his face when he was done. And he would have slept well, knowing that he had rid the world of one vile human being.

Sullivan said, "We have all the evidence we need. Now we have to get someone out here to put Mr. Blessing in a decent grave. I'll let you look after that, Moses. I'll hightail it to Richfield and get Judge Cox to swear out a warrant for Barry's arrest. If I ride hard enough, I might just be able to catch up with him."

The three men returned to the road where Sullivan mounted quickly and disappeared in a swirl of dust. Moses and Fitzgerald returned to Bloody Edwards' place. Moses had already decided that it was his responsibility to bury his friend, so he asked Edwards for the loan of a shovel. "Better make that two," the hunter said and they both rode back to the body.

Working in silence and sweat, the two men dug a hole deep in the ground where nothing could reach Charlie but the worms. Moving the body into the grave was a grisly task. Fitzgerald's help did not extend that far, so Moses had to do it by himself.

He did it slowly and gently, irrationally afraid that he would inflict even more pain on his friend. When he stooped to pick up Charlie's head he nearly blacked out from grief and horror. The only way that he could handle it was to shut his mind off to the reality of the circumstances. When he was once again conscious of his surroundings, he was shovelling dirt back into the hole. Fitzgerald rejoined him and when they had finished, Moses tied two branches of a tree together in the form of a cross and placed it at the head of the grave as a temporary monument. The hunter removed his hat and said a small prayer, then the two men rode back to Edwards' place. Moses declined the Cockney's offer of one of his infamous lunches and continued on to Barkerville.

Over the entire distance his thoughts were full of "could haves" and "should haves" and each led to a place called guilt. Had he acted differently, he might have prevented Charlie's murder. Damn him for being so blind! And damn Barry for the devil that he was! As he rounded Richfield Mountain to the creek, he was resolved that there were two things he must do.

After returning the horse to Mundorf's stable, Moses went directly to his shop. Though there was still time left in the workday, he did not bother turning over the "Closed" sign. Instead, he re-locked the door, went directly to his room in the back, pulled off his shoes, and ate some stale bread that he had purchased at the bakery yesterday. He was not very hungry, but he needed something in his gut. Then he got from the cupboard a bottle of brandy that he kept on hand for medicinal purposes, stretched out on his bed and, just as he had done once before when he felt so desperate, drank himself into oblivion.

The following morning he performed the second task, bleary-eyed and hung over. He visited a carpenter and ordered a simple marker for Charlie's grave. Then, as punishment, he went to work.

Three days later, first thing in the morning, he was at Mundorf's again, hiring a horse. Then he went to the carpenter's, picked up the marker, and rode up the long road that led out of town. People he knew paused along the boardwalks as he rode solemnly by, but did not call hello. It was their way of acknowledging a man's grief.

At Charlie's grave, Moses embedded the base of the marker in the ground and packed earth around it until it felt solid. This done, he removed his hat and stood at the foot of the grave. He was satisfied with his work. He bowed his head and since he was not a religious man and did not know any formal prayers, he had gone to the library and found some lines by Wordsworth for his friend. He recited them aloud:

> The good die first,
> And those whose hearts are dry as summer dust
> Burn to the socket.

His horse nickered, as if the animal recognized his voice, but other than that the forest was still. He had never known such silence, nor that it could be so full of heartbreak.

That was all he could think of to do for his friend, and having done it, he rode back to Barkerville, so firmly in sorrow's grip that when he arrived he was scarcely aware of the journey that had brought him home.

Over the next few days Moses was barely able to think straight through his anger and grief. He was haunted by the image of Charlie's body and plagued by self-recriminations. He knew it was not doing him or anyone else any good, but was unable to stop himself. He talked about it with Rebecca, who once again provided a voice of reason.

"It's decent of you to bear the burden of responsibility for Charlie's death," she said. "I'm sure that if he could speak from the grave, he would be grateful, but he just might want you to place at least some of the responsibility on the man who killed him. That's where it really belongs. Listen, my dear, your rage is the result of your guilt feelings, nothing more. But if you can accept that when it comes to fate there is no guilt, I think you'll find your rage subsiding."

Moses sat with Rebecca in her parlour drinking tea. It was a small room in a small house, hardly worthy of the name, but it was where Rebecca entertained her guests so she called it a parlour. Not that she entertained many guests — in fact she had very few — but the term allowed for a bit of social protocol that was hard to come by in a mining camp. He watched her as she poured the tea, a plump, matronly woman near the end of her childbearing years, who never spoke of ever wanting any.

Her presence on the creek was one of the things that made living here worthwhile for Moses. He had never known a woman so sure of her place in the world, someone who had long ago figured out the maze of life and was walking unerringly toward the exit. He admired her greatly for this. He also admired her intelligence and the fact that she was not a hostage to the conventions of their time. She was different, which was one of the things that had attracted him to Sarah, and he enjoyed being with her. Indeed, he cared so deeply for her that he wondered if at his age such feelings might be called love. If so, it did not matter, and even if she felt the same it was irrelevant. She was Isaiah's wife and that's all there was to it.

Moses' thoughts were interrupted by a knock on the door. Rebecca opened it to John Sullivan.

"Good evening, Mrs. Gibbs," he said. "I'm told that Moses is here."

"Indeed he is," said Rebecca. "Please come in."

Sullivan removed his hat and entered. He looked tired and he was.

"Hello, John," Moses said. "Good to see you back. I hope you are the bearer of good news."

Sullivan sat down in the chair Rebecca offered and said, "The best, Moses, and the worst. I caught up with your wealthy plantation owner and he's now in jail here in Richfield."

Moses leapt from his chair. "Hurrah for you, John! I reckoned that if anybody could catch him it was bound to be you. I want to know every detail!"

"I thought you might and you, of all people, deserve to be the first to know. After I left you and Fitzgerald, I rode as fast as I could back here and got an arrest warrant, then took the Antler Creek trail over Bald Mountain." This was the truncated mountain that could be seen up the valley from Richfield. "I figured that if I rode hard I could beat Barry and the *Enterprise* to Soda Creek. She's usually held up for some reason or other, but as luck would have it, she had made that run on schedule and Barry was on the stagecoach for Yale a full day before I arrived. There was no way on God's green earth that I was going to be able to catch him with that much of a head start, and I was at a loss over what to do.

"I didn't see it right away, but the answer was staring me right in the face: the telegraph! It's mainly used as an information line on the comings and goings of the stagecoaches, but I used it to catch a criminal. Ah, the wonder of it, Moses! As Barry was rumbling along in the coach, oblivious to the fact that the law was on his tail, my message passed him on a thin wire, travelling faster than any coach can go. It arrived a half-hour before the stage pulled in to Yale and Barry had no sooner stepped down from it than the constable there had him collared. Not surprisingly, he gave a false name." Sullivan beamed. "I tell you, Moses, it's an amazing thing. A marvel, even in these modern times!"

"Did Barry have anything to say for himself?" asked Moses.

"That he was innocent of the crime." Sullivan paused and looked Moses in the eye. "And that you did it."

CHAPTER FIFTEEN

Moses looked at Rebecca. Her mouth had fallen open in shock. He should have been surprised by the accusation but he was not. In any other place, particularly in the United States, he would have been alarmed, perhaps even frightened for his life, but it was not a concern here on the creeks.

"What do *you* think, John?" he asked the policeman.

"I think anybody's capable of murder given the right circumstances, but these weren't your circumstances. This was a murder for robbery, and no other reason. As near as I can tell, you didn't need the money."

Moses nodded in agreement. "You're right about all of us being capable of murder. These last few days I've been consumed with devising clever ways to give Barry a slow, painful death if I ever ran into him."

"Well, I can't say that I blame you, but the law doesn't look too kindly upon revenge killings. Best you stay away from the jail and let Judge Begbie give Barry his due process."

After Sullivan had left, Rebecca echoed Moses' own thoughts. "You can thank your lucky stars," she said, "that you're not in San Francisco. The whites there would have found it very satisfying to pin the murder of one of their own on a black man. They would have had you swinging from a makeshift gallows by now."

Moses' vengeful mood lessened, now that Barry was in jail. Unfortunately, the next assizes were not until the following summer, so he'd have to wait until then to see justice done. The wait, however, would be worth it. He would testify and that would be his revenge. And if Barry was hanged, so be it.

The snow came late that winter and with it the valley fell quiet once more. Barkerville was not quite as isolated now that the road from Quesnelle Mouth had been pushed through all the way and, except during severe storms, mail came fairly regularly. Moses received two letters over the winter to which he had been looking forward. The first was a response to one that he had sent George Blessing shortly after Charlie's body had been found, informing him of his brother's death. George begged Moses not to blame himself for the tragedy. Only one man was to blame, he wrote, and that was the murderer. All else was happenstance. Coming directly from George, the words helped lighten Moses' conscience a little.

The second letter came in February and was from Gibbs. Moses tore it open eagerly. As he had expected, there was much happening in the life of his old friend.

"My Dear Moses:

"I expect that as I write this letter you are snowbound so I shall not mention that the flowers are already in bloom here.

"First and foremost, I must tell you that Maria and the children have gone back East to Oberlin, I believe for good. Is this the end of our marriage? I cannot say. What I can say, with no small degree of certainty, is that Victoria had become a great source of discomfort for her. She grew tired of being excluded from the social circles to which, given her education and class, she both aspired and was entitled. Here was an intelligent woman of good breeding who, because of her color and the obsolete attitudes of others, always found herself on the outside looking in. For shame! Unlike me, she was unable to assert her rights and has fled instead, to be among her own people. She will be happier there.

"I, of course, admit to not being the best of husbands. As you well know, once I sink my teeth into something I have a devil of a time letting go, much to the detriment of those about me. So I am a bachelor in a large, empty house, save for a manservant who maintains it and keeps me from starving. Still, there are compensations.

"You will be pleased to know that I was elected to city council last November. I have even served time as acting mayor during the incumbent's recent illness, and there are many, beyond myself, who insist I was more deserving of the job! I don't need to tell you, of all people, just how huge a step forward this is, for all black people. I am proud to stand at the vanguard of such great social change. I regret to say, though, that some of the opposition to my running for council came from other coloreds, most born in the West Indies. They believed that such offices should be open to British-born coloreds only. I am convinced that they lacked your entrepreneurial spirit and were jealous of our accomplishments.

"There are other problems, of course, which have nothing to do with race, and everything to do with gross incompetence. Whereas the city strives to move forward with the times, we are stymied by a higher level of government that sits like a nightmare on the energies of the people. As I've told you more than once, the legislature is a sham, totally unfit for an intelligent community in the nineteenth century. Governor Kennedy is the personification of official imbecility. If you thought that amalgamation of the two colonies was frightening for the governor and his cronies, the idea of Confederation scares them half to death. They would preserve the rottenness of the present system for their own benefit, to the detriment of us all. But their time has come and I now believe that Confederation will win the day. All the good businessmen in town are for it, which is enough of an endorsement for me. So look for an end to this present government's autocratic rule, at least if I have any say in the matter. Better to proselytize from the stump than drown in the swamp.

"You must find your way down to Victoria soon. With Maria gone I need your ear to bend even more. You must also pass on my best wishes to Mother, Rebecca and Isaiah, and tell them that their impossible relative will write soon.

"I remain your respectful servant,
Mifflin."

It was good to know that Gibbs was still in fine form, and Moses went immediately to share his letter with Rebecca, Isaiah and Maria, all of whom bemoaned their relative's lack of enthusiasm for writing personal letters, and congratulated Moses on his good luck.

Just when it began to seem that winter had come to the creeks to stay, the sun grew warmer and the snow began to melt. As water poured from the roofs of the buildings, miners poured onto the creek, shaking the town from its lethargy and starting off another season's excavation, another toss of the die in hopes of coming away with a great fortune. Moses always looked forward to this time of year, to see new faces and old familiar ones, but he had to wait until July before the face he really wanted to see finally arrived in town.

That one belonged to Matthew Baillie Begbie, and when the judge donned his robes and wig, and rapped his gavel sharply to bring his court to order, it was the sound for which Moses had waited patiently for almost a year. There were a few civil cases to be handled, mainly disputes over claims that Judge Cox could not resolve, before the criminal cases came before Begbie. There were only two. The first was Nikel Palsk, the Nicomen Indian who had murdered the miner near Soda Creek and had escaped from John Sullivan's custody after nearly killing him. The case was cut and dried, for the man had had an accomplice who testified against him in exchange for a life sentence. Begbie concurred with the jury's verdict and said he would sentence Palsk after Barry's case was heard. Word flew down the creek that, before the summer was out, Richfield would probably witness its first execution — perhaps two of them.

When, on the morning of Thursday, July 4, 1867, James Barry's trial for murder came before the court, work on the creeks ground to a halt. The courtroom was packed, as was the expanse of open ground flanked by government buildings; these included the jail and police barracks, Judge Cox's house, the courthouse itself and, slightly above them, on the hillside, Begbie's residence. Upwards of 200 people choked the area, all eager to keep abreast of the proceedings and to be among the first to hear the verdict. Begbie strutted in and took the bench, ascending to it like a king to his throne, and the crowd fell silent in deference. Barry sat in the prisoner's dock, stony-faced, as the bailiff read the indictment. Begbie then asked him, "How do you plead?"

"Not guilty," said Barry.

Moses needed every ounce of his strength to refrain from standing up and shouting, "Liar!"

In short order, a jury of 12 men was selected and the trial got under way. Opening remarks by the prosecutor, H. P. Walker, were lengthy as he covered every detail connected to the murder. He concluded by saying that he would be calling witnesses who would demonstrate to the court, beyond a shadow of doubt, the culpability of the defendant.

Counsel for the defence, A. R. Robertson, then rose and made his opening remarks, but they lacked substance and were weak by comparison. When the lawyer finished, Moses looked at the jury to see if they were as unimpressed as he was by Robertson's remarks, but nothing showed on their faces other than attentiveness. The court called the first witness.

William Fitzgerald, the grouse hunter who had found the body and subsequently helped Moses bury it, took the stand. He said that the body was lying in a clump of bushes behind a small hummock. It was badly decomposed, and the skull was four or five yards from the trunk. He could see a hole in the back of the skull that looked like a bullet hole. While he had never seen a bullet hole in a skull before, the signs, it seemed to him, were unmistakable. Walker then produced several items for Fitzgerald's examination. They included the gold pen and silver pencil set, the sheath knife and the wallet embossed with the initials C.M.B. When asked, Fitzgerald agreed that they were the items he had found near the body.

Robertson took the floor and questioned Fitzgerald's ability to say that the hole in the skull had been made by a bullet, and not by some other means, an animal perhaps, after Mr. Blessing's death by accidental means.

"I doubt that, sir," said Fitzgerald. "It was much too clean. Too round."

"But you've never seen a bullet hole through a human skull before, is that correct?" asked Robertson, trying to create doubt in the minds of the jurors about the credibility of the witness.

"That's correct, sir."

"Then it could have been made by an animal."

"Well, if I can't say one sir, then I can't really say the other, can I?"

The spectators burst into laughter and Begbie banged his gavel for order. "Silence! You will appreciate the gravity of these proceedings," he told them, "and save your laughter for the saloons. Otherwise this courtroom will be cleared."

Not a soul doubted him, and silence reigned as the bailiff called Moses to the stand. He told the court how he had met Blessing in Victoria and had travelled upcountry with him as far as Quesnelle Mouth. He recalled their meeting with Barry and the subsequent arrangements between Barry and Blessing, and the doubt the latter had felt about them. Moses also established that his friend had had about $50 or $60 in his wallet.

"Besides expressing his doubts, did Mr. Blessing say anything else to you before he left?" asked Walker.

"Yes, sir. He asked me to remember his name should anything happen to him."

"And was that the last time you saw Mr. Blessing?"

"Yes, sir. I inquired at Mr. Edwards' roadhouse and at Macafferty's in Van Winkle if anyone had asked for me, and was answered in the negative." Moses went on to describe his subsequent meetings with Barry, the reporting of his suspicions to the police, and his fortuitous encounter with the Hurdy who was wearing Blessing's gold stickpin.

Walker then produced the same items of evidence shown Fitzgerald, as well as the stickpin, and asked him to identify them. That done, he turned Moses over to Robertson.

In a way, Moses felt sorry for Robertson. The man had a devil for a client and nothing to work with, and everyone knew that the law usually came down on the victim's side.[1] The lawyer seemed as if he were just going through the motions.

"Mr. Moses," he asked, "is it true that Mr. Blessing was a self-confessed 'itinerant,' a man with few responsibilities and even fewer ties, who was known to come and go as he pleased?"

"Yes, sir."

"And just as he left you to travel with Mr. Barry for a time, is it not possible that he also left Mr. Barry to travel with someone else?"

"Yes sir. That is possible."

"Thank you, Mr. Moses," said Robertson, sitting down.

Other witnesses were called for the prosecution. William Fraser testified that he had travelled with Barry from Yale to Quesnelle Mouth and that Barry had admitted to being dead-broke and even asked him for a loan. Fraser also said that Barry carried a gun. George Gartley had travelled with Blessing from San Francisco to Victoria and identified the gold stickpin as belonging to the victim. A saloonkeeper in Cameronton testified that Barry had spent lavish amounts dancing with Hurdies in his establishment and that he had given one of them the stickpin that was produced as evidence. A miner named Stark said that he had seen Barry and Blessing together at a roadhouse 13 miles east of Quesnelle Mouth. The last witness was John Sullivan, who testified that he had gone to Yale to bring the prisoner back, and on the return journey Barry had denied killing Blessing. The gambler had said that because Blessing had developed sore feet he had left him behind, and that he had plenty of his own money and therefore had no reason to kill Blessing. He had also accused Moses of the crime, which, added Sullivan, was patently absurd.

After a two-hour recess for lunch, witnesses for the defence were called but they were unable to provide any evidence that could clear Barry's name and prove his innocence. Then for the sake of the jury, Begbie summed up all of the evidence that had been presented throughout the day, and said to them, "Gentlemen, this case now rests in your hands."

As there was no jury room in the courthouse, the panel retired to Judge Cox's residence to decide Barry's fate. In less than an hour they were filing back into the courthouse, faces grim, and Sullivan was retrieving Barry from the cells. Begbie ascended to the bench and called the court to order. The verdict was "guilty of murder."[2] Audience noise rose like an ocean swell and Begbie banged his gavel for silence. When he had it, he said, "This court will reconvene tomorrow, July 5, at 10 o'clock in the morning, at which time I will pass sentence." Another rap of the gavel and the session was done for the day.

After supper Moses sat with the Gibbses and filled them in on the proceedings at the courthouse. None of them had attended the trial, Rebecca because she preferred to avoid what she called the "sordid affairs of men."

"You might not think them so sordid," Moses chastised her, "if it were Isaiah or me buried out there by Bloody Edwards' place."

At 10:00 A.M. sharp the following morning Begbie was on his bench calling the court to order. Barry was brought in with Palsk, who would also be sentenced. The two men stood before the judge. He said to Barry, "Do you have anything to say as to why sentence should not be passed upon you?"

Barry was as staid and emotionless as he had been throughout the trial. He said, "I have nothing to say except that I never committed the murder that I've been charged with. I don't remember travelling with Blessing until I got to the 13 Mile House. That's where he overtook me. I travelled only about three-quarters of a mile with him and then we parted. I never saw him again. I passed three or four Chinamen on the road and came on to Van Winkle that night. This is all the statement I have to make."

There was dead silence in the courtroom. Begbie addressed Barry and said, "I concur with the verdict of the jury; it is one given after due consideration of the whole circumstances. It is clear that you started with the murdered man from Quesnelle Mouth; that you knew he had money; that you were penniless; that you were seen at the 13 Mile House in his company; and again seen with him a short distance from the spot where the body was afterwards found, and that the man was never again seen alive. You had money when you came on the creek; you were in possession of a nugget belonging to the murdered man, which you disposed of to a witness which has not been produced.[3] You were found in possession of a weapon that would produce the crime. I can no more doubt your guilt than if I had been an eyewitness to it. I have no doubt that you seduced your victim to leave the road and perpetrated the crime; and that you did it for the sake of booty, the most sordid of all motives; that you reveled for months on the proceeds and then left; that you gave a false name when apprehended. You have given no explanation regarding the nugget, and none to the disappearance of Blessing, and you have appeared perfectly indifferent.

"It has been proved that you did not work or do anything to get money. It is impossible to conceive of a crime more wanton or atrocious than that which you have committed. I can offer you no hope of mercy."[4]

Before continuing, Begbie ordered Palsk to rise, and asked him if he had anything to say as to why sentence should not be passed upon him. Palsk cursed all King George men and fell silent.[5] Begbie said to him, "Beside you stands a man with no common tie of blood or colour, who slew a man, actuated with the like pernicious avarice. The same fate that dogged your footsteps awaits him." Then, addressing both men, he added, "You have both dyed your hands in blood and both must suffer the same fate. The law for the savage as well as the Christian is death for death. My painful duty now is to pass the last sentence of the law on you, which is that you be taken to the place whence you came and from thence to the place of execution, there to be hanged by the neck until you are dead. And may the Lord have mercy on your souls." [6]

There was complete silence in the courtroom, and not until Begbie ordered the prisoners taken away did the place erupt in pandemonium. Moses' feeling of vindication was as profound as the shattered silence.

∞∞

Three weeks later, on the eve of the executions, Moses walked up to Richfield to watch the gallows being built. Long before he reached the area of the courthouse, he could hear the hammering of the carpenters as they worked. He hoped the sound was punishing Barry. By the time Moses arrived, the structure was nearly finished. It stood in front of the courthouse, and looked sturdy despite being put together so hastily. But it was only temporary and would come down directly after the executions. He watched as the bolt holding a trapdoor wide enough for two men to drop through was installed, and ropes were hung from an overhead frame. Gunnysacks filled with enough gravel to simulate the weight of the men were tied to the ropes and the bolt was drawn. Everything seemed to work to the executioner's satisfaction, and there was nothing left to do except wait for the dawn.

Moses decided to stop in at the Gibbses on the way home and, after only a moment there, wished that he had not. Rebecca was angry and upset over the impending executions.

"Frankly, Moses," she said, "I am disappointed in your response to these sadistic proceedings. Weren't you the one sickened by public executions in San Francisco and Victoria? This will not bring Charlie Blessing back. I thought you, of all people, would be able to rise above the need to take an eye for an eye and a tooth for a tooth. It's primitive, and I am truly saddened that you are no different from the rest in this regard."

"I would not expect you to understand," Moses said. "I wouldn't expect any woman to understand. This is an affair for men. You said so yourself."

"Yes, but that doesn't make it right. And if I'm not mistaken, I used the word 'sordid.'"

"I once felt as you do, but that reaction is typical of people who are onlookers. If either of those criminals had murdered one of your loved ones, you'd probably let the trapdoor go yourself. Believe me, Rebecca, the human race will not miss these men."

"That is simply not true. Life is sacred, Moses. *All* life. You are killing them for no reason other than a petty revenge disguised as moral indignation. Someone inflicts pain and suffering on you so you inflict pain and suffering on him. It makes no sense to me, and diminishes us all in the end. What's more, you talk so much about the importance of dignity for black people, but what on earth is dignified about involving yourself in this affair?"

"It has nothing to do with dignity. The law says 'death for death' and it was written by men — good Christian men — more erudite than you or me."

"It's not even civilized, let alone Christian, and if such a law is Christian then it pleases me that I have chosen not to follow such a doctrine."

Moses left in a bad mood. He should never have dropped in to Rebecca's in the first place. All it accomplished was to upset them both. But on the road down to Barkerville he convinced himself that he was right: Barry was getting what he deserved and that's all there was to it. By the time he reached home he'd put the altercation to the back of his mind and was thinking about tomorrow instead. When he climbed into bed he slept the sleep of the just.

He awoke shortly before five in the morning, his mind instantly alert. The air was chill and he dressed hurriedly, then struck out for Richfield without eating anything. On his way up, he met others coming out of their houses to bear witness to the valley's first executions. People greeted each other but beyond that, little was said. By the time Moses arrived at the courthouse, a sizeable crowd had already gathered. A short sideroad that led up to the terrace with the government buildings was packed, as was the road below that led to Van Winkle and beyond. People moved aside to let Moses through, feeling that if anybody deserved to be up front, it was he. At 5:30, Sullivan and a small group of men came out of the courthouse. The policeman held in his hand the death warrant, in an envelope sealed with black wax. They entered the jail and several minutes later came out with Barry and Palsk. The prisoners were shackled in irons, at both wrists and legs, and could only shuffle as a result. Barry seemed about to faint and had to be supported, whereas the Nicomen was defiant. Once he was on the scaffold, Barry spoke his only words of the morning. Addressing the crowd, he said, "I can only hope that no one present this morning will ever be placed in this awful position." He was close to tears.

As a final humane gesture, Sullivan removed Barry's leg and wrist irons. When Palsk's leg irons were removed, he became agitated and had to be restrained. His wrist irons were left on. He cursed loudly, which reddened the faces of the more pious men in the crowd, and demanded that he be shot rather than hung. Nooses were fitted around his and Barry's necks, and hoods were placed over their heads. Palsk protested the hood, saying that he wanted to make sure the King George man dropped with him, but he was ignored. Then without ceremony, the bolt was drawn and the trap fell open.

The crowd gasped. The two men dropped through and the snap of their necks breaking came right on the heels of the trapdoor thumping against the scaffold supports. The bodies bounced off each other twice, once hard, and again, gently, then swung slowly in space, until all movement stopped. The crowd was mesmerized and no one moved; there was not a murmur. The valley had not been this quiet since men began living in it. People began drifting away, singly, in pairs, then in larger groups.

Moses stayed, rooted to the spot. Dr. Bell pronounced both men dead at 6:30, and Moses watched as their bodies were cut down and placed in roughly built coffins, loaded on a wagon and taken away to the cemetery nearby.[7] Already workers were removing the scaffold, and by 7:00 it was gone. Other than the trampled ground, there were no signs that two lives had been snuffed out in seconds only an hour before. All that remained was the terrible knowledge of it in the minds and hearts of the witnesses.

Moses finally turned his back on the site, strode through Richfield and went briskly down the road to Barkerville. He felt out of sorts, completely at odds with himself when he should have been exultant; triumphant that justice had been served. Instead, he felt more like crying.

CHAPTER SIXTEEN

Dazzling curtains of light hung high in the northern heavens, flickering and shifting as if caught in some cosmic breeze. The mountains loomed like ominous shadows against the starry night, and in the valley along the creek, Barkerville settled in for the night. Shop windows were dark but coal-oil lamps shone in multi-paned windows of cabins, and here and there on the side slopes, cabin windows were lit up like stationary fireflies. Sparks flew from chimneys and floated down onto rooftops as dry as parchment. The drought the valley was experiencing was on everyone's lips these days; no one could remember a summer as dry as this one had been. It was now the middle of September and there still had been no rain.

Sounds rose from the buildings as people finished a busy day: here a clatter of glasses, there a cleared throat, somewhere a stove fire being stoked and filled with logs and a metal door clanging shut. The sound of laughter and dancing, amid strains of a piano, issued from Barry & Adler's Saloon and the boots of stragglers going home drummed along the high boardwalks above the dirt street, baked hard over the arid summer.

To the east, the mountain rim gave birth to a sliver of moon, but the northern lights were the first thing to greet Moses as he left his shop for a walk before bedtime. Though he had seen these mysterious lights many times, he was still awe-struck by their beauty and never grew tired of the show they put on. Yet there was something about them that suggested a world on the verge of an unimaginable cataclysm.

It was not usually his custom to walk this late at night but he had felt restless and thought some exercise would do him good. He turned south, toward Richfield, rather than north toward Marysville, so that he tackled the upward gradient with fresher legs. The air was chilly and his breath came out as ghostly white puffs. He passed the Occidental Hotel, a fruit store and then the Bank of British Columbia. Beneath his feet, the road was bone-dry. The whole town was bone-dry for that matter, and he worried about fire, especially now with the cold nights, and stoves blazing longer and hotter. He did not subscribe to the notion held by many townsfolk that the wood with which the buildings were constructed was a special variety that would not readily burn. He thought such beliefs the height of naivete, for it was mostly pine. While it might have been resistant to burning when the buildings were first erected and the wood was green, it had dried out long ago and the town was now a tinderbox, just waiting for a careless move to send it up in flames.

By the time he had reached Barnard's Express office he could no longer see the lights at the lower end of town, for they were hidden by a slight curve in the road. He passed another saloon — the town had 12 of them — from which the sound of a fiddle and banjo emanated, and his nostrils were assaulted by a strong smell of stale alcohol. In Chinatown he caught a whiff of opium. He left the commercial part of Barkerville behind and walked on the hard-packed road, past single-room log and frame cabins to his right and the ravaged creek to his left.

Along this stretch of road were some of the original claims that had stirred the hearts of people thousands of miles away, causing them to pack up and leave home and loved ones. First was the Diller claim, which in a single day had given up 200 pounds of gold to its owners. Then there was Stout's Gulch, the first real producer in the valley. Ned Stout, the man who had staked it, was one of the most fearless men that Moses had ever met; he had been hit seven times by arrows during a fight with Indians in the Fraser Canyon and lived to talk about it. A little farther along the road was Twelve Foot Davis' claim, named for Henry Davis who reckoned that the original claim along this stretch, staked by somebody else, was 12 feet longer than the 100 feet it was supposed to be. Davis staked a claim on that 12-foot section and was soon $12,000 richer. Moses reckoned they ought to have called him Eagle-Eye Davis.

Lamps burned on all these claims as miners worked round the clock, getting in as much digging as they could before winter arrived. There were still people on the road and he greeted them as he passed. A trail branched off to his right, up to the cemetery where James Barry had been buried in an unmarked grave slightly more than a year ago. Moses had not wholly come to terms with his feelings in the aftermath of the executions; he supposed, though, that Rebecca had been right all along. And when he visited Charlie's grave last May, on the second anniversary of the murder, he was surprised at how quickly the old feelings of guilt rose to the surface and seeped through the cracks in his resolve not to blame himself for his friend's murder. He still wished that he could go back in time to Quesnelle Mouth and have the opportunity to stop Charlie from travelling with Barry.

In Richfield he saw that a lamp was burning at the Gibbses, but the curtains were drawn. It was too late to stop in; they were probably all preparing for bed, anyway. Just below the courthouse, he turned in his tracks and retraced his route to Barkerville and, despite the number of times he had made the walk, he was surprised at how quick the return trip was by comparison. Overhead, the northern lights disappeared as if someone had snuffed them out. By the time he was letting himself into his shop, many of the lights in town had also been extinguished, and the valley was falling silent, save for the creaking of water wheels in the distance and the gurgle of water down the long wooden flumes. It'll be frozen in the morning, Moses reckoned, for the air was still and icy now, and was bound to get even colder during the night. He had a stiff brandy to fortify himself, then banked down the fire before turning in. He lay awake for a long time, unwilling to let sleep hasten tomorrow's coming. He could not fathom why.

In the morning, as an aura of grey light formed above the eastern ridges and began building skyward, dimming the stars and bringing human movement along the creek, a bitter wind, colder than mountain water, spilled down the valley. Icicles, thick and long, hung from the flumes. Eventually the sun itself rose above the line of mountains and obliterated the stars completely. It shone down on the town and though it lacked the intense heat of summer, it continued to suck moisture from the wood buildings, just as it had done for weeks now. Fires were stoked up again to ward off the early morning chill. Sparks from hot chimneys drifted onto rooftops like autumn leaves and glowed there for a while before dying out.

Moses awakened early, still feeling unsettled, and went down to the Cosmopolitan for breakfast. Outside, he was disappointed. He had hoped for rain or snow but the sky was the same river of blue above the valley that it had been for weeks now, and looked unchangeable. At the restaurant, he ordered beefsteak and eggs, and exchanged comments about the tedious weather with the waiter. When the meal came, he realized that he did not have the appetite to eat it. He picked at it for a while, then pushed it aside. Apologizing to the waiter for the waste of good food, he paid his bill and went to work.

About 2:30 that afternoon, he was just finishing with a customer when he heard yelling from outside, and saw people running. He and the cape-covered man ran to the door and out onto the boardwalk. His heart jumped into his mouth. Across the street and a few doors up, a huge column of smoke, bent by the wind, was rising from the roof of Barry & Adler's Saloon. Flames were shooting several feet into the air. As Moses watched in horror, a gust of wind sent them leaping over the narrow street to set the Bank of British Columbia on fire. Then the buildings flanking the saloon began to burn. Moses' customer tore off the cape and ran home while Moses himself rushed back into the shop to save what he could.

He flew into his living quarters and grabbed a jacket hanging from a hook on the wall, then pulled a blanket from his bed and threw it over his shoulder. Returning to the shop, he gathered up his barber's tools, tore his wedding picture from the wall, and wrapped everything up in the blanket. He could hear the flames hissing and the wood crackling, and knew that his barbershop and home, and probably the entire town, were doomed. Carrying the blanket over his shoulder like a sack, he ran out the front door and jumped from the boardwalk to the street with a jarring thud, thinking that he was far too old to be doing such things. The heat of the fire chased him as he turned and ran down the road toward the north end of town. Others were doing the same thing, some carrying huge loads of personal items down into the dried-up creek bed where they would be out of the fire's reach. Moses took his load there, too, and then pitched in to help, carrying everything from carpetbags stuffed with clothing, to tables and chairs. When it was no longer safe, everyone headed down into the creek bed where they huddled together with the goods they had managed to save, and watched as their town went up in flames and smoke.

The fire had started near the centre of Barkerville and spread first toward the north, or lower, end of town. There, 50 kegs of blasting powder were hastily removed from one of the buildings and placed down a dry mineshaft for safekeeping. Up at the south end, the fire was held at bay for a while by men standing in the Barker flume and throwing water down on the buildings, but they fought a losing battle and were soon running for their lives. At one point, flames rose up in a huge wall that roared like a hurricane over the hissing and crackling. There was a tremendous explosion in one of the dry-goods stores when the fire reached several five-gallon tins of coal oil. Blankets and bedding were blasted 200 feet in the air, and a tin lid came to rest five miles away, at Grouse Creek. The cabins on the hillside were soon part of the conflagration, and it was fortunate that the slope above had been stripped of trees, otherwise it would have burned too. As it was, sparks flew up onto the ridge behind and set the trees there ablaze. By 4:00 P.M., the fire had done most of its work in the town and now huge flames danced along the crest of the ridge that stood out starkly against the sky. It looked like the rim of hell. At 4:30, all that remained of Barkerville and the hillside was a charred, smouldering wasteland. The crowd stood in stunned amazement.

How different was this, Moses wondered, from a hurricane rumbling over Grand Cayman? Not much, he reckoned. Not only had he traded one island for another, he had also traded one disaster for another, and once more was forced to start all over again.

Many of the townspeople made lean-tos among their piled-up household furniture, and slept in the freezing cold that night, but Rebecca and Isaiah had come down from Richfield to insist that Moses take advantage of the settee in their parlour until he decided what he was going to do. Rebecca was concerned that he might be thinking of leaving, rather than starting anew here, and was relieved to discover that the thought had never crossed his mind. While watching the fire, he had heard others say that starting first thing in the morning, they were going to clear away the rubble and begin rebuilding, and he fully intended to join them.

Thus the resurrection of Barkerville began. There were still wisps of smoke rising here and there among the blackened ruins as new lumber from Nason's Sawmill was delivered and stockpiled. The mill, up on Mink Gulch, a mile or so above Richfield, could produce a thousand board feet an hour, and even though their regular price of $80 per thousand shot up overnight to $125, that was the law of supply and demand and only a few people were deterred. Debris was soon cleared away and foundations were laid. This time the main street was made wider so that the town would be more spacious and a similar conflagration less likely. The new buildings would be farther apart, in some places with enough space to allow for cross streets, and all would be built at the same height off the ground to make the boardwalks even. Very quickly, walls rose on the foundations, and roofs rose from walls. Within a week, 30 buildings lined the street and foundations were in place for many more.

Everyone speculated on the cause of the fire, but Moses heard from a reliable source that the culprit was a miner trying to kiss a Hurdy. Apparently, he bumped into a hot stovepipe and knocked it against a canvas ceiling that instantly ignited. Moses kept this information to himself. There was genuine fear that there might be a lynching if the townsfolk ever found out who it was.

Moses' new building was now on the opposite side of the street, its back to the creek. By the time he had ordered a new barber's chair, and furniture and dry goods for his private quarters, he was as low on money as he had been during those first days in San Francisco. It did not concern him. This was home and there would always be enough work for a man of his profession; people would always need haircuts. Still, there were moments when he thought it would be nice if the laws of supply and demand applied as stringently to barbering as they did to the sawmilling industry.

Paradoxically, as the new town rose from the ashes, the economy of the valley was declining. The ground had already given up most of its gold and many miners were pulling up stakes and leaving, some for home, others to seek their fortunes elsewhere. Yet many would make this valley their home. Moses, of course, already had and he settled into a rhythm that took him from one season to the next. And as the seasons tumbled down the years, he was content.

CHAPTER SEVENTEEN

I f any single person had his finger on the pulse of the town and knew how it was faring and what was going on, it was Moses. He kept a diary, and while it was largely testimony that most days passed uneventfully, some things were important to him and deserved mentioning: pack trains coming and going, stages arriving on time or late, men and women leaving for, or coming from, the lower country. He noted that two horses burned to death in a fire up on Conklin Gulch; a man drowned in a flume; and a bull puncher had his feet crushed under the wheels of his freight wagon when a dog frightened his oxen. One day, he received by mail a box of assorted perfumes that he had ordered from the coast; another day, an eclipse of the sun darkened the town at mid-afternoon. And because such events were rare, he recorded that a man was arrested for fighting, and that a store was robbed and the loot found in a nearby tunnel. He wrote down the births of children; and sometimes their entry into the world brought their mother's departure; other times they were born only to die themselves. A six-year-old boy died, Rebecca fell seriously ill once and recovered, as did Isaiah, and these were all recorded. There were brief mentions of nights at the Theatre Royal, and the arrival on the creek of new Hurdy Gurdy girls, the details of life in a mining camp so far from civilization that it had become civilization itself for those who called it home.

He kept in touch with his old friend Mifflin Gibbs and in 1870 received a rare letter from him. Gibbs had just returned from the Queen Charlotte Islands where he had overseen the building of a tramway for a new coal-mining operation, and though he had been asked to stay on as mine superintendent, and had done so for a while, the rainy islands could not keep him. Back in Victoria, he was sent as a delegate to the 1868 Yale Convention, which helped define the terms that would bring British Columbia into Confederation. When he lost his seat on council in 1869, there was nothing to keep him in the colony any longer and he had decided that he would not stay on. He was going home to Philadelphia, and then perhaps to Oberlin to rejoin Maria; he did not know. In his letter to Moses he said, "It is not without a measure of regret that I leave Victoria. The geniality of the climate has been exceeded only by the graciousness of the people, despite the political problems and those experienced by Maria and other black women. I myself, though, have been successful in this town and have had political opportunities that might not have been available to me elsewhere. But love of home and country is asserting itself and I feel it is time to go."

It was typical of Gibbs, this departure. To fight like hell for achievements other men would not think possible, and then leave once they were attained. There was no one on earth quite like Mifflin Gibbs, and that was an indisputable fact. Moses wondered if he would ever see him again.

About the same time that Gibbs left the colony, Rebecca, Isaiah, and Maria quit the creeks and moved to Victoria. Moses thought that part of the reason might have been his relationship with Rebecca. He and Isaiah had had a bit of a falling-out over it when Isaiah called it odd. Moses knew that he did not suspect an affair, and that he was probably just envious of the fact that Rebecca could talk to Moses in a way that she could never talk to him. The two men patched it up to some degree but the result was that Moses did not drop by as often any more. Even so, it was a sad day in his life when they left. There was no one he could talk to as intimately and honestly as he could to Rebecca, and after she rode out of town on the B.X. stage he missed her before the dust was even settled.

Moses had gone up to Richfield to see her off and afterward went into the nearest saloon to have a drink. He was joined by a strident Englishwoman named Mary Higgins who seemed intent on drinking herself into oblivion. Mary had not been in town long, but her drunken and lascivious behavior had already raised many eyebrows along the creek. Moses could not have cared less. Over the next two weeks, the only time he and Mary did not have a drink in their hands was when they were sleeping or fornicating. He stayed with her in her tiny miner's cabin on the edge of town, did not open his shop, and only returned to Barkerville to get money to buy more liquor. Somehow, in their alcoholic haze, they managed to get married, an act that sobered them up completely. But they were not as good with each other sober as they were drunk and their partnership was little more than a verbal mêlée that the whole town knew about. Then one day, without any notice, Mary packed her bag and left. Moses tried to tell himself that he cared, but he could not find that feeling anywhere within. He went back to work and it was a while before he felt comfortable enough to look his friends and neighbours in the eye. The last he heard from Mary was a letter saying that she was returning to England.

It was not bad news as far as Moses was concerned. The bad news came sometime later. One afternoon, just as he was leaving Barry & Adler's Saloon, someone handed him a letter from Isaiah. He knew that there was only one reason Isaiah would write him and, with some trepidation, he tore the letter open right away. The news was just as he had feared. Rebecca had taken ill and died. She had not suffered, Isaiah wrote, and passed away quietly in her sleep. They buried her in the new cemetery at Ross Bay. With Rebecca gone, Isaiah and Maria were planning to rejoin Mifflin and his family in Oberlin at the first possible opportunity. Moses stood there for a long time, holding the letter as it fluttered in the wind. Then he let it go and while it danced away down the street, he did an about face and returned to the saloon.

Oberlin was a name that Moses had heard often. It was a small town about 30 miles from Cleveland and its college, linked to the Underground Railroad, had graduated many blacks. One of these graduates moved to Barkerville in 1875.

He was Dr. Bill Jones, a dentist and, like Moses, a man with humble beginnings. Jones' father had been a slave in North Carolina who, with hard work, was able to buy his freedom. Convinced that the road to freedom for all blacks lay in education, he founded a school for that purpose. The whites, however, saw the threat that such institutions posed and burned him out. Undeterred, Jones' father started again. Equally undeterred, the whites burned him out again. After the third time, he gave up and moved to Oberlin where he could at least see that his own children were well educated.

Though Bill Jones was nearly 20 years Moses' junior, the two men got along famously, their common backgrounds a wellspring for conversations that would occasionally last deep into the night. Moses was the first to take advantage of Jones' services and had him extract a bothersome tooth. Best of all, though, Jones taught Moses how to play chess and the two friends spent hours at it, in the evenings and on Sunday afternoons. Every now and then, someone in great pain from an abscessed tooth or some other dental malady would interrupt a game, and Jones would have to leave for a while. Moses always seized this opportunity to study the board and plan his next move, and the next after that, and they always led to a checkmate, at least in his mind. But when his friend returned it was always Moses who was checkmated. He made it a goal in life to one day beat Bill Jones at the game of chess.

During the same year that Jones came to town, Moses was a witness for a saloon owner named Sam Greer who sued another man for "debauching" and "making a whore" of his wife while Greer was out of town for an extended period. Moses had seen Mrs. Greer coming and going from the defendant's house at all hours of the night, and felt obliged to say so. He still harboured guilt feelings over his own tryst with Constance and did not want to see Mrs. Greer get away with her misdeeds. Despite his testimony, Greer lost the suit.

Bob Stevenson left Barkerville for good in 1877. Having grown tired of a bachelor's life, he went off to marry a teacher down in Victoria and to pursue other mining interests. Moses travelled to the coast with him and attended the wedding in late July. It filled him with sad memories. Before leaving for home, he hired a carriage to take him out to Ross Bay Cemetery to visit Rebecca's grave. He had the driver stop along the roadside so that he could pick some wild flowers for her.

The cemetery sat on a gentle slope above the bay where the sun sparkled off the blue water, and he thought it was as fine a place as any to spend eternity. The caretaker told him that he would find her grave in the Anglican section, but he walked among the headstones there twice before he found it. He supposed he did not really *want* to see it because of the finality it would bring. He crouched and placed the flowers against the marker and, unsure what else to say, recited a verse that he remembered from Rebecca's poem "The Old Red Shirt."[1]

> Far from these mountains a poor mother mourns
>   The darling that hung by her skirt,
> When contentment and plenty surrounded the home
>   Of the miner that brought me the shirt.

Back at his hotel, he heard that James Douglas had died. Moses waited in town for the funeral and joined the great crowd that spilled out of The Church of Our Lord, up and down Blanshard Street and across Humboldt. He did not follow the procession out to the cemetery. Instead, he went back to his hotel to pack and left for home the next morning.

By the 1880s the population on Williams Creek had dropped from a few thousand to a few hundred. Moses' business dropped off accordingly, but since he was the only barber in town now that Dixie had gone, he made enough to get by. When there was extra money, he invested it in various claims, some of which brought decent returns while others did not. Over the years, though, he ran a little ahead of even and managed to put a bit of money aside. With fewer things to invest it in, combined with the fact that he was not getting any younger — he was now 65 years old — he decided to do something with it. He wrote Gibbs and said that he would like to come for a visit if Gibbs was not too busy. His friend wrote a short note back, "Come ahead. If you wait until I'm not busy we'll never see each other again."

When Gibbs left Victoria, he had returned east and rejoined Maria and the children in Oberlin. He studied law at the college there and, after graduating, moved around the country for a while before finally settling in Little Rock, Arkansas. He hung out a shingle in 1873, and before long he was elected municipal judge — the first black man in the U.S. to achieve that status. Since then, he had been heavily involved with the Republican Party and Reconstruction, and was a continuing delegate at presidential conventions. Moses was not the least bit surprised by Gibbs' stellar career and was pleased for his friend. But people changed and he hoped that the intervening years would not mar their reunion.

He sailed from Victoria to San Francisco and scarcely recognized the place, it had changed so much. He rode a cable car for the sheer novelty of it, then took a ferry across the bay to Oakland where a train whisked him to Sacramento, following the route of the old Underground Railroad. There were more towns along the way now, and farm after farm stretched across the distance, but he thought he recognized the place where the Turners had hid in the bush. After 30 years, they still held a special place in his heart, still brought tears to the corners of his eyes. And the sorrow of their lives still made him angry.

Though he had seen them from afar, the jagged peaks of the Sierra Nevada Mountains were breathtaking in close-up, as the train gained 7,000 feet in elevation over 70 miles and squeezed through gaps blasted in the rock that were not much wider than the track. The fire-hot deserts beyond were fearsome places and he wondered how the American overlanders had ever survived them. East of the Continental Divide, the great plains were as empty as the ocean, and the tall grass, not yet seared by the sun, waved in the relentless wind. The train pounded across the rolling landscape in the stifling heat, making good time, and pulled into Omaha, Nebraska, five days after leaving Sacramento. Moses boarded a paddlewheeler and sailed down the muddy Missouri River to the Mississippi and south to St. Louis. He thought of Charlie much of the way. Another train took him from St. Louis to Little Rock, a pretty town on the Arkansas River. He had wired Gibbs of his arrival time and his friend was at the station to greet him.

Gibbs had not lost much to the years. He was approaching 60, so there were a few more wrinkles on his face and his hair was turning grey, but there was still that great energy, still that determined look in his eyes. The two men delighted in their reunion, then Gibbs steered Moses to his carriage, sitting outside the station, which took them to Gibbs' palatial home overlooking the river.

Maria was as happy as Moses had ever seen her. Only the oldest child remembered his "uncle," but Moses revelled in the family's company and stuffed himself on Maria's home cooking. During his stay, he saw more of Maria and Little Rock than he did of Gibbs, who was extremely busy. Gibbs often worked late, and when he was home, messengers frequently came to the door with some piece of news that could not wait until he was in his chambers. Nevertheless, he gave all of his spare time to Moses.

They went to a soirée attended by many of Little Rock's most prominent citizens, both white and black. Moses felt underdressed and out of place the entire evening despite his experience at similar events in San Francisco and Victoria. He put it down to too many years living with the informality of Barkerville.

The times Moses enjoyed most were the evenings of conversation on Gibbs' verandah, as the heat of the day let go of the land and the cool darkness of evening descended upon them. They sat in padded willow-branch chairs that Maria had ordered from a store in St. Louis. Between them was a table that held either a bottle of fine imported whiskey or some exotic liqueur, depending on their tastes. There were also two glasses, two ashtrays and the men's pipes. They drank and smoked and talked, while the aroma of tobacco smoke mingled with the sweet scent of flowers, and mockingbirds sang their warbling, fluid songs in the garden. They reminisced about San Francisco and the Underground Railroad, and about Victoria and Sarah. Both men fell silent at the first mention of her name, then Gibbs thanked God that incidents like the one that had turned her life into a living hell were now a thing of the past. They argued at length over politics and on some things had to agree to disagree. Moses was surprised that his friend had grown critical of the ex-slave population. Gibbs insisted that he had worked hard on their behalf during Reconstruction and now it was their turn. Yet most of them seemed lost in the doldrums. Their lassitude in an era of abundant opportunity troubled him.

This was a more conservative Gibbs than the one Moses had known. It seemed to him that Gibbs had come to believe, like many men from humble beginnings who achieved a measure of success through hard work, that everyone else could do the same. He was rigid and uncompromising in this view. In response, Moses said, "For Heaven's sake, Gibbs, bend a little. Not everyone can be as driven as you are. Then again, you never were a man of patience, were you?"

"There is no time for such luxuries," Gibbs said.

He spoke briefly of his satisfaction that British Columbia had joined Confederation, and of the small part he had played in it. In his opinion, the economic future of B.C. would be better in the hands of enterprising Canadians than it would have been in the hands of an anachronistic, self-serving British monopoly.

On most nights, Gibbs would steer the conversation around to his conviction that Moses should leave Barkerville and move to Little Rock.

"I tell you, Moses, this is a glorious country with an unlimited future! It has its share of barbarians and philistines, of course, but what country hasn't? At least you'll find no malaise here among its administrators. The race is on, my friend, and there's room for many winners."

Moses imagined himself on top of a mill wheel, running to keep pace with its turning. The idea of a barbershop in Barkerville was much more appealing. "The race doesn't interest me anymore, Gibbs," he said. "Besides, Cariboo gets in your blood."

"If I can be candid," Gibbs said, "you confound me, Moses. You have a natural intelligence that could bring you much gain in this country, yet you choose to live in a backwater that's snowbound for half the year. I find that incomprehensible, particularly when this country offers everything a man could want."

"But few things that I *need*. I'd be just another black face in the crowd here, but in Barkerville, everyone knows me and I know everyone, and many of them are my friends. Most of them have forgotten the colour of my skin, Gibbs, and that's no small achievement in any coloured man's life. Only a fool would willingly give that up."

Gibbs said nothing but it was clear to Moses that he thought that only a fool would stay in such a place.

"I'm a simple man, Gibbs," Moses went on, half defensively. "I look around me, and everything that you would consider a sign of success and prosperity would be a burden to me. Don't take me wrong. I would not deny you your need, or right for that matter, to aspire to such things, but they are not for me. Believe me when I say that I am happy you've been able to carve a niche for yourself; happy that you've achieved success and respect in your own way, but you must, in turn, be happy for me. I've done it in mine."

Moses stayed for two and a half weeks, until the ache for home was too powerful to ignore. As July turned to August, he bade goodbye to Maria and the children, and Gibbs took him to the train station. In their watery eyes and handshake was the knowledge that they would probably never see each other again.[2]

Moses was impatient to be home and the plains' western horizon seemed unreachable, the coast a geographical myth. When at last he was in Victoria, tired and stiff, he did not delay booking passage to the mainland and Cariboo. He arrived back on the creeks in mid-August, finding the valley sun-drenched and dry and the road dusty. It had been a long journey home, and the last part of it, from Quesnelle Mouth to Barkerville, was the longest. As the coach rolled down the street to the B.X. office, people saw him and waved. Others called out greetings when he stepped down from the passenger compartment. He would have asked for nothing more.

∞∞

It felt good to get back into a routine again, good to be back in the shop enjoying conversations, playing cards over at Wake-up Jakes since it had been converted from a restaurant into a saloon, and trying to beat Bill Jones at chess. It was only a matter of time, Moses reckoned.

In 1885, a new road was pushed through the wilderness from Van Winkle to Barkerville, through Devil's Canyon and alongside Jack of Clubs Lake. It entered the valley of Williams Creek from the north and replaced the old trail that came in from the south through Richfield, shaving five miles off the trip to Quesnelle Mouth.

Every May 31, regardless of the weather or how he felt, Moses visited Charlie Blessing's grave. Over time the marker he had erected for his friend weathered badly, and since he could not afford to buy a new one himself, he raised the money for it. He kept a pot in his shop with a sign that read "Charlie Blessing's Memorial Fund" and his customers contributed generously. Some of the local children helped him raise money because he had helped build their school. Before too long, there was enough to have a more fitting monument, appropriately inscribed, made in the style of the day: three 2- by 8-inch boards joined side by side with dowels and rounded at the top. He also ordered a picket fence to surround the grave, just like the graves up in the Cameronton cemetery. In 1886, shortly after his 70th birthday and on the 20th anniversary of Charlie's death, he hired a wagon and with Bill Jones drove out to Charlie's grave. Moses removed the old marker, which had all but fallen over, and planted the new one deep in the ground. Then he and Jones set the corner- posts of the fence and nailed the four pre-built sections to them. The monument read: *In Memory of Charles Morgan Blessing, A Native of Ohio, Aged 30 Years, Was murdered near this Spot, May 31, 1866.*

Jones returned to the wagon so that Moses could be alone with his thoughts. He stood there for a long time, the dank oppressiveness of the forest weighing heavily on his heart, trying to think of something profound to say. Nothing came to him that would not sound trite. He tried to recall the words that he had recited 20 years before, but his memory was not as good as it used to be. Something by Wordsworth, he knew, about the good dying young, but that was all he could remember. In the end, all he said was, "God love you, Charlie. I hope the ground has laid lightly on you all these years." Then he joined Jones in the wagon and they drove home, back to Barkerville.

In the summer of 1888 John "Cariboo" Cameron returned to Williams Creek. It was not that he had spent all of the money from the big strike in '63 and needed more; rather it was to rediscover something in his soul that had been lost during years of high living. He and his second wife checked into the Barkerville Hotel and he went right to work. Moses thought that there was something both sad and noble in Cameron's efforts, for the man did not look well at all. Three months later, he was dead.

That was the thing about growing older. Besides feeling it in your bones, and some days just plain not feeling well, there was the passing on of contemporaries to provide frequent reminders that your turn might be just around the corner. It was the saddest part of old age. The best part was spending it in a place that fit like a favourite suit of clothes. To Moses, that was Barkerville. He had been made welcome here 22 years ago, more than he had ever been anywhere else, and he felt as content as any black man whose anchor was lodged firmly in a sea of white folks. It had become his world, familiar and comfortable, where life was easy and friends were plentiful, where a stroll down the street brought a score of hellos and a dozen small conversations, and where the slightest indication that someone needed help always brought more than was needed. Over the years, he had grown to love the children on the creek and always had sweets for them when they came into his shop. He never forgot them at Christmas, either, and bought them slates to draw on and toys to play with. And when the hardness of winter turned into the softness of summer, and work on the creek began again in earnest, he thought that he would never hear a lovelier noise. It was the sound of the collective search for something better, and it was so … human. He hoped they all found what they were looking for. God knows he had, even if it was not all that different from what he had been so disdainful of as a young man.

The years had come down around Moses and piled up like a Cariboo snowfall that would never know a spring melt. Barely a day went by when he did not think of dying, that one day his flesh, his blood would be no more. Though it did not frighten him, some days it was hard to believe. His hair had gone grey, his joints were stiff and his back had a bend in it that would not straighten out. A touch of rheumatism in his right knee made it harder to get around and there was a slight limp to his walk. Gone were the days when he could walk to Richfield (which did not matter much anyway since there was not much left of Richfield to walk to) or trek up the side of a nearby mountain on a summer Sunday to take in the splendid view of the valley. Yet despite his inability to venture very far afoot, nothing stopped him from opening his shop six days a week. Indeed, he had had it rebuilt with a nice front porch smartly finished with a scalloped trim. Nevertheless, he was thankful that the really busy days were all in the past now, part of a different era, and that there was always time for a nap in the comfortable barber's chair he had bought after the fire.

One fine winter's day, when the sun was high overhead and reflected off the snow so sharply it pierced a man's eyes, Moses felt a little more tired than usual. As there were no customers, he climbed into the chair and closed his eyes. Drifting in and out of consciousness, he listened to the crunching footsteps of people in the snow along the boardwalk and the sound played like music in his ears. Typically, his mind wandered down roads travelled long ago, stopping here and there to bide awhile among good memories and bad, with old friends and family, and with Sarah. The memories forever remained, all of them, the small and large parts of his past that ebbed and flowed like the tide, remembered, forgotten, the sum of an old man nodding off in a barber's chair in a gold town called Barkerville. At times like these, a part of him wished someone would drop in to get him moving again, while another part relished the peaceful, near blissful, state of mind he was in. Sometimes he thought it might not be too bad a way to spend eternity. Suddenly he became conscious of an unusual stirring deep inside his chest. Something was poking around in there like an animal looking for food, and it scared him. He felt a large bump. Then the thing grabbed hold of his heart and sent an electric jolt through his body; a crushing pain filled his chest. He heard a rushing sound that came from far off and filled his ears, and over it or in it, he could not tell which, he thought he heard someone call his name. He could have sworn it was a woman's voice, could have sworn it was Sarah's.

EPILOGUE

Wellington Delaney Moses died on January 3, 1890, at the age of 73. Compared to John Cameron's funeral, which was larger than anything Barkerville had ever seen, Moses' was modest. But unlike Cameron's, which attracted an entourage of people who had never known the man, only his name, it was friends who gathered around Moses at St. Saviour's Anglican Church to mourn his passing. Bill Jones, whom Moses never managed to beat at chess, read the eulogy and, knowing of his friend's lack of religious faith, did what Moses himself would have done: found a poem over at the library. It was Christina Rossetti's "Remember," and Jones read it after the eulogy.

> Remember me when I am gone away,
>   Gone far away into the silent land;
>   When you can no more hold me by the hand,
> Nor I half turn to go yet turning stay.
> Remember me when no more day by day
>   You tell me of our future that you planned:
>   Only remember me; you understand
> It will be too late to counsel then or pray.
> Yet if you should forget me for a while
>   And afterwards remember, do not grieve:
>   For if the darkness and corruption leave
>   A vestige of the thoughts that I once had,
> Better by far you should forget and smile
>   Than that you should remember and be sad.

The mournful sound of the organ accompanied the pall-bearers as they carried Moses' coffin up the aisle and outside, where a horse-drawn sled awaited. Ever so gently, the men placed it on the sled, and Jones, with the rest of the mourners following, led the horse by the halter up the road to the foot of the cemetery on the hillside. Soft mantles of snow graced the grave markers, picket fences and trees; the air was still and the sky leaden. Peace lay on the land so firmly it suggested eternity. The pallbearers lifted the coffin from the sled and carried it to the top end of the cemetery where freshly dug earth stood out starkly against virgin snow. Two labourers stood respectfully by with shovels. Jones had had a wooden marker made, much like Charlie Blessing's, and inscribed simply with Moses' name and the dates of his birth and death. Below these was written, *"By leaving home, he came home."* With ropes, the coffin was let down slowly into the ground while the minister recited *The Lord's Prayer*. It began to snow, huge flakes that looked as if they might fall forever. The rituals for the dead complete, the mourners turned from Moses' grave and made their way down the hill, leaving behind them the sad sound of earth and stone striking wood.

E N D N O T E S

Part One

Chapter One

1 For example, one such site is called "The Wreck of the Ten Sails," which consists of a flotilla of 10 ships that hit the reef in succession.

2 Greytown is now San Juan del Norte; Bragman's Bluff is Puerto Cabasez.

Chaper Two

1 A person of Indian-Caucasian (usually Spanish) heritage.

2 The route Cornelius Vanderbilt intended to build was ultimately stymied by politics, and the Panama Canal was built instead. He did, however, run a steamboat operation (after clearing obstacles out of the way) up the San Juan River to Lake Nicaragua, across the lake to El Virgin, and by coach from there to San Juan del Sur on the Pacific side. This was during the years after Moses' journey.

3 The sharks were bull sharks, which ultimately became a large part of the Nicaraguan fishing industry, but are rarely seen now. Sawfish weighing 1,000 pounds were once taken from the lake. Both species apparently entered the lake up the San Juan River before an earthquake altered the landscape and cut off their escape.

Part Two

Chapter Three

1 Frederick Douglass was born into slavery, escaped and later purchased his freedom. He toured the New England states protesting slavery and helped recruit blacks to fight for the Union during the Civil War. During Reconstruction he fought for black civil rights and held various government positions, one of the first blacks to do so.

2 Although it was one of the more outrageous laws with which blacks had to contend, being unable to testify in court actually worked in one

fugitive slave's favour. A young slave by the name of Frank had been brought to California from Missouri by his owner, Calloway, and subsequently escaped. Calloway had the young man arrested, but his only proof of ownership was Frank's admission that Calloway was indeed his master. Since the young black was not allowed to give that testimony, the judge sent him away a free man.

3 Widely thought of as the boundary between the northern and the southern states, Mason and Dixon's line actually separates Pennsylvania from Maryland and West Virginia, and Maryland from Delaware. In other words, the line runs both east and west and north and south. It was created because of boundary disputes between those states.

Chapter Five
1 McGloin, John B., *San Francisco, The Story of a City*, p. 65.
2 Stanley, Jerry, *Hurry Freedom*, p. 58.
3 Kilian, Crawford, *Go Do Some Great Thing*, p. 20.
4 Ibid., p. 19.
5 Ibid., p. 21.
6 Stanley, Jerry, *Hurry Freedom*, p. 67-68.

Part Three
Chapter Six
1 The letter is as quoted in *Go Do Some Great Thing*, p. 54.
2 Ibid., p. 54.

Chapter Seven
1 The letter is as quoted in *Go Do Some Great Thing*, p.124
2 Ibid., p.120.
3 Ibid., p.123.

Chapter Eight
1 Pethick, Derek, *Victoria: The Fort*, as quoted on p. 195.

Chapter Nine
1 It wasn't until 1864 that a women's medical facility was built. Till then, the hospital was for men only.

Chapter Ten
1 Usually, runaway slaves from the west side of Chesapeake Bay were channelled by their conductors through Baltimore. Met on the out-

skirts of town by some form of transportation, they were taken to a safe house, where a new conductor would lead them to Philadelphia. It had always been dangerous work, but it became even more so with the passage in 1850 of a new Fugitive Slave Act, which stated that runaway slaves, even if they had made it to free soil, could be captured and returned to their owners. It also made it possible for any black anywhere in the United States to be accused of being a runaway slave and taken south into captivity. Because blacks could not testify or give evidence in court, this section of the act held terrifying ramifications for every free black.

2 Howard Estes was one of a handful of blacks who homesteaded on the Saanich Peninsula. His daughter, Sylvia, married a man named Louis Stark, and they and their two children moved to Saltspring Island to become among the first pioneers there.

Part Four
Chapter Eleven

1 Dr. Chipp reported their findings in the June 6 edition of the *Sentinel.* It is now known, of course, that the real problem was contamination of the creek water by adjacent toilets. That the disease had all but disappeared was more likely due to the fact that most of Williams Creek had been diverted, and drinking water was coming from a source farther away.

2 William Rennie eventually married and lived in Barkerville until 1884, after which he disappeared from the record. A photograph of him remains, taken in Barkerville as he stood among his fellow Masons. A close-up reveals a face of heart-rending bitterness, a face that seems angry with the world, but in all likelihood is angrier with its owner.

3 As quoted in *Go Do Some Great Thing*, p. 90.

4 Skelton, Robin, *They call it the Cariboo*, as quoted on p. 127.

5 Compton, Wade, *Bluesprint*, as quoted on p. 65.

6 Ibid., p. 52

Chapter Twelve

1 Arthur Edward Kennedy, royal governor of Vancouver Island from 1863 to 1866.

2 Gibbs refers to Frederick Seymour, governor of British Columbia, who eventually became governor of the united colonies and died of alcoholism.

3 Pemberton ultimately succeeded, and John Butts was sent home to Australia.

Chapter Thirteen
1 Dickens, Charles, *American Notes*, pp. 143-44.
2 Cook's Ferry is now Spences Bridge.

Chapter Fourteen
1 Williams, David R., *The Man for a New Country*, p. 73.
2 In his work on Begbie, David Williams says that problems similar to that which confronted Begbie come before modern courts, too, where "courts of appeal sometimes overturn jury verdicts for the same reason that Begbie did — the sworn evidence does not support the verdict." *The Man for a New Country*, p. 73.
3 Ibid., p. 100.

Chapter Fifteen
1 According to David Williams, "... it must always be remembered ... that the opportunities for a successful defence in a murder trial were far more limited than they are now, since the weight of the law tended to favour the prosecution, i.e. the victim." *The Man for a New Country*, p. 137.
2 Williams also writes that during these times "no gradations of murder such as those developed in this century [20th century] existed ... " *The Man for a New Country*, p. 137.
3 In all probability, the Hurdy Gurdy girl.
4 *Cariboo Sentinel*, August 12, 1867.
5 A native term for Englishmen.
6 *Cariboo Sentinel*, August 12, 1867.
7 The Richfield Cemetery was never maintained and no markers remain.

Chapter Seventeen
1 Visitors to Rebecca's grave will find a new marker, on the back of which is the poem in its entirety.
2 Gibbs continued on in Little Rock, the recipient of various patronage appointments because of his staunch support of the Republican Party. In 1897, he became the U.S. consul in Madagascar. After his return to Little Rock three years later, he became president of the Capital City Savings Bank. He visited Victoria briefly in 1907 and died in 1915. The first black high school in Little Rock was named after him.

BIBLIOGRAPHY

Published Sources

Compton, Wade, ed. *Bluesprint: Black British Columbian Literature and Orature*. Vancouver, BC: Arsenal Pulp Press, 2001.

Dickens, Charles. *American Notes, and Reprinted Pieces*. London, UK: Chapman & Hall, publication n.d.

Downs, Art. *Wagon Road North*. Surrey, BC: Heritage House, 1993.
———. "Paddlewheels on the Frontier." *B.C. Outdoors Magazine*. Cloverdale, BC: 1967.

Gregson, Harry. *A History of Victoria 1842–1970*. Victoria, BC: The Victoria Observer Publishing Company, 1970.

Henderson, James. *Jamaica and the Cayman Islands*. London, UK: Cadogan Books, 1996.

Higgins, David William. *Tales of a Pioneer Journalist: From Gold Rush to Government Street in 19th Century Victoria*. Surrey, BC: Heritage House, 1996.

Kilian, Crawford. *Go Do Some Great Thing, The Black Pioneers of British Columbia*. Vancouver, BC: Douglas & McIntyre, 1978.

Lapp, Rudolph M. *Blacks in Gold Rush California*. New Haven, CT: Yale University Press, 1977.

Lester, Julius. *To Be A Slave*. New York: Scholastic Inc., 1968.

Marryat, Frank. *Mountains and Molehills*. New York, NY: J.B. Lippincott Company, 1962.

McGloin, John B. *San Francisco, The Story of a City*. San Rafael, CA: Presidio Press, 1978.

Muscatine, Doris. *Old San Francisco: The Biography of a City from Early Days to the Earthquake*. New York, NY: G.P. Putnam's Sons, 1975.

Paterson, T. W. *Capital Characters: A Celebration of Victorian Eccentrics*. Duncan, BC: Fir Grove Publishing, 1998.

Pethick, Derek. *Victoria: The Fort*. Vancouver, BC: Mitchell Press Ltd., 1968.

Ramsey, Bruce. *Barkerville, A guide to the fabulous Cariboo Gold Camp*. Vancouver, BC: Mitchell Press, 1977.

Sadlier, Rosemary. *Tubman: Harriet Tubman and the Underground Railroad*. Toronto, ON: Umbrella Press, 1997.

Skelton, Robin. *They call it the Cariboo*. Victoria, BC: Sono Nis Press, 1980.

Stanley, Jerry. *Hurry Freedom, African Americans in Gold Rush California*. New York, NY: Crown Publishers, 2000.

Streissguth, Thomas. *The Transcontinental Railroad*. San Diego, CA: Lucent Books, 2000.

Twain, Mark. *Life on the Mississippi*. New York, NY: Bantam Books, 1963.

Williams, David R. *The Man for a New Country: Sir Matthew Baillie Begbie*. Sidney, BC: Gray's Publishing Ltd., 1977.

Williams, Neville. *A History of the Cayman Islands*. Grand Cayman: The Government of the Cayman Islands, 1970.

Wright, Richard Thomas. *Barkerville, Williams Creek*. Williams Lake, BC: *Cariboo*, Winter Quarters Press, 1998.

Newspapers

The Cariboo Sentinel

Unpublished Sources

Moses, W. D. "Diaries, 1865 – 1889," A01046 – A01047, British Columbia Archives.